HERS

THE FIGHT CLUB, BOOK FOUR

BECCA JAMESON

ACKNOWLEDGMENTS

To my editor, Lisa Dugan, and my publisher, Georgia Woods, for all their patience brainstorming with me to make this series shine!

To all my fans who love and support this MMA series. I adore you! Thanks for your continued words of encouragement.

CHAPTER 1

Thwack.

Kayla flinched. She couldn't help it. No matter how many times she watched someone get flogged, she jerked with every crack of the whip.

Her skin tingled as she leaned against the corner of the wall and gripped it with both hands. She felt the flush that rose quickly up her cheeks as Gage expertly swatted the naked submissive two more times and then soothed the pink lines running along the woman's butt with his fingers.

Kayla squeezed her legs together, well aware of the reaction toward Gage that left her wet, needy, and panting. She ignored those results, as always, and concentrated on the intense feeling of relief she would be able to obtain if she let Gage flog *her*.

She craved the submission. The release. It was imbedded deep inside her. She'd known it for several years, at least as long as she'd been aware of the fetish world. Hell, she craved the sex too, but that was an entirely different topic. And Kayla intended to keep the two desires separate, mutually exclusive. She had to for self-preservation.

She'd done two spanking scenes with him recently, and she knew he was interested in doing more with her, but she was hesitant. He'd pursued her on several occasions. She feared his interest lay a bit deeper than what she was willing or able to give him.

Right now, Kayla wanted to do a scene. It had been a few weeks since she'd done a scene with Gage. The first time, she approached him. He readily agreed to spank her and set her up on a bench to do so. It was the best domination of her life. She was shocked by the contrast with her former Dom.

The second time, he came to her. The twinkle in his eye told her he was interested in more than just a scene. That scared her to death. Almost as much as the flogging she watched intently now.

Gage swatted the sub several more times, reaching lower to cross her thighs with pink lines. The woman moaned. She held firmly to the rope loops at the top of the St. Andrew's cross and leaned into the cross with each swish of the flogger.

Kayla watched every reaction, her attention flitting from Gage to the sub and back, over and over. The submissive let her mouth fall open and her head dip back. Her shoulder-length, brown hair hung loose across her back. She dipped one knee forward with each swat. Her legs had started at shoulder width apart, but they'd inched closer.

Gage lowered the flogger and leaned toward the submissive, whispering in her ear. The woman nodded, her mouth closing, a small smile tipping up the corners.

Kayla's pussy leaked. There was no denying she wished she could be at the receiving end of this flogging. Was it

Gage? Or did she simply want to be flogged? It had been years since she'd allowed herself to do anything so intense. Not since Simon.

Just thinking his name made her stiffen. *Asshole.*

Gage proceeded, and the woman on the cross hummed as lines of submission multiplied across her pale skin. Every few strikes, he paused to stroke the woman's skin. He had the perfect combination of caring and domination.

As he finished and wrapped the submissive in a blanket, Kayla took a deep breath. She needed this. She needed the release a flogging would bring her, something more intense than a simple spanking. All her pent-up anxiety would ooze from her body if she could only bring herself to ask someone to flog her.

Not that there were choices to be made. The only man she trusted right now was Gage, and that trust was dubious. Hell, he had no idea she paid such close attention to him. At least she didn't think so.

What she knew for certain was he was kind and gentle while yielding his flogger, something she needed and craved. The fact her pussy clenched every time she watched him was inconsequential. He didn't need to know he had that effect on her. She had no intention of pursuing that side of things. She could fuck anyone. But this, this domination, was a different story. She would never permit a random Dom to flog her.

Of course, the fucking part was ludicrous also. She hadn't had sex since Simon either, and she had no intention of giving that piece of herself away to anyone. It was one thing to let someone ease her stress with a spanking. It was an entirely different thing to open herself up to someone emotionally through sex. *No thank you.*

There was nothing random about Gage. He worked at the police department where she was a secretary. And the reality

3

was, Kayla trusted cops. Her dad had been a cop. He'd been killed in the line of duty right after she graduated from high school, but she'd spent her life hanging around the station. The chief of police, John Edwards, was like a second father to her. She adored him, and she was blessed that he not only took her under his wing, but took her back into the fold without a question when she returned to Vegas two years ago.

Even though Gage was a K-9 trainer, not a police officer, he had the aura of being an upstanding citizen by default. The fact that he worked for the department made her feel safer with him than any other Dom.

At least a few times a day she interacted with him, exchanging pleasantries when he passed by the front desk. Even though she didn't know him well, which was her fault for remaining distant, she knew he was a good guy. Everyone in the station adored him. He treated his dog as if the German shepherd were royalty. And on more than one occasion the chief of police had given her a look that said she should go after him.

Ludicrous. She wasn't interested in going after *anyone*. But if Chief Edwards gave him the stamp of approval, she knew she would be in good hands.

"Kayla?"

She jerked her head up when she heard the deep voice that reached inside her and made her body vibrate. Apparently she hadn't been paying attention because the woman he'd flogged was gone, and Gage now stood inches from her, his brow raised in question. "Oh, hey. That was lovely. I enjoy your work." She said the first thing that popped into her mind, wanting to kick herself afterward.

He smiled. "Lovely?"

She winced. "You know, nice." *Yes, because that's so much better.*

4

"Did you want to do a scene with me?" he asked, stepping closer. He reached out with one hand and set it on hers, peeling her fingers from the corner of the wall, obviously more aware of her rigid stance than she was.

She lowered her gaze. *Do it.* "That would be nice." *There's that word again.* She lifted her face and met his gaze. "I mean if you don't have anyone else scheduled, I'd appreciate a slot of your time tonight."

He lifted one side of his mouth higher. "A slot of my time?" He chuckled. "Kayla, all you have to do is ask. I'm all yours." He squeezed her hand and finished prying it from the wall. "What did you have in mind?"

She glanced around him toward the vacated cross. *Where did the woman go?*

"You want me to flog you? Like I just did for Kristen?" He still held her hand, and he lifted his other hand to nudge her chin up with one finger.

She met his gaze and swallowed back her fear, hoping to replace it with courage. "Yes, Sir."

He set his thumb on her chin and held her. His gaze narrowed. "Have you been flogged before? I've never seen you do that."

"Yes, Sir. It's been a while." *Years.*

"And you're sure you're up for it?"

"Yes, Sir."

He glanced at the clipboard on the wall behind him. "Well, it looks like no one else has scheduled this area right now."

She nodded, stepping back a pace to dislodge his fingers. She needed to lower her gaze and regroup. It was happening fast. That was a good thing. The more she thought about it, the more likely she would be to chicken out. "Please, Sir." Her voice was weak. It matched her resolve. But she pulled her shoulders back and stood taller to make up for her voice with her stance.

~

Gage stared at the woman before him. He'd pursued her for weeks. He was drawn to her at first by her smile. It lit up the room, though she didn't smile often. Her long blonde curls bounced when she walked, and he would swear she was a true blonde. He hadn't had the opportunity yet to be certain, but his heart pounded at the possibility he might get his wish tonight.

Kayla didn't talk much. They worked at the same police station, so he saw her nearly every day, but they usually only exchanged a few sentences. She came to the club often, but she was quiet there also, at least quieter than most women. She had friends he often saw her hanging out with, but none seemed to be super close to her.

Kayla Temple was a mystery, one Gage had been dying to solve. She dropped into the scene from out of thin air two years ago and took up residence at both the police station and later the club, Extreme. He knew because he too had returned to Vegas two years ago. They'd started work in the police academy division within the same month.

He reached for her other hand and walked backward into the cove where the St. Andrew's cross had been vacated. The room had three sides, intentionally leaving the fourth open to viewers.

When he reached the cross, he leaned against it and lifted Kayla's chin again. This woman had a story. "You sure about this? You seem awfully reluctant."

"I'm sure, Sir. It's just been a while."

"Okay. Safe word?"

"Red, Sir."

"Good. Use it. Yellow if you need me to slow down."

"Yes, Sir."

He released her hands and trailed his fingers up her arms, noticing the goose bumps that rose in his wake. "Can I remove your dress, Kayla? I don't like to flog through clothes. I need to see my results as I go along to ensure I'm not hitting too hard or too soft."

"Um, yes." She flinched, a tiny jerk another Dom might not have noticed.

So, nudity is an issue for her. Noted. Besides not having seen her pussy, he also hadn't seen her nipples. She dressed to fit in at the club, but she never removed all her clothes. At least not that Gage had been present for.

He circled behind her, keeping both hands on her skin at all times. He'd never seen her this nervous. He'd spanked her twice, and she hadn't been so unsettled. He lifted the bottom hem of her loose skirt and pushed it up her body, intentionally keeping his palms on her skin to graze over the contours of her hips, the dip in her stomach, and then the swell of the sides of her breasts.

She lifted her arms when he nudged her biceps.

He whisked the thin, silky, black material over her head and gripped it with one hand. Smooth, pale, unblemished skin. With his free hand he stroked one finger down her spine. This was the most of her he'd ever seen. And she still wore a matching black lace thong and bra. He wouldn't push his luck with those last items of clothing, assuming she would balk at removing them.

Gage draped the dress over the back of a nearby chair and set his palms on Kayla's hips to guide her to the padded area at the base of the cross. "Reach up and grab the ropes, baby." He couldn't seem to release her, and he smoothed his palms up her body again as she followed his instructions.

She shivered, making him smile. Her hesitation was palpable.

"You okay, Kayla?"

"Yes, Sir."

Something about the way she fell into the role and called him Sir didn't ring quite right. He'd dominated many women over the last two years since he'd joined Extreme. Most referred to him as Sir. But coming from Kayla, it sounded forced. Awkward. Untrue. Not that she wasn't submissive. It was just the way she said the word *Sir* that didn't suit her.

He shook the idea away and caressed his hands up her arms, barely stroking the sides of her breasts on the way by. When he reached her hands, he wrapped his around them. "Hold on to the loops. Don't let go."

"Okay, Sir."

Finally, he released her, reluctantly. He'd dreamed of doing this with her for months. How had he gotten so lucky? He stepped back and picked up the softest flogger he owned from his bag. Her skin was so pale, and he had no intention of doing anything to change that. He wanted his marks to last hours, not days. Whenever he flogged someone for the first time, he took extra care. But with Kayla he was more cautious, in part due to her obvious nervousness and in part due to his desire to make this the first of many experiences with her.

She might think she was asking for a one-night scene, but Gage had other ideas. His cock had other ideas. The shaft was stiff and tight inside his jeans. If he didn't think she would run, he would undo the button and give himself some breathing room. But Kayla hadn't asked him for anything sexual. She'd asked for a flogging.

If he wanted things to go further, he was going to have to give the performance of a lifetime.

And Kayla seemed as though she might be receptive to the idea. After all, she'd come to him—again. And her nervousness was obvious, though it may have had more to do with the requested flogging than any actual desire to have something more with Gage.

He stepped closer, trailing the ends of the flogger up her spine and across her shoulders, watching as she shivered again. He leaned close to her face. "Spread your legs farther, baby."

She complied, separating her thighs slightly. Not as much as he'd like, but it was something.

He leaned over her shoulder to watch her chest rise and fall, his cheek next to hers, his gaze landing on her breasts. The nipples were hidden under the edge of the lace, but the creamy white skin swelling from the top made him lick his lips. For someone as petite as Kayla, she had full breasts. "Relax. How many times have you seen me flog someone?"

"Several, Sir."

"Have I ever hurt the sub?"

"No, Sir."

"And I won't hurt you either. Never." He turned to face her. Her lower lip was between her teeth, and she nodded. "Kayla?"

"Yes, Sir?"

"You don't have to do this. You look like you'd rather run from the room. If you aren't ready…"

"No. I'm ready. I want this." Her words fell out from between her lips fast. She twisted her head to look at him. "I'm good."

"Okay." He stepped back. "I'll start at the top and work my way down. You'll use your safe word if you need to."

"Yes, Sir."

He lifted the flogger and flicked his wrist, letting it land across her shoulder blades.

Kayla jerked, dipping one shoulder forward and setting her forehead against the wood of the cross.

Gage snapped his wrist again, crisscrossing the second line over the first. He immediately stepped into her space and smoothed two fingers down first one pink line and then the other. Perfect. Not as hard as he normally flogged a submissive, but hard enough for Kayla's sensitive skin. Not only was she clearly out of practice, but her skin was thinner than some people's. If he hit her too hard, the welts would last longer than he preferred.

Kayla's shoulders lowered as he took the time to trace his lines.

He waited for her breathing to resume a normal pace, and then he took a step back and flicked the leather through the air again, this time beneath the first two marks.

Kayla flinched, but only a small whimper escaped her lips.

He watched her reaction closely, deciding she could take more. He lowered the flogger to her smooth butt and swatted her two times across the center of her cheeks.

Kayla jerked forward. She released her hold on the rope with her right hand and whipped it behind her to cover her ass.

Gage took one quick step to reach her. "Baby, you can't do that. It's not safe. I need to know you'll leave your hands above your head so I don't accidentally hit them." He grabbed her wrist and lifted it back onto the cross. "If you let go of the rope again, I'll secure your hands. Understand?"

Kayla sucked in a sharp breath. She nodded. Gage was usually a good judge of where his submissive was in her mind, but he doubted himself for a moment. Was she turned on by his words? Or frightened?

Two more strikes across her ass, and he paused again to set his palm flat on one of her butt cheeks, squeezing the pink welt and massaging the sting. "Good girl. Can you take more?"

"Yes, Sir. Please." Her voice wavered. She didn't look at him.

He released her ass and stepped back. The next line landed at the junction of her ass and her thighs.

Kayla squealed and let go of both ropes to reach for her thighs.

Gage dropped the flogger on the mat behind her, grasped both wrists with his hands, and lifted her arms high above her head. He released one wrist and tugged the other toward the rope, slipping the loop over her hand and then grabbing a separate loose section of rope to wrap around her wrist. The moment he tightened the knot enough to secure her, she screamed.

"No. Stop. Stop stop stop." She tugged at her hand. "I can't. Stop... Red..." Her body bucked as she pulled harder on the hand now attached firmly to the cross. She reached with her other hand and plucked at the rope, attempting to dislodge herself. Her entire frame stiffened as she rose on tiptoes and fought for freedom. She screamed again in frustration...no...fear.

Gage did the first thing he could think of. It came naturally. He flattened himself against her back, pressing her jerking frame into the cross. He pushed one leg between both of hers to get closer, his back completely enveloping hers, one hand wrapped around her under her breasts, the other reaching up to circle her flailing free wrist. "Shh. Baby... Kayla..."

She still squirmed, but her screams settled into moans of frustration. Her breathing came heavy and irregular.

What the hell happened? He had no idea, but for now, all he could do was reassure her.

Gradually her jerking motions switched to trembling.

He held her tighter, his lips landing on her ear. "I've got you. You're okay. Shh… Relax." He couldn't undo her hand yet. He didn't have a free limb to work with. "Deep breaths. Baby, you're okay now. It's over." He loosened his grip on her wrist, gauging whether or not she could remain calm if he released her.

Her shoulders relaxed, her hand went limp, and she let out a long exhale. "I'm sorry." Her words were barely audible.

"Shh," he soothed again, his lips so close to her ear she shivered. His cock had been hard since she approached him. Now it was painfully erect against her naked ass, begging for attention it wouldn't get tonight. He didn't dare move for fear he would bring attention to his plight.

He felt like an ass for experiencing such a reaction while she was clearly freaking the fuck out. But her body… Shit. She was so fucking sexy. He'd been gritting his teeth watching her pale skin pinken under his attentions. His stiff cock wasn't something he could immediately stop when she lost it. "Talk to me, Kayla. I need to know what happened so I don't do the same thing again. No reason to be sorry. I'm the one who should be sorry. I scared you. I just need to know *what* scared you."

She still said nothing.

He lowered her hand to set her fingers on the wood section of the cross at the level of her head. And then he could finally stroke her cheek. He gently nudged her face toward his. He ducked his forehead to set against hers, wanting to hold her as close as possible. "Better?"

He almost missed her subtle nod.

"Good." He smiled. "I'm gonna untie your hand. Hold still." He watched her face for signs of stress. Seeing no immediate distress, he released the grip he had on her chest and lifted both hands to untie her wrist.

The second he freed her, she exhaled and then inhaled deeply again.

He wasn't ready to release her body, and besides, she wasn't either. Instead he ran his palms down her arms and threaded his fingers with hers, pressing them into the smooth wood of the frame at both sides of her face. "Concentrate on breathing." He breathed with her, giving her time to calm down.

Finally, she took a breath and spoke again. "I'm sorry. I didn't mean..." She stopped.

"It's okay. You're entitled to wig out. It happens." He attempted to chuckle, but it came out garbled. "Talk to me," he repeated.

When she pushed against him, he had no choice but to step back and release her.

Instead of meeting his gaze and providing him with the answers to a dozen questions swimming around in his head, she turned away from him, grabbed her dress, and fled the scene.

He stood there staring after her, shocked. *What the hell just happened?*

What made her freak out? Why did she ask to be flogged in the first place? And why did she ask *him* to do it?

He watched her retreating back, knowing there would be no answers to his questions. At least not tonight.

CHAPTER 2

Kayla nearly ran from the cove to the locker room. She shimmied into her dress the minute she stepped inside and leaned against the wall, thankful there were no other women currently around.

Deep breaths. If she'd been asthmatic, someone would mistake her gasps for an attack.

God. What the hell have I done?

She couldn't imagine what Gage must be thinking.

Ugh.

She'd thought she was ready. She'd believed she could withstand a flogging, find release from it even. It had been so long since she'd entered into a deep enough subspace to really let go.

And this was her fault. She couldn't blame Gage. He'd been fantastic—before, during, and after her little meltdown. She asked the right man to do the job, and then she singlehandedly fucked it up. How the hell was she going to face him again?

Someone entered the locker room. A woman she didn't

know smiled at her and kept walking to another row of lockers.

Kayla shoved off the wall, headed for her own locker, removed her bag, and trudged toward the entrance. She took a deep breath, said a quick prayer that Gage wouldn't be standing outside the door, and opened it slowly.

Relief. He was nowhere in sight. She easily slinked toward the front entrance and into the night. She assumed she must have held her breath on the way to her car, because as soon as she sat, she felt light-headed. Her hand shook as she put the key in the ignition. Why? She was safely ensconced in her nice reliable Camry.

She glanced out the rearview mirror, found the parking lot clear, and backed out. It wasn't until she was halfway home that she truly breathed free. What did she think would happen? That Gage would follow her into the locker room, outside, or even down the street? Screaming at her?

Words from the past slammed into her, making her eyes water and blurring her vision. She wiped away her tears with the back of her hand so she could see the road for the last few blocks until she reached her house. *Don't fall apart until you get inside.*

She stopped at her mailbox and emptied the contents onto the seat next to her on autopilot. It was what she did every day. When she pulled into her garage, she shut the garage door behind her before getting out of the car. She shuffled through her mail on the way upstairs to the main floor, cursing at the contents. Leave it to fate to turn a miserable evening into something more heinous. She tossed the mail on the floor in the kitchen as though it were diseased and made the climb to the next floor, the bedroom level of her condo. Dropping her bag, she kicked off her heels and collapsed onto her bed. She stared at the ceiling. "Fuck."

She hadn't missed Gage's hard length pressing into her butt. In fact, a part of her longed to see it. She needed to shake that notion free. No way would seeing his cock be a good plan. Seeing would lead to touching, tasting, and... mounting. None of those were good ideas. If she couldn't withstand a simple flogging without balking, not to mention how wigged out she got from the restraints, how the hell was she going to fuck someone?

"Fuck," she repeated.

Gage was surely pissed. Right? She pictured his face. He hadn't looked anything except concerned. His brow had been furrowed with worry, and he never once mentioned the hard-on he pressed into her ass.

She winced, words from her past flooding her mind. *"You fucking cock tease... You did this, bitch... Don't blame me... If you intend to be a cock tease, be prepared to suck..."*

Tears filled Kayla's eyes, and she was finally in a safe enough place to let them fall freely. She rolled onto her side and curled into a ball, her fingers fisting around a corner of her pillow.

Would she ever be normal again? No, probably not. There was no way to erase the past. The memories were stuck with her for life. That fucking asshole had scarred her in ways she would never overcome.

Gage is different. You know it.

He had backed off and let her go. Why? She wouldn't have believed a man capable of such behavior after she inadvertently rubbed against his dick and made him hard. She was always so careful not to get a man turned on. But Gage... He wasn't like other men. She hadn't done it intentionally. It seemed he'd managed it all on his own. But was she to blame? Intellectually she knew that was all crap, but history forced her to think back on the entire episode to make sure she hadn't encouraged him in some way.

Not that it mattered. She'd never needed to encourage Simon in any way for him to scream at her and blame her for his stiff dick.

But Gage had gone one step further. The man apologized to *her*. That wasn't something she could wrap her head around. He'd taken the blame.

Simon never took the blame for anything, his fault or not. Everything was always her fault. She didn't even have to be present to ruin his day.

Kayla took a deep breath and let it out slowly. She uncurled enough to pull a blanket over her and tuck her pillow under her head. She was safe. She'd been safe for two years. Simon could never hurt her again, and she'd be damned if she let anyone else take his place.

Gage dropped his workout bag on the floor next to his locker and plopped onto the bench at the gym.

"Rough night?" Rider finished tying his shoe and smirked.

"You could say that."

"Kayla Temple?"

"Yeah." Gage shifted his gaze to his locker, opened it, and stuffed his bag into the tiny space.

"I heard you did a scene with her and it didn't go so well."

"That sums it up."

"What happened?"

"Hell if I know." Gage ran a hand through his hair. "She asked me to flog her—"

"Flog her? I've never seen her do a scene like that."

"Yeah, me neither. But she asked." Gage turned toward Rider. His heart beat faster thinking about last night. He hadn't slept well, and he was going to get his ass kicked in the ring today. "I swear I took it slow and easy. I was leery. And she was fine, at first. I think I'm a pretty good judge of a woman's mental state. Or I thought I was."

"You are, dude. The best." Rider scooted closer.

"I warned her if she didn't keep her hands wrapped around the ropes above her head, I would restrain her." Gage slapped his palm over his forehead and rubbed it down his face. "I misjudged her reaction. Severely, apparently. And that isn't like me."

"Not at all. And you shouldn't beat yourself up over it either. Kayla…she has issues, don't you think?"

"Clearly." Gage rolled his eyes.

"Did you talk to her, after I mean?"

"Nope. She bolted. I tried, but she ran."

"But you're going to?"

"Of course. First chance I get. Monday morning, I guess. I don't exactly know where she lives, and I don't have her number either." Gage stood. "Let's get to the ring. Joe is probably pacing, waiting on us to get started. And I need the workout."

Rider stood. "Okay, but I'm gonna kick your ass out there today. You don't look like you slept a wink."

"I didn't." Gage pushed the door to the gym open and headed for the cage.

"'Bout time you guys showed up." Joe stood inside the fence, glancing at his watch and smirking. "Rough night, fellas?"

Rider jumped onto the raised platform first. "Yeah. Somebody failed to get laid."

Gage shoved him into the ring. "Somebody's about to get their teeth knocked out." He pulled his gloves on and then stretched his torso and legs, loosening up. "How's Emily?"

Rider smiled. "Fantastic. Don't think you can weaken me by bringing up my woman. It won't work."

"You two were able to separate long enough to come work out? I'm surprised you didn't bring her to the gym with you the way you've been plastered to her lately."

Rider bounced around, ready to spar. "Ha ha. You're just jealous. If you want what I have, talk to Kayla. I know you're interested in more than doing a scene with her. Whatever skeletons she has, flush them out and make her see you."

"Yeah. We'll see. She hardly says two words to me as it is. I'm not sure she's willing to sit down for a heart to heart." Gage bounced into the center of the ring. He stepped to one side and stretched against the fencing. Thank God for MMA workouts. If it wasn't for the satisfying release he got from sparring with Rider and the rest of the guys at the gym, he wasn't sure he'd be completely sane.

He'd only been back in Vegas for two years. Gage had enlisted in the army straight out of high school and worked for the military police. After two tours in Iraq, he'd been exhausted. When it came time to reenlist, he decided to give up the military and return home.

Within a week, Gage met Rider at the police station and found out the man was hugely involved in MMA. Gage had dabbled in the sport in the army, so it was perfect timing and good luck that landed him at the gym with five other guys from his weight class. The owner, Joe Marks, was a gem. Gage had never made a better decision in his life. Training with Rider and the other four guys in their group had been a godsend after leaving the army.

Even better, soon after meeting up with Rider and establishing their friendship, he learned that Rider and the other guys belonged to a fetish club nearby. The minute

Gage entered Extreme for the first time, he knew he was at home. He'd researched BDSM over the years, intrigued by the concept, but he'd never been to a club. His life was perfect. He had a nice civilian job as a K-9 trainer at the police station where Rider was a cop. He had the instant bond of friends, and Extreme—the best place to loosen up and be himself at the end of the week.

After burying himself in classes and research, Gage had turned out to be a damn good Dom. He got compliments from everyone, including the owner. And all sorts of women asked him to do scenes with them on the weekends. It was common knowledge he had a knack for spanking and flogging. He could ease the stress of anyone beneath his hand as though it were second nature.

And then there was Kayla. The woman had shown up out of nowhere at the police academy a few weeks after Gage's return to Vegas. He knew few details about her. She was clearly beloved by the chief of police, John Edwards, who hired her as the front desk secretary at the attached police academy where Gage's K-9 unit was also located. She was quiet and timid. She was hardworking and diligent. And she was fucking hotter than hell.

Every time Gage passed by her desk, he swallowed his tongue. He felt like he tripped over his words around her. When she smiled, which didn't happen often, he melted into the floor.

He never had the balls to approach her, and she had the most obvious barrier around her that she wore like a shield. It screamed "stay the fuck back."

Not that he didn't speak to her. He did, almost every day, in an attempt to be friendly and make conversation. But her protective shell was thick, and she didn't put off vibes that encouraged more than a professional relationship.

A few months after, when he saw her at Extreme, he nearly dropped his soda. He was pretty sure he did swallow his tongue that time, choking so badly on the sip he had in his mouth, he had to leave the room.

Kayla wasn't just smokin' hot, she was fucking out of this world.

And she'd shocked the hell out of him.

She didn't hold her head any higher than she did at work, nor did she dress as provocatively as other submissives, but her demeanor told him she was indeed submissive, or had been at one point.

Whatever her story was, Gage was intrigued immediately. And still he hadn't had the balls to proposition her. The first time she asked him to do a spanking scene, his dick got so hard he had to jerk off in the restroom as soon as it was over. She never once asked him for anything more than the release from the scene. No sexual overtures were made. So, he kept his cock in his pants and his palms firmly on her perfect smooth ass.

"Dude?"

Gage jerked his gaze to find Rider standing in the center of the ring.

"We gonna spar, or are you gonna stand there stretching that leg for the rest of the day?" His eyes twinkled with mirth. "She has a firm grip on you, buddy. You're going down."

Joe stepped closer to the center of the ring, shaking his head. "I'm losing the members of this Fight Club left and right to women. When will it end?" He threw up his hands in mock defeat. The man had dubbed the six of them The Fight Club a long time ago. And it stuck. The guys trained together and belonged to the same club, Extreme. They had each other's backs. And Gage felt like he had an extended family.

"Eh, we're still here, aren't we?" Rider asked. "I think my woman likes my abs." He clenched his stomach, accentuating his six pack, and patted himself with his gloves. "Don't want to lose this figure."

Gage rolled his eyes. "Emily? She'd fall all over you if you never lifted another muscle. Now let's fight. I have pent up energy to burn."

CHAPTER 3

Gage got to work early on Monday morning. His German shepherd, Thor, stayed right on his heels. He headed straight for the front desk of the police academy, thinking to confront Kayla and ask her to lunch.

She wasn't there yet. Marci, the private secretary for the chief of police, was at the front desk instead.

"Where's Kayla?"

Marci smiled. "Not 'good morning, Marci. So nice to see you.' Just, 'where's Kayla?'"

Gage chuckled. Marci was good natured. He knew she was teasing. "Good morning, Marci. So nice to see you. Where's Kayla?"

"Good one. She called in saying she would be a few minutes late. I'm covering for her until she gets here."

"Then I'm sure you won't mind telling me how she likes her coffee. I'm making a run."

Marci lifted an eyebrow.

"And you too, of course. What can I get you?" Gage grimaced at the way he was handling this situation.

"Sure, stud. Whatever." Marci rolled her eyes. "I'll have

mine black if you don't mind. Kayla is a frufru girl. Let me write her order down for you." Marci grabbed a Post-it note off the corner of the desk and jotted several words. She winked as she handed the note to him. "Good luck, stud. Leave Thor here with me. I hardly ever get to see him."

Gage smiled and walked Thor around the front desk. "Stay with Marci, pal. Be right back." He often took Thor with him across the street for coffee, but if Marci needed some lovin', Gage could share.

Thor retired from the military at the same time as Gage. It worked out splendidly because Gage had worked with the dog for many years and two tours in Iraq. The two of them were attached at the hip, literally. When Gage heard he would be able to adopt Thor and keep him, he breathed a huge sigh of relief. Thor was nine, but showing no signs of slowing down.

Now that Gage worked as the in-house K-9 trainer, Thor came to work with him every day. Everyone adored him, and he was the perfect example to help train the new puppies coming in. Most days Gage wasn't sure who earned his paycheck, Thor or himself.

Gage made his way across the street and back with three coffees before Kayla arrived. He left her iced, decaf, vanilla latte in the center of her desk and tucked a folded note under it. *Lunch* was all he said. No question mark. No name. She would know who it was from, and it wasn't really negotiable.

He liked Kayla. Surely she hadn't missed that detail. He'd been flirting with her forever it seemed, but the woman either never took the hint or didn't return his affections. No. That wasn't true. There was more to it than that. She was guarded. That shield of hers kept him at arm's length. It didn't mean she wasn't interested. She had no choice but to face him today, though. No way was he going to let what happened Friday night slide without addressing it.

The morning was busy. Several new puppies had been placed with handlers recently, and he spent his days training the handlers to work with their dogs. It was the most fulfilling job in the world, and he was damn glad to have spent eight years training military dogs, which made him more than qualified to take this job when he opted not to reenlist.

By the time Gage rounded to the front of the building with Thor looking for Kayla, it was after twelve. He prayed she hadn't already given up on him and left. A grin spread across his face as he found her bent over behind the desk, flipping through a filing cabinet. "Ready?" he asked without hesitation.

Kayla shot upright. "Oh. Crap. You scared me." She set one hand on her chest.

"Sorry. I thought you heard me coming. Lunch?" Thor sat next to him and wagged his tail. If Gage didn't know better, he would think Thor was excited by the prospect.

"I can't do lunch today, Gage. I'm sorry. I was late getting in. It's busy around here, and I'm struggling to play catch up all day." She pulled out a file and sat at her desk. From the corner, she lifted a brown paper bag. "Besides, I brought my lunch," she added as if that made all the difference in the world.

He leaned over the edge of the desk. "You're avoiding me."

"Nope. Just busy." Her gaze shifted away from him.

"Dinner then. You didn't bring that in a bag also, did you?"

He saw her flinch. "Gage, I can't do that either. I don't

even have a car today." She bit her lower lip as she lifted her gaze to him.

"Where's your car?"

"In my garage. It wouldn't start this morning. Luckily my neighbor was able to bring me to work. He's going to pick me up at five."

He? Some guy brought her to work? Why did that make him want to punch something? "*He* is, is *he*? Well, call *him* and tell him not to bother. You have a ride. We'll swing by your place. I'll look at your car, and then we'll go to dinner." He lifted a hand when her mouth popped open, undoubtedly with her next excuse on the tip of her tongue. "Kayla, I insist. We aren't going to walk around here for weeks on end ignoring the elephant."

She nodded, letting her mouth fall shut.

"'K then. Glad that's settled. I'll meet you here at five." He turned toward the front door. As he reached to push it open, he heard her small voice one more time.

"He's seventy-six, by the way."

He turned to face her. "Who?"

"My neighbor." She smiled broadly and turned her back to him.

Gage shook his head, his own smile spreading wider. So, she knew he was jealous. Good. Fine. Let her. She wasn't wrong.

Kayla couldn't think the rest of the day. She'd fully intended to deflect Gage's advances, but the man hadn't taken *no* for an answer. After her encounter with him at noon, she'd been a ball of nerves.

At five o'clock, she grabbed her purse from her bottom drawer and stood.

Gage rounded the corner from the K-9 unit moments later. "Ready?"

She nodded, glancing down at Thor. Her hands shook, and she clasped them at her sides, balling them into fists. *It's just a ride home...and dinner...and a look under your hood...* God, she almost moaned at the last thought.

Gage set a hand at the small of her back as he led her to his Jeep Wrangler. Black of course. And high off the ground. It suited him. And it was functional, which was more than she could currently say about her ten-year-old, midnight-blue Camry she'd bought used when she moved back to Vegas two years ago. At the time she was pressed for funds. Hell, she still was. She wondered how much this repair was going to set her back.

Gage opened the passenger door and held her arm as she climbed inside. He reached for her seatbelt next, and she batted his hand away. "I can handle a seatbelt, Gage."

"Right. Sorry." He shut the door, circled the hood, opened the rear driver's side door to let Thor in, and then settled himself in the driver's seat and turned to Kayla. "Address?"

"Oh, right." Kayla rattled off her address, and before she could give him more specific instructions, he nodded.

"Got it. I know that area." He pulled out of the parking lot and onto the busy side streets of Vegas. He took all the back roads, even some she hadn't ever figured out herself. He really did know where he was going. Neither of them said a word during the drive, making Kayla uncomfortable, but not enough to cause her to start a conversation. The only sound in the car was that of Thor breathing heavily in the back. The poor guy must have worked hard all day.

When they pulled up outside her condo, Kayla quickly opened her door and jumped down from her seat. She used the keypad on the garage door and waited for it to rise while Gage and Thor waited next to her. "You don't have to do this, you know. I can call a tow truck."

Gage frowned. "You may have to still, but let me have a look first. It could be something simple. Hate to see you waste time and money on a tow truck if it isn't needed."

"Okay." How could she argue with that logic? If the man was willing...

He turned to Thor as he rounded the car. "Sit. Stay." The dog obeyed without hesitation, plopping himself down next to the driver's side door. Gage lifted his gaze to meet Kayla's. "How old is this car?"

"About ten years. I've never had a problem with it until now."

"You've had this car ten years?"

"No. Of course not. I bought it two years ago used."

"Ah." Gage rounded the driver's side and opened the front door to pop the hood.

Kayla watched, admiring the way he wore his uniform. He wore the same thing every single day at work, but today she took a sharper notice of how he managed to fill out his black polo shirt and the way his cargo pants hung around his hips. He still had on his utility belt. Even his boots were sexy. They made him seem incredibly masculine.

She startled when he spoke again. "What did it do when you tried to start it this morning?"

"Nothing." She came up beside him and peered under the hood with him, as though she had a single clue in the world what she was looking at. He reached inside and fiddled with a few things, pushing his sleeve up above his forearm. His muscles bulged. Kayla licked her lips while she watched him work. She had no idea what he was doing, but looking at him was not a hardship.

She may have been celibate lately, but she wasn't dead.

She knew a sexy man when she saw one, and Gage was by far the sexiest specimen she'd seen in this lifetime. If only she could get that thought out of her head and stop staring.

He leaned down, and she watched his back ripple under the strain. His shirt pulled tight, and she suddenly found herself wishing he wasn't wearing the black polo shirt at all.

Gage righted himself and turned to her. "Can you try to start it for me?"

"Oh. Sure." Kayla pulled her keys from her purse and squeezed behind him to get to the driver's side door. There was barely enough space for one person, let alone two at the hood of the car, so her front brushed against his ass on the way by. She swore he stiffened his butt cheeks. She even glanced down to stare at them on her way by.

Lord, she needed to stop this infatuation she had for the man. No way was she going to take a relationship with him, or any other man, further than the occasional scene at the club. Anything else would be more than she could handle. Possibly ever.

Kayla exhaled a breath as she slid into the car and turned the key. Nothing. She stepped back out. Thor glanced up, but he never moved.

"I'm betting it's your battery. Have you ever replaced it?"

She shook her head.

"It's very corroded, and since the car isn't even trying to turn over..."

"So I need a tow truck then?"

He shook his head, holding his hands out to avoid touching anything. They were already black in some spots. "Of course not. I'll pop this one out and run it up to the parts store. They can test it and sell me a new one. Won't take half an hour." He leaned back under the hood to detach the battery.

She felt useless, and frankly she was. She knew nothing about the mechanisms of a car.

Gage popped a black, icky box out and held it up. "I'll be right back, and then we'll drop off Thor and go to dinner."

Kayla tried not to react. She didn't want to spend more time with him than necessary. She feared getting to know him any better would make things worse. She never should have approached him at Extreme in the first place. That had been her first mistake. Her second had been letting him talk her into doing it again. And the list went on…

The problem was she trusted him. Not because she knew anything about him other than where he worked, but she'd always had a deep solid trust for anyone in law enforcement. It was ridiculous. But her dad had been a cop, and she'd grown to respect everyone she ever met in this office. When she first came back to town, she was too busy and too scared to seek out a fetish club. It had taken a few months. Once she finally began to attend Extreme and realized both Rider and Gage were members, she relaxed, marginally. Her irrational self said no harm could come to her with two cops in the building.

Even though Gage wasn't a cop, he did work for the police academy. And he was sexy as all get out. It hadn't taken much for her to decide to try a scene with him. She knew he would never tell a soul. There was an ethical code at Extreme. No way would a man like Gage break it.

Now she questioned her thought process. Playing with a man like Gage meant she also had to see him at work. And clearly he was unable to leave the club at the club. Though how could she blame him after the idiotic way she behaved on Friday?

The only reason she'd returned to BDSM was to fulfill her need for the incredible release she got when she submitted to a Dom. Not sexual. She could handle that herself at home. But the physical release from a spanking allowed her to chip away at the emotional burden she carried. Every time she submitted to a Dom, another piece of her stupid past, her bad judgment, her poor choices, and the mental anguish she carried for her part in all of it slowly dissipated.

Everything about it seemed irrational. But she didn't care. She did what worked and to hell with the rest. She never crossed the line with any Dom. Never flirted. Never acted coy. Never offered more than the scene. And no one questioned her. It wasn't uncommon for subs to ask Doms to scene with them without strings. And it suited her perfectly. Any time she felt an inkling of something more —a stiffening in her belly or wetness pooling at the V of her legs—she tamped it down. It didn't happen often. It happened every time with Gage. Even last Friday night on that cross.

God. She needed to nip this in the bud.

"I'll be back in a jiffy," Gage repeated as he set the gross box on the floor behind his seat.

She hadn't realized she'd followed him to the car.

"You want to come with me?"

"No. I mean, how about if I cook dinner while you go? It's the least I can do. Thor can stay with me." *Cook? You don't cook.* She reached down and patted the German shepherd on the head.

Gage grinned. "Sounds perfect." He swung up into his car and pulled away, leaving her standing in the driveway, wondering what the hell her big mouth had gotten her into now.

The only thing she'd been thinking at the time was how

to get rid of his firm ass quicker. Cooking seemed like the most logical answer.

Kayla turned and entered her condo through the garage. "Come on, buddy. Let's go inside." She didn't bother shutting the garage door. It wasn't as though someone could steal her car.

As soon as she entered the kitchen, she grabbed the pizza coupon from the side of her refrigerator and placed an order. No way in hell was she going to subject Gage to her cooking.

~

Gage returned forty minutes later after sitting in traffic and waiting in line at the parts store. He popped the new battery into Kayla's car, found the keys still in the ignition, and started the Camry without difficulty. He didn't bother to knock as he shut the garage door and let himself into her condo.

He climbed up one story to the main level and immediately smelled pizza.

Thor lifted his head from where he lay comfortably curled on the floor next to the kitchen table, but somehow managed to snub Gage with a sigh of indifference.

Kayla stood on her tiptoes at the counter, reaching for some glasses in the cabinet. He admired her ass for a moment, knowing what the smooth white skin underneath looked and felt like intimately. He wondered if she still sported the faint lines of his flogging Friday night and hoped that wasn't the case. He didn't like his submissives to wear his marks that long. And her skin was so fair.

When she turned around, she shrieked, almost dropping the glasses she held in each hand. "Shit. Gage. I didn't hear you come in."

"Sorry. I didn't mean to startle you." He rushed forward, washed his hands at her sink, and took the glasses from her.

"Did you find a battery?"

"I did. And she started right up. You're good to go."

"How much do I owe you?"

"Not a cent." He carried the glasses to the fridge and filled them with ice from the slot on the door, noticing she had a variety of sodas on the island.

"Gage..." Her voice was exasperated. "The battery at least. Come on. You can't just replace my car parts."

"I can." He turned toward her and set the glasses on the island. "I did, in fact." He smiled and then nodded at the giant box steaming next to the sodas. "So, this is your idea of cooking?"

Kayla's face fell, and she fidgeted with several cans of soda as though it were important to line them up properly. "I... Yeah, I don't actually cook... I mean I cook, but..."

What the hell was up with her? She looked like...well, scared.

He frowned. "Pizza's good. I like pizza. I don't care if you cook. I was teasing."

"Oh." She lifted her face and pasted on a fake smile. "Good. It's my specialty."

"Perfect." Gage picked up the box and carried it to the table. He felt like he was walking on eggshells now. This woman was a pile of mysteries.

Kayla followed behind him, set the glasses down, and returned for several cans. "I have a variety of sodas."

He didn't care if he drank water, soda, or Drano at that point. He just wanted Kayla to relax. He grabbed a random can and filled his glass, keeping his gaze on Kayla most of the time.

"I wasn't sure what you might like, so I got meat lovers."

She opened the box, and the rising steam brought with it the delicious scent of sauce and pepperoni.

"I'm easy. I eat almost anything. That looks delicious."

Kayla passed him a napkin and reached for a slice. "Thanks for fixing my car. That's a load off my mind. I was afraid it would be in the shop for days and I'd be scrambling for transportation."

"No problem. Glad I could help. And you do realize I could come pick you up if you're ever in a bind like that."

She lifted her gaze. "Thanks."

They ate several slices of pizza before Gage sat back. "Talk to me."

She exhaled slowly. "Nothing to say, really." She shrugged and didn't meet his gaze. In fact, she ripped the corner of her napkin in tiny pieces, plucking away at the thin paper. "I haven't done a flogging scene for a while. I thought I was ready. Please don't read too much into it."

Don't read too much into it? Was she crazy? Gage hesitated to speak. He didn't want her to freak out more than she clearly already was. Finally, he opened his mouth. "Kayla, look at me."

She lifted her gaze, jerked it really. Her face was flushed a faint pink color.

"I know there's more to this story than you're willing to share. I also know this has more to do with the restraints than the flogging. And that's okay. If you aren't ready to talk about it, I can wait, but I want you to be honest with me. If something isn't working in the future, let me know. If I had realized you were so distraught, I never would have proceeded."

She swallowed and nodded. "Yes, Sir."

He cringed and shook his head. "We aren't role-playing right now. You don't have to call me Sir. We're just two people eating together and talking."

She sucked her lower lip between her teeth in response.

Gage leaned forward and set his elbows on the table. It brought him closer to her. He wanted to read her face. If nothing else, her expressions gave away at least part of what she was feeling. "How long has it been since you were flogged?"

"Um, a few years."

"Okay. See? Easy. We're making progress. How long since you were restrained?"

"The same."

"Okay. So, same person?"

"Yes," she whispered, flinching and drawing back from him.

Fuck. Some bastard scared her. He paused. "You were with another Dom at the time?"

"Yes." Her voice was weaker, and she stood abruptly and carried several things to the kitchen counter.

He took that to mean she was done with tonight's sharing session. *Fuck. Fuck fuck fuck.* Was she raped?

"I think Thor wants to go outside," Kayla muttered.

Gage turned to see his dog standing at the back door. Before he could get up, Kayla opened the slider and let him out. "He might take a dump in your yard. Do you have a grocery bag or something I can use to clean it up?" Gage asked as he stood.

"No worries. I'll get it later." She turned to him and pulled her shoulders back, standing at her tallest. "I'm sorry about Friday. It won't happen again."

"Kayla…" He approached her and stepped right into her personal space, making her back up, but the counter was behind her, and she ran out of space fast. "There's nothing to be sorry about. Your reactions to different stimuli are just that—reactions. You deserve validation for whatever you're feeling at any given time. I've told you that. I'm not

35

remotely angry with you. If anything, I'm rather pissed with myself for not recognizing I had pushed you too far. Forgive me?"

She swallowed, and her eyes went big. "Of course."

Jesus, had no one ever apologized to her before? He thought hard about his next words. This woman was damaged. Someone had abused her mentally or physically or both. No wonder she was skittish and quiet. She was petrified. How had this never occurred to him?

Gage reached for her face with both hands and held her cheeks, gently lifting her chin until she met his gaze. "I want to help you. It's obvious you're looking for a Dom and trying to reenter the D/s world. I assume you recognize yourself as being submissive. I also know this is hard for you. You must trust me on some level, or you wouldn't have asked me to flog you."

She nodded subtly, even though he still held her face in his palms. He didn't think she was breathing.

"How about if I agree to work with you, and you agree to let me in a little at a time?"

"Let you in?"

"Give me more information about your past."

Her eyes widened, and her mouth fell open.

"Kayla…" He set his forehead against hers. "I'm not asking you to bare your soul right this second. I'm only asking you to throw me a bone every once in a while. Can you do that? You choose when. You choose what. I won't pressure you."

She hesitated and then nodded again. "Yes, Sir."

He smiled. "Sir again, huh?"

Kayla lowered her gaze.

"You're very tense." He lowered his hands from her face to her shoulders and squeezed, mostly because it was obvious she wasn't comfortable holding his gaze any longer.

Gage pulled her into his chest and held her tight. He'd give anything to fast-forward in time to a date in the future when he would have more details about this gorgeous, damaged woman. And he would. There was no doubt he would get her to open up. But how long would it take?

CHAPTER 4

Kayla stared at Gage's chest. Damn him for saying and doing all the right things. It made it so much harder for her to separate her feelings for him from her needs. Why did the very man whom she'd chosen to trust with her submission also have to be someone she found unbelievably attractive? And why the hell had she agreed to submit to him?

She'd known him from work first, and later was shocked to see him at Extreme. The first time she ran into him there, she did so literally, coming around a corner and crashing into his solid body. He reached out with both hands to steady her on her feet. When she lifted her gaze to meet his, both of them gasped.

But then Gage smiled, and her heart melted the slightest bit after years of frigidity. His mouth had turned up on one corner that night. "Kayla," he muttered.

She'd instantly warmed, her entire body responding to the man who held her biceps in his huge palms and squeezed. The sexy K-9 director from the police academy was into BDSM?

He was perceptive enough that night to recognize when she panicked. She flinched, knowing her face had gone totally pink with embarrassment. And she stared daggers at him, daring him to say a word about her choices.

Gage's smile had fallen, and his brow furrowed. "Kayla, don't look so petrified. Code of conduct here, hon. We don't discuss what happens at Extreme outside of Extreme. Your secret's safe." He winked then. And she nearly died.

But that was separate. Unrelated to the fact he was the only man inside Extreme she trusted enough to scene with. Well, Rider, perhaps, but he had a girlfriend and was so newly into her, he barely glanced around.

The only strike against Gage was he'd been in the army. Simon was in the military. Where she totally trusted cops, she had a legitimate fear of what the military did to a man. In her experience, it altered them somehow, or else Simon had simply been a jackass to begin with and she was too smitten to notice. The idea made her cringe every time she thought about it. So she chose *not* to think about it.

Gage cleared his throat and brought her back to the present. "Do you have a fear of public scenes?"

She tipped her head back to look up. "What?"

He shrugged. "I thought maybe you were thinking about people watching you Friday night. If that's the case, we could do a scene here, where no one can watch. It might help you get over the hump."

She thought about his words. She didn't have an aversion to public scenes at all. He wasn't hitting the mark. But that didn't mean he didn't have a good idea. Perhaps doing something private would ease her back into the fetish world and keep everyone in the club from knowing she was freaked out. "We could," she muttered.

Gage smiled. "Whatever you need, I'm all yours." He

turned his body so her back hit the counter and he had her trapped against the edge.

And then Thor gave a single bark, startling her. She twisted to see him sitting politely outside the sliding door.

Gage released her and stepped away to let the guy back inside. "Hey, buddy. Find someplace to sit while I take care of this pretty lady." He scratched Thor on the head and turned back to Kayla.

"I can't believe how perfectly trained he is." She glanced at Thor. "I mean, I get it. He was military trained and now works with other police dogs, but it's still amazing."

"Yeah. He's the best." Gage stepped back into Kayla's space and planted his hands on the counter on both sides of her body. "Now, where were we?"

She grinned. "You were about to do a scene with me to prove you are the master of all Doms and can conquer my biggest fears." Holy shit. She couldn't believe she said that.

"By all means then." He stepped back and took her hand, dragging her to the living room area. "How about you lose the sassy and assume a submissive role?"

"Yes, Sir." She giggled, but then straightened her face and took the position more seriously.

Gage led her by the hand to the couch and sat, pointing at the floor. "Kneel here."

Kayla easily assumed the position she was beyond familiar with, though it had been a long time since anyone commanded her in her own home, or anyplace other than the club. She shook, but clasped her hands behind her back to steady herself.

He stroked a hand through her hair, weaving his fingers between sections of curls. "You've had a lot of practice at this. It comes second nature to you. Almost eerily so."

She didn't comment. He was more right than he knew.

"And yet, it's been a while."

"Yes, Sir."

"I suspect two years. That's when you moved back to Vegas, right? Same time I arrived."

He knew more about her than she suspected. And she wondered what rumors he'd heard around the precinct. She'd been gone four years when she returned. A few people at the station knew her and remembered her from her childhood, but everyone was respectfully discreet about her return. She didn't know if they were told by the captain to keep their mouths shut and their questions to themselves, or if they took one look at her and felt the need to zip their lips. Either way, she was grateful. The only person who knew anything about her absence was Chief Edwards. And she trusted him with her life. He would never tell her secrets to a soul.

"But you're from Vegas, originally."

"Yes."

"I think I've heard that your dad was a cop?"

"Yes. He died on duty right after I finished high school. Shot by a kid who was high and selling drugs on a street corner." She dipped her head lower after divulging that to him. Why was she so quick with answers all of the sudden? She never talked about her family.

"God, Kayla. I'm so sorry. That must have been hard."

"Impossible."

"So you left town."

She didn't move. Question and answer time was over.

"Mmm," Gage added. "Okay, I'll stop grilling you for now." He leaned forward, still twirling a lock of her hair with his fingers. "I sense the anxiety you're experiencing, and I assume you feel it most of the time. That's why you need the release."

"I guess." She shrugged. He was spot on, but she didn't want to admit it so easily out loud.

"How about we go back a step and you let me spank you? You'll get the release you need doing a scene we've already done before in a safe environment where you don't have to worry about stopping me if you need to."

She thought about that. It was a good idea. And it had been so long since she'd gotten that kind of release—the last time Gage had done it to her in fact. A few weeks ago. "That would be great. Sir."

"I'll take it slow and easy. We'll do what makes you comfortable this time. Nothing more."

"Okay."

"Kayla, can you take your clothes off for me?"

She lifted her gaze. "How about my shirt and pants?"

He nodded. "That'll work. I don't like to spank or flog anyone through their clothes. I told you that the other night."

"Yes, Sir." She stood and unbuttoned her shirt, wondering what he was thinking, praying he didn't have sexual intent. She could barely handle the idea of being spanked right now. Sex was totally out of her comfort zone. And she was very much aware that although it might seem prudent to work through her anxieties about submission in the privacy of her home, at the same time it opened the door for things to escalate.

Gage gave away nothing while he watched her remove her shirt, kick off her shoes, and then wiggle out of her pants. She set everything on the coffee table and stood before him feeling surprisingly self-conscious.

"You're shaking."

"I'm nervous." She watched his face.

He let his gaze roam up her body. He'd seen her similarly dressed before. Why should tonight be any different? "Nothing happens that you don't specifically request, Kayla. I promise you that. You can trust me."

"Okay."

"Tell me what you need."

"I need you to spank me, Sir." That was exactly what she craved. She knew the release would be the best thing for her current state of anxiety, a state she'd been in for two years if she admitted it fully to herself. Sure, she'd done a few scenes, but nothing that reached deep enough to really allow her into a deep sub space where the world disappeared and left her raw with emotions that would ooze away. She longed to feel that again. She believed Gage could do it for her.

She'd been there before. It had been years. But she'd been there. And she wanted it back.

Would he lay her across the coffee table, or the back of the couch, or his lap? She shivered at the idea of settling across his knees.

"Come here." He reached out with one hand.

She stepped up to his knees.

He set his hands on her waist. "Your nerves are palpable."

"I'm sorry." She tried to stand still, calm her racing heart, slow her breathing. She lost.

"You don't need to be sorry. Just an observation. And I'm wondering what's making you so nervous. I've spanked you twice before. You've had a setback with the flogging." He squeezed her waist, making her feel things she didn't want to feel, a tightness in her stomach that had lain dormant for so long she thought it would never return.

The memory of what it felt like to be a sexual being was so distant she barely recognized it.

"I want to be sure you aren't pushing yourself too far too soon."

She nodded. "I'm good."

"So, in the past, you've been able to enter a sub space that freed you from your stress?"

"Yes." She didn't always call him Sir, but he never commented on it. Perhaps it wasn't important to him.

Simon had insisted.

Gage was decidedly *not* Simon.

She trembled as he tugged her around to his side. "I want you to lie across my lap, baby." His voice had changed, deepened, softened.

Kayla held her breath as she did what he said. Two years she'd been without a Dom. Two years. Gage didn't know it, but he was the best Dom she'd been with in that time. Two spankings at the club, unless she counted the failed flogging from the other night. All the other Doms she'd done a scene or two with before approaching Gage hadn't held a candle to him.

Both of those spankings had been in a controlled environment on a bench. Both times she was wearing a dress and thong. Gage had pushed the dress above her butt to expose her cheeks, but that had been it.

When she lowered across his lap now, her heart pounded. Perhaps this wasn't the best-laid plan. It was more intimate, making it difficult to deny the sexual feelings she always ignored with Gage. He helped ease her across his thighs so her chest hung heavy on one side and her pussy extended on the other.

The man's thighs were hard with muscle. He didn't have soft spots on his body. She couldn't reach the ground with her hands, so she grabbed his shin, proving her point. Even his lower legs were rock solid.

He set one hand on her lower back and held her steady. With his other hand, he palmed her ass, squeezing and molding her flesh while her embarrassment rose at the exposure, assuming he was intently staring at her exposed skin. His hand smoothed down until he reached her thigh, which he continued to massage in the same way.

Kayla sucked in a breath. Try as she might to keep this experience strictly based on the release she would receive from the spanking, she couldn't control the way her pussy clenched as he stroked her thighs. Her nipples puckered and pressed against her bra. And dammit, she was wet. It was a struggle to keep from squirming and drawing attention to her plight. Her legs were separated, but not far. She wanted to squeeze them together and squelch the pressure at her sex.

"You okay?" he asked, his palm spreading wider on her lower back.

"Yes." The word was more of a breath, and she cringed inwardly thinking she sounded needy—and not in the way she'd intended this to go.

"Safe word?"

"Red."

"Use it, Kayla. Don't wait until you're falling apart."

"'K."

Gage lifted his hand, and she sucked in another breath, waiting for the first strike, willing it. She prayed for him to get on with it, hoping his spanking would distract her from the fact she was struggling to disassociate the dormant sexual longing from the present physical need for release. Weren't the two things mutually exclusive? She'd always thought so. They certainly were with Simon. The bastard took what he wanted from her both sexually and physically without a care in the world for the connection.

But now, as Kayla lay across the lap of a Dom who was nothing like her ex, the line between the pulsing need in her pussy and the desire to be spanked faded.

The first strike landed on one cheek, followed quickly by a second swat to the other cheek. Gage immediately squeezed the offended flesh, switching back and forth to soothe her skin.

Kayla bit the inside of her cheek, her eyes wide as she fought to keep from moaning.

Holy fuck. Her pussy grew wetter. She slammed her legs together as the moisture seeped into her thong. *Oh my God. This can't be happening.*

This wasn't at all what she intended. She'd managed to let Gage spank her at the club without this reaction. Hadn't she? Or maybe she'd been lying to herself. But here, in her home, across his lap, practically naked and exposed, Kayla wanted more.

She squirmed against his hand, her mind refusing to acknowledge that what she really wanted was for him to reach between her legs.

"Kayla? Baby? You okay?"

"Yes, Sir." Her voice was weak. She scrunched up her face when she heard her tone. She sounded like a woman in the throes of sex, not one enduring a simple spanking scene.

He continued to soothe her skin, his damn palm making her want even more. She gritted her teeth to keep from speaking, unsure if she would beg him to stop, or to fuck her before she lost her mind.

Gage lifted his hand finally and tapped her thighs where they met. "Spread your legs, baby. You're stiff."

Kayla's breath hitched. She was helpless to deny him. All she had to do was relax her muscles, and her legs fell open on their own, just enough to make her more aware of her pussy when the air in the room hit her wet panties. She whimpered.

"Good girl. May I continue?"

"Yes."

He lifted his palm again and swatted her ass, lower this

time, four strikes that landed at the base of her cheeks and then the juncture with her thighs.

She moaned. *OhGodohGod*. She was so aroused, she feared she might come. That floaty sensation she hoped to acquire from the spanking, the one guaranteed to accompany a rush of endorphins, was totally not what she was experiencing. Not even close.

Nope. Kayla was so fucking aroused, she couldn't concentrate on anything but the need growing in her pussy. And she had no intention of letting Gage know he affected her that way. She pushed on his shin, trying to lift off him. She needed to separate from him. Not fuck him. *Shit*.

He pressed her against his lap, however, his hand moving from her lower back to her shoulder blades. Mistaking her need for escape, he muttered, "Stay still, baby." And in an effort to keep her from wiggling off his lap, he grabbed her thigh, the one closest to him, right at the juncture to her ass and held her firmly. His fingers landed between her legs, too far for him not to notice her wetness.

Gage froze.

Kayla stopped moving, and breathing.

"Baby..."

She listened to his breaths in the still of the silent room, shallow pants that came too rapidly.

"Kayla, do you need more than a spanking?" He slowly eased his fingers lower until he cupped her pussy.

She moaned, an unintentional noise that whooshed out of her mouth without her permission, but Lord, his hand felt so good pressed against her pussy like that. She didn't answer him. But she doubted he missed her cues. They weren't subtle.

Gage nudged her legs farther apart with his pinky and thumb. "You're soaked, baby."

She bit her lip, letting her head hang lower as though in defeat, or in reaction to having been caught keeping this secret from him.

What she didn't do was leap off his lap and run. She didn't push him away or squeeze her legs together. She didn't keep him from flattening his hand over her pussy and stroking his middle finger across her clit through the thin barrier of her thong.

He kept that up, drawing lazy circles around and across her tight nub forever. Her wetness increased. She needed to come so badly, she didn't even care that this hadn't been in the plan. Fuck the plan. She squeezed her eyes together and let herself enjoy the feel of Gage's fingers working their magic across her clit, his other hand splayed on her back, holding her so firmly she couldn't move.

And then his hand disappeared from between her legs, and a sharp sting radiated up her body when he swatted her firmly at the juncture of her cheeks.

Kayla let out a sharp scream. *Holy shit. Holy shit.* She'd never felt anything like this before. Amazing. The combination of his firm hand landing on her ass mixed with the need soaking her pussy...

He spanked her a few more times, harder than before, and then when she thought she would implode, he reached back between her legs, yanked her thong to the side, and thrust two fingers into her pussy.

She didn't implode. She fucking exploded. Her body grabbed his fingers and milked them, the most intense orgasm of her life sending a massive shiver up her spine. All she knew was the way her pussy continued to pulse around Gage's hand, the way her clit throbbed in a rhythm she'd never truly known.

And he didn't stop. He kept thrusting into her, deeper, faster, harder. He added a third finger as she came down from her high, forcing the ecstasy to stay intact, driving her need back to full speed with each thrust of his hand.

Kayla panted as her arousal built back up on the heels of that fantastic orgasm. Instead of pulling away, she attempted to buck up into each thrust of his hand, wanting more, though there wasn't more to give.

When Gage's fingers disappeared from her sopping wet sheath, she moaned, but it was short lived. He immediately set all three wet fingers on her clit and pressed. After only a heartbeat, he rubbed her clit firmly. His hand between her shoulder blades stroked down to the small of her back again, the pressure of his palm holding her steady to take what he offered between her legs.

She hadn't realized she'd squirmed nearly off his lap. She closed her eyes and concentrated on the fingers. The intensity mounted with the pressure. Nothing existed except Gage and his fingers and his hands and the way he played her. And she didn't care.

On a long groan, she reached a second climax, her body stiffening as she came for the second time against Gage's hand. He kept rubbing her clit as she pulsed against him, not easing or slowing until the throbbing inside her subsided. When she finally came down from her second high, her body went limp, threatening to ooze off Gage's lap and slip to the floor like jelly. Her arms and legs shook uncontrollably.

Gage lifted her in his arms and spun her around until he had her nestled in his lap. He leaned back into the couch, cradling her against his chest.

Her damn teeth chattered as though she was cold. Or in shock.

Gage grabbed the throw from the back of her couch

and wrapped it around her, his huge arms tucking her solidly against him. He kissed her temple and then left his mouth against her face.

For a long time, Kayla fought to catch her breath and regain the ability to think. And then the reality of what she'd just done, allowed Gage to do, sank in. "Oh God." She pushed against him, trying to dislodge herself from his solidness.

He held tighter. "Don't. Don't do it. Don't make this ugly, Kayla. It was beautiful and humbling and sexy and so many other things. Don't ruin it. Stay right here and let me hold you through the crash." He kissed her temple again.

She whimpered softly, unable to fight him.

"That's it. Let it go. It was just what you needed. Might not have been what you expected, but clearly it was what you needed."

She breathed. That was all she could do as she followed his instructions, letting herself relax into his chest. His heart beat against hers, almost in sync. She closed her eyes and let her mind relax with her body. After a while, she must have fallen asleep, because the next thing she knew, Gage was lifting her. He carried her, as though she weighed nothing, up the stairs and into her bedroom. He pushed back her comforter and settled her under the sheet, tucking the warm blankets around her.

And then he surprised her by climbing over her and tugging her back against his chest, his arm across her middle, one leg wrapped across both of hers. He held her so tight, she didn't have the energy to question him. A tear leaked from her eye and ran down to her pillow. She prayed he didn't notice.

CHAPTER 5

When Kayla's blaring alarm went off the next morning, she reached over and slapped the snooze button like she did every morning of her life. After she pulled her arm back under the covers, she burrowed deeper and grabbed for that extra nine minutes of sleep.

And then last night wormed its way into her brain. Kayla bolted upright, letting the warm covers fall away. She whipped her head around the room. She was alone. She listened closely. Nothing. She glanced down. She still wore her bra and panties. Her heart pounded inside her chest now that she was fully awake. Gage. Had he left?

Shit. She tossed the covers aside and swung her legs over the edge of the bed. Her body ached, deliciously, every muscle tender from the scene. She winced as she slid off the bed, her ass reminding her of the swats it had endured at her pleading.

Kayla padded to the bedroom door and leaned into the hall. "Gage?"

No answer. She let her shoulders go slack. He'd left. She had no idea if that made her happy or sad. Facing him would be excruciating at the moment, but not facing him was equally maddening.

What the hell had happened?

She turned, shut off her alarm, and headed for the bathroom. As she flipped on the shower and waited for it to heat, she bit her lower lip. She watched herself in the mirror. Her hair was a mess, sticking out all over the place. Just fucked.

Except she wasn't fucked.

So there was that. The nicest man she'd ever been with had given her exactly what she wanted, needed, asked for, and then *not* fucked her. Was that a good thing? Or was he not even interested in her that way?

She was the one who made it clear she needed a spanking. And she was then the one who had gotten aroused and moaned against Gage's lap. She had not asked him to fuck her, and he had not taken advantage.

And now she was the one who had to pull herself together and get to work where she would have to face the object of all these unanswered questions.

And again—fuck.

She moved quickly through her morning routine, showering, drying her hair, and eating some cereal she barely tasted.

She tried not to think, but by the time she got to work, she was a ball of nerves. She slipped behind her desk without making eye contact with anyone—and then she smiled. Right in the center of her desk sat her favorite coffee. And under the coffee was a folded piece of paper. Her fingers shook as she tugged the page out from under the cup and opened it.

Lunch.

Same thing he'd said yesterday. She glanced around. No one was paying attention. She couldn't avoid him forever.

The man had fixed her car and then provided her with the best night's sleep of her life. She could surely do lunch.

After another busy morning, she had her back to the front of the office and was bent over a filing cabinet when she heard panting right before a huge wet tongue landed on her ear. She giggled as she reached out to scruff Thor under his chin. "Hey, big guy. You slipped out on me last night. Do you treat all the women that way?" The words popped out before she could convince herself to stop them. Obviously Thor's owner would be right behind him, in earshot.

She righted herself and turned around to find Gage grinning, his head cocked to one side. "You talking to my dog or me?"

She felt the pink flush that rose up her cheeks, burning her face. And she ignored him to grab her purse. "Where're we going?" she asked to cover up her blunder.

"Deli three doors down. They don't mind Thor."

"Isn't Thor allowed to go anywhere you want? He's a working dog, after all."

"Yeah, well sort of retired though, and I find it easier to avoid the stares." He shrugged and led the way out the front door, holding Thor's unnecessary leash in one hand. It wasn't as though the dog would ever wander away from Gage. The German shepherd worshipped the ground Gage walked on. He idolized him, if that were possible for a dog.

Kayla wondered what the two of them had been through together. She hadn't spoken to Gage about his time in the service, and she couldn't really ask him since she wasn't remotely prepared to talk about her past. Ever.

A bell rang above the door as they entered the deli she'd eaten lunch in so many times in her life she couldn't count them. Even as a small child, her dad had brought her there for lunch. The owners treated her like their own. And thank God she had so many kind people in her court. It made returning to Vegas after Simon so much easier. The police chief had taken her back and given her a job without batting an eye. Eva and Ward, the older couple who owned the deli, greeted her with open arms, never asking a word about where she'd been. As if four years hadn't passed since the last time she'd been in.

At first it had unnerved her the way everyone treated her with kid gloves, as if they *knew* something about her past, but then she decided not to look a gift horse in the mouth and took their kindness graciously. Lord knew she needed the friendships.

And Marci had been a godsend. Kayla'd met her on the first day back at the office. Marci was Chief Edwards' secretary, and immediately Kayla trusted the woman. The two of them were close in age. Marci was married and had a two-year-old son, but she included Kayla in many of her family's activities.

In two years, Kayla had not reconnected with any of her high school friends. She had no interest in getting together with anyone from her previous life. She couldn't begin to explain what she'd been doing since high school and frankly never wanted to share that side of herself with anyone. Including the man currently pulling out a chair for her to take a seat.

"I'll order. You keep Thor. It's crowded in here." He nodded at the menu on the chalkboard above the counter. "Know what you want?"

"A BLT would be great. And iced tea." She reached for her purse to give him some money, but he disappeared through the crowd before she could stop him. Trying to relax, Kayla threaded her fingers into Thor's hair and scratched the top of his head. The dog sat perfectly next to her, but when she stroked his fur, he set his head on her lap. If only people were that reliable.

Gage returned in minutes and settled food all over the table. He smiled as he nodded at the way she held on to his dog. "You're going to spoil him. He won't want to come home with me."

She jerked her hand free of his fur, and Thor immediately popped his head up.

Gage sat in the chair across from her at the small round table. "Kayla, I was kidding." He reached across the table and grabbed her hand to squeeze it.

"Of course." She forced a smile. If she'd stopped to think about his words, she would have realized that. But habit made her forget a man could joke around.

Thor lay on the floor between them with a sigh, his head on his front paws.

"How was your morning?" Gage asked before he lifted his sandwich and took an enormous bite.

"Good. Yours?"

"Good." He set his food down and wiped his mouth. "How long do you suppose we're going to dance around each other?"

She shrugged, picking at the top piece of bread she hadn't touched yet. She'd never been so uncomfortable.

Gage reached over and lifted her chin with one finger. His eyebrows rose. "No pressure, okay? You needed the release. I provided it. It can mean whatever you need it to mean."

Right. In her experience there was no such thing. And her pussy tingled from his touch as though he were still pressing his fingers into her. She nodded but shifted her gaze to the table.

Gage sighed. "Kayla. Look at me." He removed his fingers and lowered both hands to his lap as she jerked her face to meet his. "I'm not going to deny I'm attracted to you. You've probably known it for months. And it's been a damn long time since I've met anyone I was physically attracted to who also happened to enjoy a bit of kink. But I'm not an ass. And I want to help you. Your terms.

"Do you enjoy my company?"

She widened her gaze. How could she not enjoy his company? "Of course."

"Do you trust me?"

"Yes."

"Then how about we spend some time together? Get to know each other? What do you have to lose?"

What do I have to lose? Everything.

She swallowed through the lump in her throat. "I'm a disaster. And I'm not looking for a relationship."

"Noted."

What was happening here? "I'm not even looking for a date."

"Also, noted." The man picked up his sandwich and took another huge bite as though they were discussing a wallpaper choice. "Eat, Kayla." He pointed at her food.

She wasn't sure how she could swallow a single bite with him watching her. His frame filled the entire room. The table looked ridiculous in front of him. He wore the usual black polo shirt over a black tee that pulled tight around his muscles. And as she watched him chew, she wanted to rub her face against the close beard that covered his chin. Here she sat, having lunch with the sexiest man in Vegas, and she was too busy telling him she didn't want to date.

She squirmed in her seat, her legs bouncing under the table as she attempted to squeeze them together. And she watched as Gage polished off his sandwich and sat back in his chair, sucking down a soda.

"Baby, you haven't touched your sandwich." He nodded at her food again. "How about you eat and I tell you about myself."

She scrunched up her nose. "In exchange for what?"

He chuckled. "Not everything I give you has to have expectations of reciprocation, baby." He leaned his elbows on the table. "Have you not realized that about me?"

She should have. The man gave her two glorious orgasms last night and asked for nothing in return. Yet.

In her experience that was unheard of.

He narrowed his gaze again, so she picked up her sandwich and took a bite. It was delicious. Maybe she could eat after all. "Okay, tell me all about yourself." She straightened her spine and took another bite, her gaze locked on his dark face. His full lips made her wonder what it would be like to have them on hers, or any other place on her body for that matter. She shook the thought away as he began.

"I was born and raised here in Vegas."

"Me too."

He smiled. "Look at us sharing," he teased. "I was raised on the poor side of town, though." He grinned bigger. "My parents worked hard, but they didn't have the money to pay for college. So I enlisted in the army when I graduated from high school."

"God, you were so young. That must have been tough."

"Yes. And no. In a way I loved it. It opened a whole new world for me." He glanced down at Thor and continued, "I was interested in law enforcement at the time, so I joined the military police. I had also always been good with dogs. I had trained my own two pups growing up, loving the challenge of getting them to do the strangest things. Impressed my friends every time they came over.

"Anyway, when the army found out how I was with

dogs, they assigned me to the K-9 unit, and I became the luckiest bastard in the military. I got Thor when he was six months old. He was by my side through two tours in Iraq. When I left the army, I got even luckier and was able to adopt Thor. He's been with me almost non-stop his entire life."

"Wow. That's awesome." The man did have an interesting tale to tell, and little did he know his love for pets endeared her to him even more. Simon hated animals. Almost as much as he hated humans. Maybe that should have been a sign to her. Or maybe she shouldn't have gone into that relationship with blinders on. "Why did you leave the army? You're so young."

"I was tired. I worked hard for nine years. When it was time to reenlist, I decided to cut loose. Being in the military, well, being on the front line, it takes a toll on people. I'm no exception. I couldn't stand the thought of giving any more of my life to that sort of death and destruction." He shivered as he spoke.

"Sorry." She felt bad for bringing up such a painful experience.

"No worries. It's part of who I am. And without the army, I wouldn't be where I am today, doing what I love most in the world—training in the K-9 unit."

"You're clearly good at it." She reached down and gave Thor a pat on the head. "Why didn't you become a police officer when you got out?"

He shrugged. "Frankly, I had lost interest. There's a huge difference between the military police and a civilian officer. I knew by then I was way more interested in training dogs than handing out traffic tickets."

That made sense.

"Hey, you managed to eat." Gage reached for her wrapper and balled it up with his. "I'll keep in mind that any time you need nourishment…all I have to do is talk your ear off." The twinkle in his eye made her go soft in all the wrong places…or maybe she needed to admit the places were right.

Gage cleaned off the table and walked Kayla back across the street, Thor at his side. He leaned over her desk as she sat. "Dinner?"

"You're persistent."

"I am."

She tried to think of an excuse to avoid him for the evening. If she let herself continue seeing him this often, she might lose her resolve to keep it simple.

"Did your car start okay this morning?"

"Yes. Thank you very much. I still owe you for the battery."

"Good. You can cook for me. I'll be over around six." And with that, he sauntered off, leaving her speechless and stressed.

She watched as Thor wagged his tail, glancing back over his shoulder to look at Kayla. His owner did not.

Gage pulled into Kayla's driveway at exactly six o'clock. He jumped from his Jeep and waited for Thor to hop out behind him. The dog looked excited when he saw where they were, wagging his tail and circling Gage's legs. "Dude, you're going to give me a complex if you keep this up." He climbed the steps to her front door and rang the doorbell. Thor stuck his nose to the window as if he knew he would get a glimpse of Kayla first.

When the door finally opened, Kayla stood there nervously holding the frame, her face flat. "I told you I don't cook."

Gage smiled. At least she wasn't flat out rejecting him. "And I told you I didn't care."

Thor wasn't patient enough for this conversation from the doorstep. He pushed his way past Gage and nuzzled Kayla's hand until she smiled down and patted his head.

She lifted her gaze and rolled her eyes. "You coming in? Or just dropping Thor off for babysitting?"

Gage entered when she stepped back, and he shut the door behind him. He lifted his nose in the air and sniffed. "Wait a minute. I smell food."

"Yeah, well, I was afraid you weren't kidding about dinner, and a man your size has to eat, so I picked up Mexican on the way home. It's warming in the oven."

Gage took her hand and lifted it to his face, rubbing his close-cropped beard with the backs of her fingers as he gauged her reaction. She still wore the dress she'd had on at work, a sundress that reached to her knees. He loved it. The color, a pale pink, suited her perfectly, and the bodice hugged her chest. She'd worn a short sweater over it at work, but now the sweater was gone.

One of the bonuses of living in Vegas—the weather forced women to be sexy all year.

She didn't pull away from him. In fact, she leaned closer. "Gage," she muttered.

"Yeah."

"I can't do the girlfriend thing." She shook her head and gently tugged her hand away.

"You mentioned that." He ignored her and made his way into her home. When he reached her kitchen, he started opening cabinets and drawers until he had plates and silverware.

Kayla leaned against the island, biting her lip. Thor sidled up to her and rubbed her leg with his head until she set her hand on him and stroked his fur.

Gage removed two tinfoil trays from the oven and set them on potholders on the island. He decided to talk while he worked. "You need a Dom. I'm a Dom. You like me. I like you." He opened the foil tops, letting the steam out. "God, that smells delicious."

"I never said I needed a Dom."

"True. But you do. You've been milling around Extreme for months. I've rarely seen you work with a Dom. I bet it was tough for you to ask me to do a scene with you." He lifted his gaze to watch her expression.

She nodded. That was all he got.

"So, maybe we can eat first, and then we'll play a game."

"A game?" She stepped back, her eyes going wide.

He swore he saw fear in her expression. That didn't set well. "A verbal game, baby. Words. You sit staring at me while I try to piece together your life. That way you don't have to actually tell me anything."

"I don't like that game."

"I'm sure you don't." He forced a smile and dished up the food onto two plates. When he finished, he carried it to the table. "Sit, baby. Eat."

Kayla came to his side and took the same chair she had last night. He liked this new arrangement. He liked eating with this woman while his dog sat at her feet as though she were his new owner. He wasn't even jealous. If his dog liked someone, it said a lot about the person.

They ate with few words between them. Surprisingly Gage didn't have to beg Kayla to eat this time. He wasn't sure if she ate so slowly all the time, or just when she was with him.

When they finished, Kayla started to stand.

He set a hand on her arm. "Stay. I'll clean up."

She nodded, her eyes wide again. Shocked. Hadn't a man ever take care of her before?

Gage put the food in the refrigerator and the plates in the sink, and then he took Kayla's hand and lured her into the living area. He pulled her down next to him on the couch.

She turned sideways, leaned against the arm, and tucked her legs under her, careful to keep her skirt wrapped around her knees. Thor, having followed her, sat again at her feet, sighing as he settled his head on his front paws.

Gage turned halfway around so he faced her. "All right. So, let me get my facts straight. You were born and raised in Vegas."

"Yes, Sir."

He shook his head. "Don't do that. We're just talking. When you sub for me, you can call me Sir if you'd like. When we're just two people hanging out or eating or whatever, we're equals."

She nodded. "Okay."

Gage went back to his inquisition, hoping to gain some insight into Kayla's past. "So, your dad worked for the department until he died when you were eighteen?"

"Yeah." She lowered her gaze and fiddled with the material of her dress in her lap.

"I'm sorry. That sucks. Where was your mom?"

"She died when I was young. Breast cancer. It was just me and my dad."

"Oh, baby. I'm so sorry." Hearing that made his chest squeeze. He knew about sick parents. It tugged at his heart. He wanted to reach for her and pull her close to him, but he didn't.

When she didn't move, he continued. Better to leave that subject behind. "So you worked at the police station after your dad died?"

"Yes." The one-word answers were better than nothing.

"Did you go to college?"

"I got my associates before—"

"Before what?"

She hesitated, her fingers balling into fists. "Before I moved away for a few years."

And there was the gap. "Where did you go?"

She lifted her gaze. "I'd rather not discuss it. It's private and it's painful, Gage. Please leave it alone."

Fuck. He nodded. If he didn't respect a few boundaries, she'd never trust him. "Okay, baby. Then you came back, two years ago?"

"Yeah." Tears filled her eyes, and she wiped them with the back of her hand.

Fuck fuck. "Chief Edwards gave you a job."

"He did. He's like a father to me. Thank God." Her cheeks were pink, but the tears stopped.

"When did you first dabble in BDSM?"

She opened her mouth, and then she paused. It seemed she was thinking of the best way to answer, probably without giving too much away, but not wanting to lie to him. He liked that. "When I moved away."

"Ah, and it was good?"

"At first." She unfolded her legs, twisted her body, and stood. She stepped over Thor and began to pace. Thor lifted his head and wagged his tail, but he didn't get up. "Look, Gage. This isn't going to work. I'm not giving you more than that. I can't. I won't. And it's not fair to you. I'm sorry I approached you and gave you the wrong impression. I didn't mean to lead you on. I only wanted to do a scene."

Lead me on?

The woman had no more led him on than she had spit in his face. Something in her mind was seriously twisted. "Kayla." He waited for her to stop pacing and look at him.

"You've done no such thing. You did *not* lead me on by asking me to do a scene. It's customary to do such a thing, and it has nothing whatsoever to do with the way I feel about you."

She flinched and stepped back.

Fuck. Again, fuck. He shouldn't have said that. He was pushing. "What I mean is that I would do a scene with you any day. I would do a scene with nearly anyone who asked me if I thought it was the right thing for them. I'm incredibly sorry for misjudging you the night you asked me to flog you. That was the first time I've ever agreed to do something I shouldn't have. The reality is I knew better. I could tell you were hesitant. My judgment was clouded by the fact that I wanted to do anything you asked me, even against my instincts.

"I was overjoyed you approached me, and I should have known better. Read you better. Paid closer attention. I'm so sorry, baby." He stood and shuffled closer to her. When she didn't move, he set his hands on her shoulders and waited for her to lift her gaze. "I was attracted to you, and I let that cloud my decision to flog you. I knew better."

She shook her head. "How do you do that?"

"Do what?"

"Turn something that was my fault around and make it yours?"

Now he smiled. "Baby, no matter what, and above all else, as a Dom it's my responsibility to see to the needs of a submissive in my care. Not hers. You have every right to be angry with me for what happened Friday night."

"Me?" She widened her eyes incredulously. "Are you kidding?"

"Nope. My job. If you give me a second chance, let me in, I promise to make sure nothing like that happens again. Whatever issues you have, we'll work through them. When you're ready to tell me more about your hiatus from Vegas, you will. I'm asking for that chance." He bent his knees to get level with her face.

She shook her head. "I can't do that to you."

"Do what?"

"Lead you along thinking I'll ever be ready to give you more."

"My risk. Not yours." He stepped closer until his face was inches from hers. "You said yourself you felt safe with me. Can you deny you're interested in me?"

"No, but—"

He cut her off. "Then I can work with that. Spend some time with me. If all it amounts to is you conquering some of your fears, it will be time well spent. If you fall head over heels in love with me and can't stand to be without me even for a minute, time well spent."

She flinched. "Been there done that. Got the scars to prove it." She shook her head. "I can't jump into this with you. Not now. Probably not ever. It's too fast. I don't have a good track record making rash decisions."

Ouch. She said everything and nothing at the same time.

"Kayla, I'm not asking you to move in with me and declare your undying love. This may be Vegas, but I'm not planning to drag you to some Elvis church, either. I'm talking about getting to know each other. Safe. Sane. Consensual." He reached with one hand and tucked her curls behind her ears.

She leaned into his touch.

Thank God. She was leery. He got that. But she was also interested.

"You've known me for two years. Have I ever given you any reason to believe I wasn't one of the good guys? I get that someone fucked with you. That's clear. I'm not him. I swear I'll prove it."

She gave him a wan smile. Thank God. It was better than nothing.

"Listen. I promise not to pressure you to do anything. I'll take my cues from you. Whatever you need from me, it's yours."

"Who are you?"

He smiled. "Gage Holland." And then he glanced at his watch. "And I'm late." He released her reluctantly, stepping back a few paces. "There's one thing you need to know about me, if you don't already."

"What?"

"When I'm not at work, I'm usually at the gym. I fight amateur MMA on the side."

"What's that?"

"Mixed Martial Arts." He grinned. "Love it."

"Like boxing?" Her shoulders relaxed.

"Sort of. But rougher. Less rules."

She smiled. "Huh. That, I'd like to see." She softened more under his touch. Good. Great. Excellent. He'd found a topic that didn't make her skittish.

He nearly collapsed. The woman wanted to see him fight? His heart beat faster, and his cock jumped to attention. She was full of the unexpected, and the idea she wanted to come see him made him hornier than hell. "Anytime you want. But right now, the guys are waiting on me to work out. They'll give me shit for weeks if I don't come because I'm with a girl." He chuckled. It was true.

"What guys are those?"

"Well, the owner of the gym, Joe Marks, calls us The Fight Club. And honestly, you probably know almost all of us, because the six of us dubbed The Fight Club also belong to Extreme."

"Really?" Her face lit up more. "Intriguing. Who are they?"

"Rider, for one."

"Rider? Huh. Guess I can see that. You two look almost the same."

Gage lifted an eyebrow at that comment. "You have the hots for Rider too?"

She giggled at that. Her voice sounded like music. She was always so serious. He wasn't sure he'd ever seen her let go. Finally, a subject she found interesting. Who would have thought? "Of course not. Besides, he has a girlfriend."

"Yes. Emily. Attached at the hip." He eyed her closely.

She grinned wider. "No, I don't have the hots for Rider, as you put it. Stop looking at me like that."

He shook his ridiculous jealousy away and continued. "The other four members of our so-dubbed fight club are Rafe, Mason, Zane, and Conner. If you hang around me long enough, you'll meet them all. I'm sure you'd recognize them."

"Is Rafe the one who got married a while back?"

"Yep. He's the one. Katy. You've probably seen her too. Small, about your size, curly brown hair a bit shorter than yours."

"Oh, right. I've met her. She's sweet."

"That she is. And super fucking intelligent too. She's a lawyer."

Kayla's shoulders slumped. "Ugh. My current goal is to get back in school and finish my first degree. I can't imagine how much work and how many years it would take to reach that."

"You're going back to school?"

"As soon as I can afford it."

"That's awesome. I'm sure you'll do excellent at anything you set your mind to." To hell with the guys. They could harass him for a month if they wanted. He had Kayla engaged, her eyes twinkling with interest in several subjects for the first time. No way was he going to leave.

"You need to go." She glanced at her own watch. "What time are you supposed to be there?"

"Now." Ugh.

"Go." She pointed at the door and then turned to look at Thor. "Does Thor go to the gym?"

"Not usually. I'll run him by the house."

"Leave him here with me. We'll go out back. I can throw a stick."

Gage froze at that idea. It would mean he had to come back. God bless his dog. "You don't mind?"

"Not at all. Love your dog."

"You'll think about everything I said?"

"Sure."

"I might be late."

She shrugged. "I'll live."

He hesitated a moment and then decided to go for it. He stepped into her space again, hauled her against him, and kissed her forehead. It wasn't her lips, but it was a start. He released her just as fast, knowing if he didn't, he never would. As he headed toward the door, he turned to Thor. "Be good, buddy. I'll be back."

CHAPTER 6

Kayla sat on the back patio on her favorite chair, her legs curled under her, her head tipped toward the clear night sky.

Thor lay at her feet panting from the two thousand times he'd run across her tiny lawn and brought her back the only stick she managed to find in the yard. She didn't even have a tree. More like an oversized patio with a few feet of grass around it.

She couldn't believe what had happened in the last few days. How had she gone from permanently lonely and depressed to having a huge sexy boxing guy pleading with her to give him a chance? And what was she supposed to do with that?

He said he didn't care how long it took her to open up to him about her past, but he didn't realize the time frame on that was two hundred years. Was it possible he could live with that?

Of course not. Who was she kidding? No one could accept those conditions. That's why she didn't pursue relationships. There would never be a way to avoid discussing a four-year hole in her life.

She took a deep breath and let it out. For the first time in…forever, she felt like maybe she could give herself another shot at life. Gage made her see that. Even though she couldn't possibly continue this farce with him, at least she knew she could come out of the fog and find some sort of happiness.

She was twenty-six years old. She could never be what someone else deserved or needed, but if there was anyone on the planet she wanted to spend time with, it would be Gage. Hands down. His sexy self had starred in more than a few of her dreams since she'd first met him two years ago. But date him? Submit to him? Could she do it?

Could she not?

She'd essentially been seeing him for two days. It seemed like longer. He'd wormed his way into every aspect of her life quickly. Hell, his dog was running around her yard. She'd shared several meals with him. They were already an item.

The sliding door opened behind her, and she turned to find the very man in her thoughts stepping outside. "Woman, you leave your front door unlocked?"

She smiled. That was the first thing he had to say to her? She didn't respond. "You're back."

"And you leave your front door unlocked." He took the seat next to her, pulling it to her side.

"Only when a two-hundred pound hunk of muscle is going to return for his guard dog, and I'm sitting out back."

"Well, it isn't safe. Don't do it." He glanced at the small table next to her where her phone sat. He picked it up and handed it to her. "Put my number in there. And then send me a text so I'll have yours. Next time I'll call when I'm almost here instead."

Next time. She hadn't consented to that verbally yet.

He rattled off his number, and she quickly sent him a text. The vibration of her text hummed in his pocket, but he didn't retrieve it right then.

Thor lifted his head briefly, but then he set it back down. "You wore my dog out."

"I did."

"Thanks. Now I don't have to take him for a walk tonight. More time with you." He turned back to face her.

Suddenly she felt nervous, like a teenager on her first date.

"Did you think about what I said?"

"Yes."

"And?" He leaned forward, brushing a lock of hair from her cheek and tucking it behind her ear.

How was she supposed to say *no* to that? Everything he did was tender and sensitive.

"I suck at relationships."

"I don't." His confidence was swift and startling.

She met and held his gaze in the dim light coming from the kitchen.

He watched her intently, waiting. Not pressuring her with words, but nudging her all the same with his incredible presence and the way he looked at her.

"I'm rusty. And I haven't been with a man in…"

"Two years?"

"Right. About that."

He smiled broader. "So you'll give me a chance?"

She nodded, her bottom lip making its way between her teeth. No way in hell could she turn him down. Her resolve melted in the face of his intense stare. "Like a date?"

"Dating. Like a couple."

She curled up her nose. "You want to have a relationship with me?"

"Of course."

"I don't know, Gage. That's a lot. It's so fast." She curled her fingers into fists, hoping the bite of her nails digging into her palms would ground her. Her heart beat faster, considering what he was offering her.

"We've known each other for two years."

"In passing."

"Long enough for me to know I like you and you to know I won't hurt you."

"I can't date you, Gage. I can't date anyone."

"Ever?" He narrowed his gaze.

"Well, yeah." It sounded stupid when put that way.

"Never. You're never going to date anyone again."

"Right." Her voice was softer.

"Kayla, that's jacked up." He set his hands on his jeans and rubbed his palms. "Do you like me?"

"Of course." She sucked in a breath when she blurted those words too quickly.

Gage leaned forward until his face was inches from hers again. "Look, I know you have issues. Hell, we all have issues. I'm asking you to set them aside and take a chance." He paused and then continued. "I'll make you a deal. I won't so much as mention what happened to you while you were away from Vegas. If it's that painful for you, let's set it aside indefinitely. I also won't pressure you to sleep with me. Take all the time you need. Or if it never feels right, don't take that step. We'll go our separate ways.

"But let me be your friend and sometimes Dom. We can hang out together, eat meals, go to movies, whatever. And in between we can go to the club or do some D/s scenes at one of our houses. Whatever you want."

She hesitated. It was impossible to tell this man *no*.

There was no other person she'd rather dominate her at the moment, and she needed that. There was also no other person she wanted to spend time with outside the office and the club. And frankly, she needed that too. But what he was proposing was above and beyond. "So, you'd take a risk like this, hang out with me, dominate me, befriend me, with no promise of more?"

"Yes." He didn't hesitate.

"Why?" Even though she thought she was losing her mind considering this proposition, she found herself propelled to accept. *He's not Simon... He's not rushing you, pressuring you... Dragging you to the altar and out of town...*

He lifted one hand and cupped her face. "I believe you're worth it."

A flush stole its way up her face, making her skin burn. She had the urge to turn in to his palm and kiss his hand.

Seconds went by. He waited.

"Okay."

The way his face lit up made her sure of her decision. She was nervous as fuck and had no idea how to go about dating someone, let alone a giant Dom, but her heart told her to try.

Gage reached down and hauled her off her chair and into his lap. He nuzzled her neck with his face. "You won't regret it. Swear."

When he lifted his face again, he met her gaze. "May I kiss you?"

She melted, her body oozing into his lap like honey. *The man asks for permission to kiss me?* Two seconds into this new relationship and she was a blithering idiot. All she could do was nod.

His lips met hers, his gaze still holding her hostage. Soft, gentle, and so fucking fantastic. At first he nibbled across her mouth, and then he angled to one side and deepened the kiss, his tongue stroking the seam of her lips. He didn't pressure her in any way, but she opened to him, craving more than he was giving. In fact, she slipped her tongue out to meet his first, delving into his mouth and tasting him for the first time. Mint...and Gage. Pure Gage. The best flavor she'd ever had. He'd gone out of his way to suck on a mint on the way to her house. Just in case...

Simon had never bothered to adjust his breath for her. At least not after the "honeymoon" stage. She'd hated kissing him. And hated it more and more as the years wore on.

Kayla broke the kiss with that bad memory tainting her. She shook the thought of Simon from her head, literally, and unfortunately, made Gage think her weirdness had something to do with him.

He squared her shoulders and lifted her chin. "Sorry. Didn't mean to pressure you."

She shook her head again, harder this time. "No. That was...perfect. I just... It's not you."

"'K." He set his forehead against hers. "Good." He pulled her closer.

She could feel his cock pressing against her hip and sat very still.

"I need to go. You need to get to bed."

She pulled back, stunned. He would leave with his cock like that?

"What?"

"Nothing." She shook her head again. She was making herself dizzy.

"You're going to be a mystery every minute, aren't you?" He smiled. There was no malice in his statement.

"Probably."

He narrowed his gaze. "How many men have you been with?"

She opened her mouth, not to speak but because she couldn't believe he would ask that.

This time he shook his head. "Don't answer that. Sorry."

She swallowed. She needed to grow some balls and give him a few tiny details. If she didn't, this would never work. "One. And he was an ass."

Gage froze, his eyes darting back and forth staring into hers.

She worked hard to hold his gaze so she could watch his reaction.

"Fuck."

That wasn't quite what she expected, but she agreed. "Yep."

He took a deep breath. "Well that explains a lot. No wonder." He lifted his hands from her arms to her face and held her cheeks. "I promise you this will be different. I'm not an ass. I *am* a Dom. And I think you like that part, but I'm not an ass. If I ever do anything, no matter how small, you don't like, you'll tell me and I'll stop." He narrowed his eyes again, as if making sure she understood.

She nodded slowly. She couldn't believe this guy. Was he real?

"Kayla, I don't know what the fuck happened to you, but I can tell I won't like it. Keep it to yourself for a while. It's a good plan. I'll want to know. Later. But for now, just knowing you've had a rough past is enough. It affects how I handle you. Thank you for trusting me enough to tell me that."

She decided to speak up. "See, I don't really want to affect how you handle me. I'm a grown woman. I don't want kid gloves."

He grinned. "And when it's appropriate, I'll keep that in mind." That was all he said.

Jesus. She was in so much trouble. Already she'd

divulged way more than she ever expected to tell any human in this lifetime. She'd agreed to make something of this relationship with Gage not ten minutes ago, and she was in so deep she wasn't sure she would ever escape.

She also wasn't sure she ever wanted to.

Gage drove home with his hands gripping the steering wheel as though it might fly out the window if he didn't hold on tight. And it was entirely possible. The windows were down, after all. Partly because Thor loved to sit in the front seat with his head halfway out the window, and partly because Gage needed the cool night air to keep from combusting.

He'd left Kayla on her doorstep, kissing her several more times until he needed to practically run for his car before he lost his resolve to leave at all. The last thing she needed was for him to pressure her to sleep with him. And by that, he wasn't thinking of the kind of sleeping he'd done next to her last night.

Nope. His mind was swimming with thoughts of having her naked body beneath his, writhing in need.

He would. God, he hoped he would. But he needed to take things slow. Give her a chance to catch up. No way would he make love to her until she was flat out begging him. To do otherwise would be insensitive.

He needed to win her heart over by proving he was not the asshole who'd taken her virginity and damaged her beyond recognition.

He wondered, not for the first time, what she'd been like before she left Vegas. He knew for a fact whatever she'd been through had occurred during those important years in her early twenties. Wherever she'd been. With whatever jerk she'd been with.

He pulled into his driveway and shut off the engine. For a minute, he stared out the windshield, still thinking. Kayla was finally his. At least for now. And that was something.

Deep breaths. He needed to get acquainted with his hand soon before his balls protested. He'd taken a shower at the gym before returning to her, but now he needed another one. Cold. And that wouldn't even do it.

Finally, he opened the door. Not because his mind had stopped running away, but because Thor nudged him with his wet nose as if to say, "What gives, man. Let's get out."

Gage let the dog out, waited for him to do his business in the front yard, and then let them both into the house. The dog hung his head as they made their way back to the bedroom. "Dude, I miss her too. Let's see how long it takes to convince her to sleep over, yeah?" He smiled down at the dog, who had no idea what his owner was talking about.

Thor wagged his tail and lifted his face. He didn't actually understand English, did he?

The cold shower did nothing to help ease Gage's stiff cock. Nor did the hand job under the cascade of water. When he lay down naked on his sheet, not bothering to pull anything over his still-heated skin, he stared at the ceiling for a long time.

It was late. That didn't change how fast and furiously his mind raced.

Someone had hurt Kayla, damaged her, permanently. He was certain the scars were deep.

And not just someone, but the only someone she'd ever been with.

Fucking bastard. Was it one time? Or over the course of months, or even years?

He cringed, knowing deep inside the answer to that question was years. She'd been gone from Vegas four years. *Four years.* That long? That was a long time to live under the thumb of a bastard Dom. And he didn't doubt the man had been her Dom. She'd said she started submitting at the same time she left Vegas. Which left only one option. She'd left Vegas with a man, a Dom, trusting him, maybe even in love with him. And he'd destroyed her, torn her apart piece by piece for several years.

Where was he now? Had she run away? Was he looking for her? She didn't seem to have that sort of fear. And that surprised him. If she was that skittish after the cruel experience...if the fucking asshole who'd done this to her was that vicious...why had he let her go?

Unless he was dead.

Gage bolted upright, gasping for oxygen at the idea. Had she killed him?

Instead of feeling fear over the concept, he smiled. He sure fucking hoped so.

Not that he wanted the authorities after her. Of course not. Just that he didn't want the jackass coming for her. In fact, he hated that he'd left her alone even tonight.

And he needed to get over it. Because no time soon would he be entertaining the idea of sleepovers. His cock couldn't take another night like last night, lying next to her with sheets and shirt and jeans and her damn thong between them.

He lowered himself back to the bed. Relax, Cujo. *She wouldn't be working for the police station if she was on the run or in trouble with the law.*

So, maybe she hadn't been arrested at all. Self-defense. *Or maybe she didn't kill anyone, man. Wild enough imagination?*

Whoever the guy was, he couldn't possibly be a threat

now. She'd left the fucking front door open and hadn't even flinched when Gage returned from the gym.

At least there was that. One less thing to worry about.

He flopped onto his stomach and held the pillow under his head. He closed his eyes, but all that got him was images of Kayla—the way she smiled before he left for the gym, the way she tipped her face to meet him when he returned, the way she opened her mouth to accept their first kiss.

He ignored the parts where she'd been skittish. He would erase those memories from her past and from their future.

Thor huffed on the floor beside Gage. The dog seemed in tune with the situation, as though he was as exasperated as Gage was with this new line of events.

Kayla was his. He would court her like a true gentleman and earn her trust, as a man and as her Dom. It would take time, but he had all the time in the world.

In order to take his mind off Kayla and face a bit of reality, he reached for his cell phone and hit the top button on his favorites list. He knew his mother would still be up. She was a night owl. Plus she hardly slept at all since Dad had his stroke.

"Hey, sweetie. How are you?" she answered.

"Good. How's Dad?"

"The same. He's resting. He doesn't sleep well, but the doctor gave him something new to help him relax and sleep several hours at night."

"What about you? Are you getting enough sleep? I worry about you."

"I'm fine." He could hear the smile in her voice. She was the strongest woman he knew. And he loved her more than anything.

"Are you eating? Do you want me to pick up groceries again and bring them over?"

"That'd be great. But only if you're coming anyway. Don't go out of your way."

"Of course I'm coming. I'll be there tomorrow night. Same as always." He spent Wednesday nights with his parents every week. And usually Sundays. It was hard seeing his dad lying in bed, a shell of his former self, but Gage put on a brave face and talked to him for hours anyway, telling him about his work and his fighting.

Until the stroke, Jed Holland had been a man to be reckoned with. Always a strong Alpha sort, Gage never doubted where he got his dominant tendencies. He had no idea what sort of relationship his mom, Aletha, had with her husband behind closed doors, but he suspected they weren't strictly a vanilla couple.

Aletha loved her husband, and she doted on him as much now as she ever had, even though his mobility was compromised. He still got around some, and his mind seemed to be sharp, but his speech was altered, and the left side of his body was uncooperative.

"I'll make dinner."

"Of course you will, Mom. I wouldn't even argue." He smiled. He'd offered to bring takeout many times, but his mom always turned him down. "See you tomorrow."

After his mom said good-bye, he hung up and set the phone on his bedside table. He rolled over and hugged his pillow under his head again.

Sleep was a long time in coming, but he finally slipped into dream land.

CHAPTER 7

True to his word, Gage gave her time and space. He didn't pressure her. He was attentive, sending texts and calling nearly every night, but he didn't come over or suggest going out.

All she could think about was the kiss he'd given her the last time they'd been alone together. His lips, the gentle way he held her, the look in his eyes when he finally pulled back… It all combined to leave her curious and frustrated.

She wanted more.

But he didn't offer more. Not for over a week. Not until she was chomping at the bit to see him again. Not until her body nearly ached to have his fingers on her, *in her*, again.

Halfway through Wednesday a week later, Kayla got a text from Gage. First, he'd left her coffee again. And then he left her alone all morning, as usual. In fact, she didn't see him once. The coffee was the only way she knew he was in the building. He beat her to work and gave her space, like he'd done every day for over a week. Bless him. And damn him.

She pulled out her phone to read the text.

I have a fight Friday night. If you want to come, I'll hook you up with the other women.

She smiled. As ridiculous as it seemed, she was actually intrigued by this side of him.

She texted him back.

Sounds fun.

Really? You're an unusual woman…

She grinned again.

I assume that's what attracted you to me in the first place.

Nope. It was totally your cooking.

Now she laughed out loud. And right at the moment Marci walked by her desk. "Kayla? You feeling okay?"

"Yeah, why?" She turned to face one of her only friends.

"I've not seen you smile like that, let alone laugh, in the two years I've known you." Marci leaned over the desk.

Kayla couldn't wipe the grin from her face. "Yeah, well." She shrugged.

"There's a man."

Right at that moment Gage walked through the lobby, and Thor bounded around the corner to plant his paws in Kayla's lap.

Marci righted herself, her smile growing wider. "I see." She walked away.

Gage looked at Kayla, cocking his head to one side. "She sees what?"

"Who knows?" Kayla lied, burying her face in dog fur. "You just texted me like two seconds ago."

He leaned his hip on her desk, smiling. "You'll go? To the fight I mean?"

"Of course." She scratched Thor's neck and lifted her face to Gage.

"Will you accompany me to Extreme afterward?"

"Sure." She cocked her head to one side. "What's this about?"

"Like as my date? My submissive?"

"Ah." She smiled. "So, you're claiming me. Is that it? You're worried about me being okay with you claiming me in public?" She tried to look at him with humor, but inside she was nervous as hell. She'd agreed to date him, though. So, she assumed that would include trips to Extreme. And she was more than ready to see him again. If his plan had been to court her until she caved, it had worked.

He glanced down at his thigh and picked at his black cargo pants. "Perhaps. I'd like that. But I wanted to make sure you were okay with it."

Kayla leaned back, her hand still buried in Thor's fur. She spoke softly. "I'm good." And she smiled. It actually felt genuine. For the first time in years, she smiled without forcing it and knowing it would appear fake.

Being at the club with Gage, as his date, his submissive, it felt right. It would be comfortable. She wasn't sure how she could ever fully give herself to him, but as long as he was willing to keep things at her pace and not question her to death about the four years she wasn't in Vegas, she was content.

The rest of the week flew by for Kayla. Gage slipped by her desk a few times a day and sent her several texts, but he didn't pressure her, nor did he see her outside of work.

That alone spoke volumes. He was a patient man. Was it still too fast? Perhaps, but nothing like what she'd experienced with the only other man she'd fallen for. Simon didn't given her an inch from the moment she met him. Not to breathe or to think. He swooped in and took over her world without hesitation. Manipulated her.

By Friday night, Kayla was a mess trying to get ready. Three women were picking her up, and she had run around her condo for an hour changing and changing again. What did a woman wear to a fight? And then how did that translate to the club after?

It didn't help that the stack of mail she'd picked up earlier clearly included the usual dreaded envelope she hated receiving. She'd stashed it under some junk mail and ignored it, not wanting to start the evening out on a sour note. Later.

When the doorbell rang, she was completely flustered. She opened it with a smile, but her hands were shaking and sweaty.

"Hi." The first woman stuck out a hand. "I'm Jenna." Her long dark hair and big green eyes were striking. She wasn't much taller than Kayla, but she carried herself as though she were, with confidence and spunk. She motioned first to the woman next to her. "This is Katy."

Katy reached out her hand. "Nice to meet you." Katy was darker complected with deep brown eyes and unruly brown curls that escaped around her face from a barrette.

The third woman spoke from Katy's other side. "And I'm Emily." Emily had blonde curls a shade darker than Kayla's. And she was the shortest of the bunch.

Kayla stepped back. "Come in." She held the door wider until they were all inside as she assessed what they were wearing and then glanced down at her own clothes. "Maybe I'm overdressed?"

Jenna spoke. "Heavens no. You'll see every sort of clothing at these things. That jean skirt is perfect. Don't change a thing."

The other three wore jeans and cute tops. Kayla felt a little overdressed next to them. "You're sure?"

"Yep." Katy nodded. "We should have thought to call you earlier. Gage gave us your address, but not your phone number. I've been so busy this week, I dropped the ball on that one. Sorry. But you look fantastic. We usually take a bag of stuff to change into after the fights if we're going to the club, which is what tends to happen on Friday nights when there's a fight."

"Good. I was going to ask that. I'm sure I've seen all three of you there on occasion, and never dressed in jeans." Kayla turned toward the stairs. "Give me a sec to get my stuff. I'll be right down." She took the stairs two at a time, grabbed the items she would wear later, and tucked everything into a pink shoulder bag. Lastly, she slipped her feet into black heels that could easily be worn all evening and headed back down the stairs.

The woman were all smiling. "You look perfect," Emily said. "And I'm so glad Gage is finally dating. Now we can double date, and he won't be hanging around like a third wheel." Her voice was jovial and sweet, and she put Kayla at ease.

"So, what are these fights like? Exciting?" Kayla asked as she let them all out the front door.

Emily responded with a *yes* at the same moment Katy and Jenna both gave a resounding *no*. All three giggled.

Emily grabbed Kayla's arm as they walked toward the car. "We might be in disagreement. You'll have to make up your own mind. I love the fights. I think it's exhilarating watching my man pummel some poor guy to the ground."

Katy turned back to look over her shoulder. "It sucks

royally when the other guy wins, though. And then there's the blood and…just…ooh." She shivered as she spoke.

Jenna laughed. "Not a huge fan either. But the boys love it, and Katy and I make an appearance now and then to be supportive. To each his own. These things are crowded and loud and smelly." She curled up her nose. "But we do have a great night at Extreme afterward. Almost always."

"Except when they lose," Kayla added, assuming that was the determining factor.

Emily shrugged. "Depends. Sometimes even then. None of The Fight Club lose often, but it happens."

The drive to the arena took about ten minutes. Katy drove, her shiny red Honda making Kayla glad her car was in the garage so no one could see it. It was old. There was no doubt about that. But it worked, now that it had a functional battery, and it was all she could afford if she was going to save her money to go back to school.

It was absurd for her to compare herself with anyone. But she knew these women all had college degrees and good jobs. She wanted that for herself. And she would have it too. The damnable detour her life had taken shaved years off her life, literally, but she was back on track and fully intended to pull herself together.

The girls were right about one thing. The noise level in the arena was impressive. It hit Kayla head-on as soon as they opened the door. And it was crowded, like shoulder-to-shoulder crowded. There was no way to communicate over the shouting when they first entered, but luckily Emily grabbed Kayla's hand and led her through the throng to some unknown destination.

As soon as they got to a place where Kayla could see the stage, her eyes bugged out. Two huge men fought each other, sweat pouring off their bodies. One had a swollen eye with a crack in the corner that bled. No matter what she expected to see, nor how many things she'd seen on television, this live, in-person pandemonium was shocking.

"Is it always this crowded?" She leaned close to Emily's ear to be heard and nearly shouted.

Emily shook her head. "Not always. This is a bigger fight tonight. There are a few important names here and a demo at the end of some professionals."

"So these guys aren't all professional?"

"No, none of The Fight Club guys are. They're all amateur." Emily's lips brushed over Kayla's ear as she yelled. It was the only way to be heard.

They kept walking. Finally Jenna, who led the group, stopped several yards from one corner of the stage, or whatever it was called.

Kayla watched intently.

Katy angled to her side and spoke into her other ear. "The fenced area is called the cage."

"Cage. Got it."

"This is a higher weight class just finishing. Then we'll move on to the middleweights. All of The Fight Club are middleweight."

Kayla nodded.

Katy stopped talking while the announcer bellowed several things through the microphone. Then she continued. "When it's their turn, they'll come to this corner between rounds."

Ah, so that was why they'd chosen this location.

"Not that we'll be close enough to say anything, but if you like to watch sweaty men get their brow wiped down, this is the place to be." Katy giggled. "There are worse things, I suppose."

Katy's obvious distaste was comical. She curled her

nose up repeatedly, but she still seemed to be supportive and present for Rafe.

Jenna leaned closer. "I think Gage is actually up first in their weight class, so that won't be too long."

Kayla grew nervous as she watched two more fights. She slowly picked up on the jargon by listening to the announcer. By the time Gage stepped into the cage, she had at least a modicum of knowledge about the sport.

She was not, however, prepared to see his bare chest for the first time. How the hell had she not seen him without a shirt on for so long? Not even at the club. He always wore some sort of black shirt, either a polo or a T-shirt that stretched across his expansive pecs so perfectly she almost drooled. But this...this was unexpected.

The most elaborately designed tattoo circled both his biceps, something geometric. Above the design on his right biceps was an inscription. And another one rested on the left side of his abs. She couldn't read the words clearly from where she stood, but she fully intended to get a much better visual in the near future.

And then he turned around. One shoulder blade sported a beautiful red, white, and blue fallen soldier tattoo with a boot, a helmet, a rifle, and a flag.

Kayla swallowed back the burn in her throat that told her some members of his team had not returned from combat. Not that she hadn't imagined this to be the case, but with the proof staring her in the face, she felt his loss deep in her gut.

She flinched when the announcer called Gage's name. "And now for the first of the middleweight contenders. In the blue, weighing in at one hundred eighty-two pounds, we have Gage 'The Ranger' Holland..." He continued listing Gage's accomplishments as well as those of his opponent.

Kayla pulled from her reverie and found herself inching forward, trying to get closer. She watched Gage bounce around in his corner, his back to her. She didn't think he'd seen her, but that was probably just as well since she felt kind of foolish, like some sort of groupie.

When the bell rang and the fight started, Kayla flinched. The opponent swung fast, knocking Gage to one side with a hit to the side of his head. She must have screamed, or growled.

Emily giggled in her ear. "He's okay. It's normal. Gage takes a while to get in the groove. He likes to let the other guy throw a few punches first so he can learn his style. He'll get a handle on it in a minute."

After a few more punches and kicks that did no real harm, Gage swept his foot out and knocked his opponent to the ground.

Kayla jumped so she could see better, as illogical as that was since it lasted less than a second. She found herself pushing through the crowd until she came within a few feet of the stage. There were chairs, but no one was sitting in them. She found Gage on the ground wrestling the other guy as though trying to pin him.

Emily must have made her way to the front in Kayla's wake. She was right next to her in a heartbeat, her hand on Kayla's arm. "That's called a takedown. He'll try to get the other guy to a point where he either can't get up or the referee calls it."

Whatever it was, it was intense. Gage was on top of the other man, straddling his body. The guy was bucking against Gage and defending his face against the blows. Suddenly he twisted to one side and managed to throw Gage off. In seconds, they were both standing once again, circling each other. They each threw several punches and kicks. When Gage grabbed the guy around the neck and fought to take him down again, Kayla fisted her hands together in front of her. The entire thing was exhilarating. She felt the stress as though she were actually in the ring.

"That's a clinch hold," Emily explained.

And then the bell sounded, and Kayla watched as the two men separated. Gage turned and headed in her direction, but she didn't think he saw her. When he reached the corner, a man wiped his face and squirted water into his mouth.

"That's Byron. The cornerman. He works with all the guys."

Kayla nodded.

"They fight for three five-minute rounds with one-minute breaks."

"How do they win?"

"Either one guy knocks the other one out, the ref calls it, or the losing man taps out. If none of those things happen, the referees judge based on some enormous point system I haven't managed to understand, but it's usually obvious who has had the most takedowns, holds, jabs, all of that."

The bell sounded again, and both men bounced on their feet toward the center, circling each other in a sort of dance.

Kayla held her breath as Gage kicked his opponent high, across the stomach. The guy barely flinched, not surprising since they both had abs made of steel. "God, is there anything they can't do?"

Emily nodded against Kayla's shoulder. "Yep. No eye gouging. No punches to the groin. Certain strikes to the head and kidneys aren't allowed. There's a long list, believe it or not. It always looks like anything goes when watching, but not really."

Kayla stood rigid as she watched Gage throw a right

hook that knocked his opponent back several steps. He followed it with several left punches to the guy's chest and arm. And then Gage circled the man while he was trying to get control and wrapped one arm around his neck in a tight grip from behind.

"That's a choke hold. Gage is good at it. He'll take the guy down to the ground in no time." Emily clapped. "Go, Gage," she yelled. She really was the only one out of the women who found this invigorating.

Sure enough, within seconds Gage had his opponent on the ground and then slid over his chest, completely in control. After incapacitating the man, the referee stopped the match.

The booming voice came through the speakers again. "And the winner of this first middleweight match is Gage 'The Ranger' Holland."

Gage bounced into the middle of the ring and waved at the crowd.

Kayla was shocked when he turned to face her, waved, and winked. She had no idea he'd known if she was even there, let alone where she was standing. Next, he disappeared at the gate on the other side of the cage.

Jenna stepped up behind Kayla. "Mason is next. Think I'm gonna be sick."

Kayla twisted to see her expression and knew she was sort of kidding. "That was awesome. You don't think so?"

"Ugh. Not so much. But I'm here. I try my best to put on a brave face."

"Where did Gage go?" Kayla asked.

"Locker room," Katy said. "He'll probably come out here in a while since he was the first of the guys. Usually we go hunt them down, but it's early."

Kayla watched the next match while Jenna held her breath and sometimes put a hand in front of her face to peek through her fingers. Mason was also a strong fighter. In fact they called him "The Bullfighter." He fought all three rounds, but he won.

The next two contenders weren't anyone the women knew, so they relaxed a bit. It was hard to talk over the noise, but in between shouts of encouragement and boos of disappointment, Jenna told Kayla about the floral shop she owned. Kayla also learned more about Katy, the lawyer, and Emily, a high school librarian. They all seemed to know already that Kayla worked with Gage at the police station.

When the next match started, a hand landed on the small of Kayla's back, followed by a chin on her shoulder from behind. "What'd you think?"

She twisted to find Gage's face an inch from hers. Immediately every part of her body went on alert. He smelled fantastic, like soap and shampoo and Gage. His hair was wet and dripped onto her shoulder. He wore his usual black jeans and tee. "Loved it." She smiled. "And congratulations."

"Really?" He glanced at the other women.

Emily giggled. "She did. Thank God. Now I have someone on my side," she teased, hip-bumping Katy next to her. She twisted to the ring as they called the next fighters, including her man, Rider "The Enforcer" Henderson.

Kayla watched, glad for the heels she wore that allowed her to see slightly better than without them. She was constantly aware of Gage's presence at her back, though. He righted himself, but his hands held her waist on both sides, and his mouth tickled her ear repeatedly when he told her little details about Rider's skills.

"Wow. That's an amazing tattoo," Kayla said as Rider

turned away from her and she saw the expanse of wings across his back.

"So, you like tattoos?" Gage's voice was teasing. His hands slipped around her until he held her firmly against his front, both arms crossed under her breasts.

She couldn't breathe, and it had nothing to do with how tight he held her. She couldn't concentrate on anything except how good it felt to have him behind her, touching her so reverently. Like a real date. Surrounded by his scent and his frame, she lost track of what round Rider was in. She never answered the question about tattoos, but she did remember the details of the display on Gage's body. And she hoped to soon see the words across his arm and six pack in the near future.

"He's something, isn't he?" Gage asked.

He might have been, but Kayla's vision was clouded. And it didn't improve any when Gage stroked the underside of her breasts with his thumbs. She took a deep breath and tried to stand taller and maybe dislodge him, but he simply chuckled and held her still. "So wiggly," he whispered in her ear, his breath making her shiver. "Stay still." He squeezed her firmly, and she lifted her hands to grasp his forearms as his thumbs stroked higher against her chest until he suddenly flicked them both across her nipples.

Kayla gasped, her nails digging into his arms.

"Put your arms down, baby," he muttered. "Watch the match."

She jerked her gaze toward the ring, not having realized the world had ceased to exist as she fell under Gage's spell.

"Arms, baby. Put them at your sides. Submit to me."

Here? She lowered both hands, but as she did so, a knot formed in her belly, and her pussy grew so wet she could feel the moisture gathering in her thong. Suddenly she wished she hadn't chosen the jean skirt.

Gage yelled something out to Rider she couldn't hear. To anyone else, she knew it would appear he was watching his friend fight with all his attention. But Kayla knew better. It was a show. The man mastered her in the crowd. His fingers worked magic on her nipples until they were so stiff they ached. He flicked them repeatedly, and whenever no one was looking, he pinched them, hard.

Kayla melted. If he let go, she was sure she would collapse to the floor.

Their first sort of official date had just begun, and already he had her in a state of arousal to rival any other date she'd ever been on. Not that there had been many. She'd been with no one since Simon and only a few men before him, none of whom she'd slept with. Simon had been a piss-poor excuse for a date after about a month of luring her into his web.

Had he ever been as attentive as Gage? She couldn't remember. In the early days, she was so enamored, she would do anything for him. She was a virgin, even though she was almost twenty. And Simon played her so well, she never recognized the signs until it was too late.

Was she a poor judge of character? She thought about Gage, the way he looked at her, held her, made her so horny she couldn't think straight. He managed that nearly every time they were together. Had it only been two weeks? She'd fallen hard. Just like she had for Simon...

Kayla stiffened. Worry ate at her and dampened the good feelings flooding her body. What if Gage was no different? After all, he was doing some of the same things Simon had in the beginning. Overly attentive. Focused intently on her needs. Saying all the right things.

Shit. She needed to slow this down before she made

poor choices. She shoved the obvious differences from her mind—the fact that he hadn't pressured her since she'd agreed to date him, the fact that he hadn't had sex with her even though he'd slept with her in his arms, the fact that he'd taken such care with her when she'd stopped their scene instead of continuing to whip her and paying no attention to her needs. Still she worried.

The match ended as Kayla stiffened further.

Gage leaned to her ear again. "You okay, baby?"

She nodded, too quick, too hard.

He released her and took her hand. "Come on." He lifted his gaze to the other women. "We'll be back." And then he led her away, totally the Dom. He didn't ask her opinion. He simply pulled her by the hand.

He isn't Simon. Not even close. Don't read so much into this.

When they left the main arena and stepped into the lobby, the crowd thinned. The noise level lowered as the door shut behind them. People stood in long lines for snacks or the bathroom, but the hustle and bustle of the spectators was greatly reduced.

Gage pulled her across the pathway and leaned against the wall, situating her between his spread legs and taking her face in both palms. "Talk to me."

She lifted her eyelids. "About what?" God, had he really read her that well?

He narrowed his gaze. "Come on, baby. You froze, like something triggered a reaction you didn't like."

She chewed her bottom lip between her teeth until Gage stroked over the offended flesh with his thumb and tugged it free.

"You okay now?"

"Yeah."

"I get it, you know. More than you think. You've been through something horrible. I'm not stupid. And I'll do my best to make sure I catch your cues and stop when you need me to. But I'm fighting an uphill battle without all the cards."

"I know." Not that she intended to give him anything else to play with, but she understood. Her shoulders slumped. There was no way for this to work long-term. Her past was too painful to share with anyone, and Gage was too astute to let it slide forever. But, God how she wished she could keep him. He was fucking sexy as hell, and he treated her like a queen—when she wasn't busy wigging out wondering about his intentions.

Gage let out a slow exhale. He set his forehead against hers. "I can also read from your reaction that you think I can't take the heat."

She smiled wanly. He was spot on. She knew he couldn't take the heat, at least not forever.

He grinned wider. "I can, Kayla. And I'll prove it to you."

She nodded subtly against his forehead. "There are some things I'll never discuss, Gage."

His gaze nailed her, eliminating everything else happening around them to just dull noise. "Let's worry about that later, way down the line."

She nodded again, but she wasn't sure he understood how important this was to her.

"I'm so glad you came. I wanted to share this part of me. Did you really enjoy it?" Bless him for changing the subject.

"Yep. But I don't think Katy or Jenna are very fond of the sport."

"Nope. Not a bit. But they come occasionally for moral support. Most times they go to dinner or the movies while we fight." He set his thumb on her lower lip and stroked back and forth, distracting her even though he continued speaking as if nothing about his action was making her arousal shoot through the roof again. "Emily enjoys it, though. If you want to come, you're welcome anytime. She usually watches. You can exchange numbers and join her in the groupie section." He grinned.

Kayla tried to catch most of his words, but she was far more interested in the heat rising across her chest from his thumb toying with her lip. In fact, she couldn't stop herself from reaching out her tentative tongue and flicking it across the pad.

Gage groaned. He released her face with his other hand and smoothed it down her back, pressing her into his crotch. His cock bulged at her belly. There was no way to miss it. "You're gonna kill me." He rolled his head back against the wall and then released her, setting her away from him a few inches. "Let's get back inside."

Kayla followed behind him in the same manner they'd exited, him holding her hand in a way that was more possessive than guiding. His pressure on her fingers was more than gentle casual handholding, but not enough that she couldn't yank free if she wanted.

He asserted his dominance with her in a way that was private, between the two of them. The average person around them wouldn't notice.

When they reached the other women, Katy's husband Rafe was about to start. Gage made fun of her as she winced before the first punch was thrown.

Katy scrunched up her nose. "Why on earth do you men find it necessary to pummel each other to death for fun? I'll never understand."

Gage settled behind Kayla again. He kept both hands on her waist, spreading his fingers wide enough for it to seem like he touched her everywhere all at once, but he didn't resume torturing her nipples into stiff peaks. Not that he had to touch the tips for them to swell and stiffen. He did that simply by being in the room. But at least she was able to watch the last fight with some level of concentration.

When it was over, at least the middleweight portion, Gage led them all toward the lobby, through an unmarked door, and down a long hall toward the locker rooms. One by one the other three guys emerged.

Kayla was fascinated by how much they each adored their woman. Considering she knew they were all Doms, it was intriguing how they interacted with each other and their submissives. Each man had subtle moves that demonstrated what Kayla knew to be true about their relationships, but nothing that would let anyone else around in the loop.

There were also two more men who came out. Gage introduced her. "The rest of The Fight Club. Zane. Conner. This is Kayla."

Kayla shook both their hands. She recognized Zane as the man who fought as she was leaving the arena to talk to Gage. She must have missed Conner altogether. He was taller than all of them and older, maybe late thirties.

The ten of them left through a side door and agreed to meet at a local outdoor taco stand for a late night snack before going to Extreme.

Kayla rode with Gage. Nerves got ahold of her. She tucked her hands under her thighs to keep from fidgeting. It was strange being out with Gage as his date this first time. She'd known him forever, but this was different. He easily laid claim to her in a way no one could deny, and it was at once daunting and exciting. There was nothing awkward about the way he always had a hand on her somewhere, and even kissed her temple on occasion. It was comfortable. But was it too soon?

If this idea crashed and burned, which she had every

expectation it eventually would, she'd never be able to step foot into Extreme again. And she liked the club.

She fought to keep her negativity at bay, smiling and making conversation with everyone while they ate tacos and stuffed themselves full of chips and salsa.

By the time they arrived at the club, Kayla was more or less at ease with the group. As usual, Frank was situated at the door to Extreme. For as long as Kayla had been coming there, he'd been the front line. He nodded at all of them and gave Kayla a double take when he realized she was with the group. He smiled on her way by.

The usual man was also at the front desk, Harper. He shook the men's hands and nodded at the women. He too raised an eyebrow when he saw the way Gage held Kayla's hand, but he didn't say anything.

Kayla separated from Gage in the hall and followed the women to the locker room to change.

It felt strange coming to a place she'd been to more times than she could count over the last few years and yet doing it on the arm of a Dom. Not just any Dom, but Gage. She quickly changed into the sexiest dress she owned, wanting to impress him. It was a deep purple and it fit skintight, draping over one shoulder. It was made of two types of material in the same color. Half of it was a solid fabric that spiraled around her body, sweeping over her shoulder, across her chest, and then circling one hip to come around the back and encase her bottom. The final section reached around the front just far enough to cover her sex. In between the solid material was a mesh in the same shade of purple.

When Kayla stepped in front of the mirror to slip her black heels back on, she paused for a moment. She'd purchased the dress on a whim over a year ago, but she'd never actually worn it to the club. She loved how it fit and how she felt in it. But was it too much for tonight? The most provocative part was that she couldn't wear anything under it. No bra. No panties. Either item would show, and likewise it wouldn't take a rocket scientist to realize she wore neither.

Kayla was still staring at herself, pondering her choice when Emily came up behind her. She whistled. "Shit, girl. You look fantastic."

Kayla flushed. "You think? It's not too much?"

Katy stepped around the corner next. "Damn. Too much? Too much what? Material?" She fingered the strap at Kayla's shoulder. "That is smokin' hot on you. Gage is gonna drop his eyeballs."

Kayla squirmed, tugging on the hem. She wasn't quite as sure. It wasn't that she didn't agree with the other women's assessment. She did. Even her boobs looked fantastic the way they were encased behind the solid purple, leaving little to the imagination. But was this a good choice for tonight?

Not that she could back down. She didn't have any other options besides the jean skirt she'd worn at the arena.

Jenna stepped up next. "Don't doubt yourself on this one. It's perfect."

Kayla turned and smiled at the women. "Thanks. For everything. For taking me with you and treating me like one of the gang. I appreciate your friendship, even before I've earned it."

Jenna dabbed at her eyes. "Stop it. I'm gonna cry."

"Yeah," Emily added, "Gage has had the hots for you for a long time. If he likes you, we knew the rest of us would too. You have nothing to prove."

He's had the hots for me for a long time. And everyone knew about it? Wow.

"Let's go." Katy turned to head for the door.

Kayla followed the others, taking the rear, hoping like hell she was making the right choice.

Trusting Gage with her body was easy. She already knew he was a fantastic Dom and an upstanding citizen. She could submit to him easily. But trusting him with her heart? That was an entirely different thing. She didn't trust anyone to that level. Because she didn't trust herself enough.

CHAPTER 8

Gage was stunned speechless when Kayla walked toward him. He'd never seen her in anything close to the dress she wore. Sexy didn't begin to describe her. In fact, he stared at her from his seat with his jaw hanging open.

Finally, he found a brain cell and jumped up from his seat.

"I told her she rocked this dress," Emily said from the other side of the table.

Gage heard Emily giggling, but he didn't take his gaze off Kayla.

The woman bit her lower lip in between her teeth on one side.

He wrapped an arm around her middle and hauled her in close. He set his lips on her ear and whispered for only her to hear. "You look amazing, baby." He flattened his hand and ran it down her back and across her ass to prove what he already knew—she wore nothing underneath the dress.

Gage swallowed as he stepped over one chair so Kayla could take the seat he'd been in.

She sat, but timidly, crossing her legs and tugging on the hemline of the dress. There was no way her ass was covered against the chair, making Gage stifle a moan.

He'd lusted after this woman forever it seemed, and here she was on his arm at his club wearing the sexiest dress in the room.

She lowered her gaze to her lap and fidgeted with her hands until he set one hand over hers and squeezed, holding them both with his own. "I got you a water. Wasn't sure what you might want."

"Water's good. Thanks."

They hadn't discussed the particulars of what their roles would be with each other, and Gage found himself not giving a fuck as long as she was next to him. He'd always thought he needed a nice submissive woman at his side, but suddenly that didn't seem as important as having Kayla at his side. She was certainly submissive, but not like other women. She wasn't a twenty-four-seven type of submissive for sure.

Gage wanted her more than anything, but he also didn't want to fuck this up. And forcing her to be demure didn't suit her. He would do any scene with her she requested, but he couldn't visualize pulling her around by a chain or having her sit at his feet. He wanted her to be whole. She'd been through something very traumatic. Whatever it was, he wanted to eradicate it.

One by one, the others drifted away to dance, chat with other couples, or do a scene.

When Gage was finally alone with Kayla, he turned to face her. He still held her hands in his, stroking her fingers with his thumb. "You're nervous."

She lifted her gaze and licked her lips. "Yeah. Is it super obvious?"

"Not to anyone else, probably." He winked. "I'm astute."

"That in and of itself makes me nervous. Nothing gets by you."

"Relax. Tell me, what makes you nervous? Are you uncomfortable with anything I've done?"

"No. Of course not." She shook her head.

Determined to lessen the mystery, he pressed further, "Are you afraid of doing a scene with me?"

"No."

"Last time we were here, it didn't go so well. We don't have to do anything at all. If you want, we can just sit here and talk. Or we can dance. Or we can procure a public scene, or even a private one if you'd like. Your call."

She balled her fingers tighter. "I don't know what I want."

The honesty he saw in her wide eyes when she lifted her head brought him down a notch.

"Perhaps you'd like me to take the reins and Dom for you for the rest of the evening. Take the choices out of your control?"

She sucked her bottom lip under in a way that made him fight against a groan. "That would be nice, Sir."

Instantly she was in the role.

"Trust me to make good choices, okay?"

"Yes, Sir." Her head tipped down in the way of submissives. Her shoulders visibly relaxed.

Damn.

Everything with her was a guessing game, but he clearly judged this one right. She needed to submit, let someone else control things. Not make any of her own decisions for a while.

He could do that.

Fuck, yes. He could do that.

He just hoped he could control his dick at the same time and not scare the shit out of her.

~

"Let's dance." Gage stood, managing to lift Kayla with him simply by gripping her fists.

She easily moved beside him, relaxing into the feel of his hand at the small of her back as he led her through the bar area and toward the dance floor.

She'd never danced with anyone at Extreme before. Dancing always felt more intimate somehow. Absurd considering she didn't hesitate to lift her skirt for a spanking, but nevertheless, the closeness of moving to the music with a man made her feel completely different.

With Gage, that difference was easy. He stepped onto the floor, folded her hands over his shoulders, wrapped his own around her middle, and swayed to the slow song that played in the background.

There were dozens of people on the floor, some moving more than others. Many were simply making out in their spot. Kayla ignored them to be in the moment with Gage. She let her gaze land on his chest and wished she'd chosen another spot immediately. His black T-shirt was tight across his pecs, and those pecs were damn fine. She almost moaned thinking of seeing them bared earlier at the fight.

"Look at me, baby."

She lifted her face, glad for the reason to shift her gaze, but concerned about what she would find when she met Gage's. Or worse, what he would read in her eyes.

"Love the dress, baby."

"Thank you, Sir."

He chuckled. Though she had no idea why he found it funny when she called him Sir.

He pulled her closer and tipped his head toward hers. "You're not wearing anything under it."

She held her breath. Would he think it was an invitation? She stiffened. How stupid of her. Of course he would. And hell, subconsciously it probably had been.

"Don't freak. I'm just making an observation. It's sexy as hell." He stroked her hip through a section of the dress that was mesh, almost see-through. "The color makes your skin creamier."

She didn't respond. It was hard enough to hold his gaze. The intensity always present in him made her squirm inwardly. Her pussy grew wet at the tone of his voice.

Gage's gaze turned darker, his eyes narrowing. And he backed her up until she landed against the far wall. It was darker in the corner away from the center of the room. "I just had a revelation."

"Oh." That couldn't be good. His revelations were always way too accurate.

"When you submitted in the past, did it always involve spanking or flogging?"

"Usually."

"For punishment?"

She swallowed. Fear crawled up her spine. She didn't move or respond.

Gage waited for an answer, taking a deep inhale.

"Not in the beginning," she finally muttered. And that was true. In the early days, she loved the way Simon treated her. He'd bind her to their bed and fuck her until she cried out with her orgasm. He would arrange her just how he wanted her and make her beg for release. That was how she knew she enjoyed the kink. And then things gradually changed…

Gage shifted his gaze back and forth between her eyes, from one to the other. He held her hips tighter and stroked her hipbones with his thumbs. "And then things changed." He didn't ask a question. He simply made a statement.

She nodded. Things changed all right. For the worse. Slowly, over time, until she couldn't recognize herself anymore, and she didn't know when it happened. There was no defining moment when she stopped being one person and became another. It just happened. Exactly as Simon intended. With precision and the passage of time.

"I think your understanding of submission is not only skewed, but doesn't suit you."

"What do you mean?" she whispered, not at all sure she wanted to hear his response.

"I mean, you think you're a pain sub. You think you need the pain to get release."

She furrowed her brow, puzzled. Wasn't she?

"I disagree."

What did that mean?

He licked his lips, drawing her attention to the fullness of them and wishing he would stop talking and use them on her. And where the hell did that come from?

He didn't seem poised to continue, and that made her tense. "Aren't I?" she prompted. She *did* get release from a spanking. Hell, she could also get it from a beating, but she wasn't going to state that out loud.

"I'm not saying you don't enjoy being spanked, or even flogged. I'm just suggesting you consider another possibility."

"And that would be?" She felt like she was working hard to pull this out of him. Something she wasn't at all sure she wanted.

"Sex."

"What?" The word slipped out unbidden.

He smiled. "When you submit to me, your body responds sexually, baby. I don't hear you screaming out with any non-verbal cues that insinuate you need a good flogging. I only get the feeling you need to come."

Her body went rigid. So many thoughts raced through her mind as Gage lifted one hand from her hip to below her breast. The other he caressed up her body, past her traitorous breasts to her neck. He wrapped his fingers around the back of her neck and tipped her head back so she looked at him.

Her heart beat faster. She breathed harder. And the ball growing in the pit of her stomach suddenly increased to twice the size, tightening her pussy unimaginably. Her ears were ringing, but she still didn't know quite what he was suggesting.

"Think about it, baby." He stroked her chin with his thumb. "Last time you submitted to me you wanted me to spank you, but why?" He waited for her, as if her mouth would work to form words.

She gulped as she parted her lips with no particular idea how to respond. "I like it, Gage. I like the way I can sort of leave my body and tip into a different dimension. It lets me release my stress."

"I hear you. And I'm sure that's true, but isn't that just a substitute for what you really want?"

"What do I really want?" She shouldn't have asked that.

He leaned in closer, his lips only a breath from hers. "To come, baby. Hard. It's a different release, and you don't like to ask for it, but I think you're more of a sexual submissive than a pain sub."

She inhaled sharply. Her eyes widened farther. *Shit. No.* It couldn't be. She shook her head.

He lifted his hand and flicked his thumb across her nipple.

She buckled, her knees unable to hold her up as she moaned. She grabbed his waist with both hands to keep from collapsing, but she needn't have done so. He had her. He knew.

His knee came up between her legs, and he pressed his body into her, pinning her to the wall.

His gaze held hers.

She couldn't look away. She wanted to, but something about him pinned her eyes to his just as her body was pinned to the wall.

And damn, what if he was right?

"It's okay," he soothed, his thumb caressing her chin again. "So many people are sexual submissives. It's not as though you should be ashamed of such a thing or think of yourself as weak."

His words caressed her senses just as his thumb caressed her cheek.

"We can do a pain scene if you want. I can spank you until you either come or slip into a deep subspace. But wouldn't it be better if you let me push you over the edge with my fingers inside your pussy? My thumb on your clit? The release isn't less. It might even be more."

She breathed heavily, her arousal not only flooding between her legs, but soaking Gage's knee at her crotch. She wasn't even wearing panties. Why had that seemed like a good idea?

He toyed with her nipple while he watched her, his thumb drawing circles around the tight nub until all she could focus on was the need for him to flick his finger over the tip.

She shivered. When she couldn't hold his stare any longer, she lowered her face and set her forehead against his chest. Sex wasn't supposed to be in this equation. She'd done scenes with other Doms without feeling anything close to what she felt every time Gage entered a room lately.

There was no denying she needed to come. She wasn't sure about his general assessment of her needs, but right that moment all she knew was arousal like she'd never experienced. And she would do anything to get relief. "Please," she whispered.

"Please what, baby?" He pinched her nipple then, shocking her with the unexpected.

"Oh, God, Gage, I'm so aroused. When you talk to me like that…" She let her head fall back against the wall and rolled it along the cool surface.

"I know, baby. Let me make you feel good."

"Yes." She could barely hear the word and wondered if she'd even said anything, but she must have because she immediately found herself released from the pressure against the wall.

Gage wrapped one arm around her and led her across the dance floor and through the crowd.

She felt drunk, though she'd had nothing to drink.

When she found herself at the entrance to the locker room door, Gage pinned her against the wall again and held her face. "I could make you come right here, in a public scene, or even in a private room down the hall, but I think it would be better to take you home."

She widened her gaze, her mouth falling open. He was going to leave her hanging like this and drop her off at home?

He smiled. "You misunderstand."

And then she realized her error. He hadn't meant to insinuate he would leave her, just that he would care for her in private. She nodded.

"Can you get your stuff from your locker? Or do you want me to have someone else do it?"

She blinked several times. "Right. My bag. Yes. I can get it."

"Good girl. I'll give your thirty seconds." He swatted her ass just enough to get her to move.

Kayla slipped through the door to the locker room, wondering how she managed to get her legs to follow instructions. Whatever kept her upright was a miracle. She beelined for her locker and grabbed her pink shoulder bag with her earlier clothes and her purse in it. She was back at his side in less than thirty seconds.

He smiled and took her hand to lead her through the crowd and out the entrance. Moments later, as though in a daze, she found herself in the passenger seat of his Jeep. This time when he reached across her to buckle the seatbelt, she didn't flinch. Her fingers probably couldn't have taken care of the simple task.

Gage climbed into his side of the car and sped away from the club. "Spread your legs, baby. Lift your skirt for me." He didn't glance her way, and his voice sounded so calm, much calmer than she felt.

As though his instructions were the most important commands in the universe, she did as he said, lifting her dress up under the lap belt and opening her thighs. She looked down to see her legs shaking, and she braced her feet on the floor to stave off the need consuming her.

"Touch yourself, Kayla. Stroke your fingers through your pussy for me."

She reached between her legs with a hand that shook as badly as her legs and stroked through her labia, drawing out more of her wetness.

Gage stopped at a light and reached for her wrist, drawing her hand up to his line of vision. "Let me see, baby." He moaned when he saw her moisture glistening on her fingers. And then he shocked her more when he drew them to his mouth and sucked both fingers in between his lips. "Mmm." He pulled them back out and licked up one and down the other.

The light turned green. How the hell was he watching

the road? He was, though. He released her wrist and resumed driving with both hands on the steering wheel.

"Go on. Do it again, baby. Keep yourself aroused."

She obeyed, adding a "Yes, Sir." When she pressed a finger into her tight channel, she bucked off the seat, straightening her legs and her entire body.

Gage stopped the car at another light. He grabbed her wrist again. Instead of bringing it to his mouth, he lifted it to hers. "That's enough playing. Taste yourself, baby."

Kayla shivered, but she followed his instructions. She'd never tasted her own flavor before. It was heady and arousing. She sucked her fingers clean, learning her blend of salty and sweet, much like a man's come.

When she pulled her fingers from her mouth, Gage spoke again. "Keep your hands away from your pussy now, baby. Set them on your thighs."

She gripped her thighs tight. "Yes, Sir." What she really wanted to do was finish herself off. But he knew that.

"Good girl." He turned to smile as he pulled into a driveway finally. It wasn't hers. She swallowed. "Your house?"

"Yes." He turned off the engine and lifted her closest hand to his face. He kissed each finger. "Okay?"

"Yes, Sir."

"Take a second. Think about this. If it's too much, we can go to your place. But the result will be the same."

She swallowed.

"I'm not going to fuck you, Kayla. That's not what this is about. But I want to make you come under my command so you'll know how good it can be. More than once, baby."

She clamped her legs together and squeezed them as she groaned against her will.

Gage smiled again, a dimple she never noticed before puckering his right cheek. "That's my girl." He twisted around and jumped from the Jeep so fast she barely had time to think before he opened her door and reached in to unlatch her seatbelt. He lifted her from the car and set her on her feet, grabbing her bag from the back. "Can you walk?"

"Yes, Sir." But her thighs rubbed against each other as she made her way behind him to the front door.

All she knew about his house was the front was a dark stone. Even when she stepped inside, she knew nothing else.

She heard Thor padding across the hardwood floor toward them, but Gage hushed the dog with no more than a whisper.

He didn't turn the lights on. He didn't even take a step away from the door before he dropped her bag and lifted her off the ground to cradle her against his chest. He kicked the door shut behind him and took long strides toward a hall to the right and then into the first door on the left. Immediately she knew it was his bedroom. It smelled like him, his own brand of Gage scent, maybe his aftershave or soap or shampoo or a combination of all of those mixed with his personal scent. Either way, she felt more drugged by every breath she inhaled.

And heaven knew she was in a trance she never wanted out of.

CHAPTER 9

Gage set Kayla on his bed, never happier that he hadn't made it that morning. He didn't have to pull back any sheets or the comforter, because everything was at the foot of the bed where it had landed when he got up or at some point last night.

"Kayla, look at me." He flipped on the bedside lamp, illuminating her in a soft glow.

She brought her eyes to center, but they were glazed. She smiled. Her gorgeous curls fanned out around her face on his pillow. He almost groaned.

"You with me, baby?"

"Yes, Sir."

"I'm going to rock your world, but I'm gonna do it with my hands and my mouth, not my cock. Got it?"

"Yes, Sir." She opened her mouth as if to say more, but then closed it. Thank God. If she begged him to fuck her at that point, he wasn't sure he could turn her down. And that wasn't at all what she needed. She wasn't ready. She would regret it later.

Gage did strip off his shirt, though. And Kayla's breath

hitched as she got her second look at his chest. Her gaze wandered over his chest and biceps. "The geometric bands around your arms are sexy as hell." She tipped her head to one side, trying to read his right bicep.

He grinned and turned a bit so she could see better. "Spec ops I run toward gunfire," he said. That part was in all caps. And then he turned the other way and lifted his arm so she could see his six pack. "Brothers are Never Forgotten."

Kayla nodded. "Let me see your back."

Gage turned around and let her gaze at the fallen-soldier tattoo across his shoulder blade. And then he kicked off his shoes, climbed onto the bed, and kneeled between her legs, pushing them open with his knees. He set his hands on her thighs and smoothed them up her legs until they were under the material of her dress. "I want to see you, baby. All of you."

He pushed her dress up over her sex and then her chest before tugging it over her head and tossing it aside.

She took his breath away. He'd waited so long to see her naked, totally bare to his gaze. He'd seen a lot of her, but there was no comparison to completely stripped for him.

Her nipples puckered as he looked at them, the pink tips straining into the air. He let his fingertips graze over the tips and down the bottom swell of her breasts as she squirmed beneath him. "Hold still, baby. Let me explore." As he smoothed his palms over her belly, it dipped. She wiggled again.

Lower still, until he held her thighs with both hands. He gripped them with just the right amount of pressure and opened them wider, eyeing the blonde curls that covered her sex. So often he found women shaved bare or with nothing but a landing strip. But not Kayla. She was natural, and he liked it. He released one thigh to thread his fingers into the curls above her clit. When he tugged, she dug her heels into the mattress and lifted her hips.

He smiled. To command her to remain still would be futile. She would fail and be frustrated, and he didn't want that. So, he did the next best thing and flattened himself between her legs, gripping both thighs and holding them wide, effectively immobilizing her with nothing but his hands. "You won't be able to follow any instructions I give until you've gotten the first one out of the way. I'm going to suck until you come, baby." He didn't wait for a response. Instead he lowered his face, flicked his tongue over her clit, and then dipped into her pussy. He groaned against her skin, realizing immediately that the vibrations set her on edge.

Kayla let out a sharp scream. Her body stiffened. Her hands flew to his head and threaded into his hair.

Gage stroked his tongue up her slit and sucked her clit between his teeth.

That was all it took. Kayla came hard against his face, her swollen nub pulsing against his tongue more times than he could count. Finally, she released the tension from her body and lay limp against the bed.

When he lifted his face from between her legs, he found her panting. Her fingers released his head and fell to the sides. He loved the post-orgasmic look on her—chest heaving, pink splotches on her skin, mouth hanging open, hair spread across the pillow.

His cock ached, but he would ignore it for now. "Lift your hands above your head, baby. Grab the headboard."

She tipped her head toward him, blinking through her confusion.

He would have chuckled if she weren't so precious.

"Grip the rungs, baby," he repeated, softer.

She lifted shaky arms and followed his directive. Her breasts rose higher on her chest as she obeyed him.

"That's my girl. Hold on for me. Don't let go."

She nodded.

Gage closed his eyes and inhaled deeply of her scent. He nuzzled her pussy again, rubbing his nose in her curls until he groaned from her smell alone. She used a girly shower gel, and he loved it. The sweet taste of her come still on his lips and tongue made the moment perfect.

And he intended to take her to that height again, slower this time, and under his direction.

He lifted his face and stared at her pussy. "Legs wider, baby."

She let her knees flop open farther. They bounced against the mattress, and he was certain they were shaking.

When Gage stroked a finger through her folds and dipped it into her tight sheath, she moaned.

Good. It would be easy to take her back to the peak. Instead of playing with her pussy more, he inched up her body until his belly pressed against her sex and his mouth aligned with her nipples. "So pink." He toyed with one, gently pinching and twisting it. "I love the way they respond to my touch."

Kayla moaned, her head tipping from side to side. When one hand flew down to grab his head again, he pulled back.

"Hands stay on the headboard, Kayla. That's my command. You'll leave them there, or I'll stop. Understood?"

"Yes, Sir."

"You aren't ready to be restrained by me yet. The only leverage I have is my touch in exchange for your obedience. If you don't surrender to my demands, you won't get the relief you need."

"Yes, Sir." Her voice was breathy.

"Your job is to keep your fingers wrapped around the spindles. If you can do that, I'll take you places you've only dreamed of. I think you'll find this kind of release more satisfying than the rush from a spanking."

"Okay."

He pinched her nipple and she flinched. He repeated the action, gripping firmer and tugging outward. Each time he pulled, the tip became more distended. Kayla lifted her chest into his palm, silently letting him know she wanted more. Her legs clamped tight along his hips.

Dear God she was gorgeous.

"That's it, baby. Just feel my fingers on your tit." He cupped the second breast and then released the first and switched.

Kayla whimpered. Her head tipped back, exposing more of her neck.

"Ah, baby. That feels so good, doesn't it?"

She didn't respond. He hadn't intended for her to be able to.

He increased the pressure, squeezing, pinching, twisting, until she writhed beneath him. Her nipples were so responsive. She had no idea she was getting the same endorphin high she got from a spanking or flogging.

When her entire body stiffened, he released her breasts and scooted back down her body. She would be too deep with need for him to avoid getting kicked, so he didn't settle his face at her pussy this time. Instead, he planted one arm over her hips to hold her down, nudging her thighs wider and bracing them open with his body, and then thrust two fingers into her channel.

Gage stifled a groan. His cock pulsed against his jeans, threatening an orgasm without contact. Her pussy was so damn tight. Not surprising really, since she hadn't had sex for two years, but still. The tight warmth made him even hotter.

He fucked her hard with his fingers, turning his hand so his palm was up and stroking over her G-spot. With each thrust, he thumbed her clit. He lifted his face to watch her expressions. "Good girl. Keep holding the rungs. Don't make me have to stop."

Her lips tucked under her teeth, and she suddenly stopped breathing.

He smiled.

Two seconds later, she shattered on a scream. Her pussy gripped his fingers tight, squeezing them as though pleading with them to stay inside her.

Gage kept pumping, letting her ride the high for as long as possible. He didn't slow until she shivered and her body loosened up against the mattress. And still, he ended with his fingers deep inside her, twisting gently, keeping her aware of her tightness. His hand was soaked with the force of her orgasm. And he'd never been so fucking happy. Even without his own release, she was totally worth it.

Kayla settled into the mattress. Her face came to center, and she slowly smiled. "Gage." She drew out his name as though it had far more syllables than the one.

"Yeah, baby." He grinned back, still stroking her inside.

"I need you."

He watched her face as she gave him her gaze.

"Please, Gage."

"No, baby. You're in a subspace. Similar to what would happen if I had spanked you. I'm not going to take you for the first time like that."

A low moan from her lips made him fight his resolve. He slipped his fingers from her pussy and sucked them clean one at a time. He'd never get enough of her flavor.

When he finished, he rose above her on his knees, still

settled between her thighs. He popped the button on his jeans, his poor cock nearly bursting to get out. It was a miracle he hadn't come already.

Kayla watched, her gaze lowering from his eyes to his hands.

He lowered the zipper and sprang free. He needed to come. There was no way he would fuck the gorgeous submissive beneath him tonight, but that didn't mean he couldn't reach orgasm. And judging by the look on her face, she was perfectly content with what he was doing. He eased the denim down his hips a few inches to completely release his erection, and then he grabbed the shaft with his hand and stroked from the base to the tip.

His legs shook. He'd never been so fucking horny. And normally when he jacked off, it wasn't with a real live sated woman beneath him staring at his every movement, licking her lips, and squeezing the rungs of his headboard.

Well, never.

Gage watched Kayla while he increased his pace, cupping his balls in his free hand and circling his cock with the other. He gathered the wetness leaking from the tip as he worked, spreading it down his shaft to lubricate it.

He wasn't going to last. It had been so long since he enjoyed a woman. And Kayla had just rocked his world with the gift of submission she'd given him. He was too worked up to last.

When his vision blurred and the world ceased to exist around him, he knew he was too far gone. He stroked harder, faster, firmer, and then he came on a long groan. He tipped his head down to watch his come jut out in long lines across Kayla's belly and chest.

And bless her, she didn't flinch. In fact tiny noises came from her lips, indicating she enjoyed the experience.

As he finished, spent and wobbly, he released his cock

and set both hands alongside Kayla's torso to hold himself up and to give himself the best vision of her sexy body covered in his semen. It took him a moment to catch his breath. "Baby, that's the hottest thing I've ever seen, you on my bed, submitting to me with my come all over you."

She whimpered again and licked her lower lip.

Gage lifted one hand to gather his semen on the tip of his finger. He lifted it to her lips, and she greedily sucked his finger into her mouth. His cock bobbed at the sensuous way she suckled him, her tongue swirling around his finger in a way that made him want those lips wrapped around another appendage.

He popped his finger reluctantly from her mouth and lifted onto his knees again. "Don't move. I'm going to clean you up." As he climbed across the bed, he wondered if his legs would hold him. Luckily, they did, barely. He padded to the bathroom, tugged off his jeans, and washed himself. He grabbed a clean cloth for Kayla, wetting it with warm water and returning to find her in the same position. The only difference was her head turned toward the adjoining bathroom.

She giggled when he set the cloth on her belly and cleaned up his come. The sound made him hard all over again. Ignoring his plight, he tossed the washcloth aside, flipped off the light, climbed onto the bed, and pulled the covers from the end of the mattress up over them both. "Let go of the rungs now, baby."

She lowered her arms.

Gage gathered her small frame against him, her back to his front. He wrapped one leg over both of hers and tucked his top arm around her body to cup her breast.

Kayla sighed.

He kissed her temple and then nudged her hair from her ear with his chin. He set his lips on her earlobe and nibbled around it until she wiggled. "Thank you, baby. That was so fucking hot," he murmured.

She relaxed into his embrace. "You were right."

"About what?"

"That was the same high I get from a spanking. Only better."

He grinned against her face. "Told you."

"I'm ruined."

"Nah, you're just entering a new phase. And I'm glad. If the idea of being swatted in some way or restrained is too much for you right now, at least you know you can submit to me without all that. Let yourself go. Let me bring you to orgasm instead. Same endorphin rush. Same end result. No bad memories to ruin the experience."

Kayla stiffened subtly in his arms.

Wait? Why didn't anything he'd just done to her elicit a single response to her past? "Kayla?"

"Yes, Sir."

"It's obvious to me that while you were away you had a bad experience with a Dom, but please tell me the guy did more than restrain you and beat you." He held his breath after he spoke.

Kayla didn't move an inch. She didn't breathe either for the longest time.

"Fuck," he finally muttered. He pulled her closer, as if that were possible. Did some rat bastard not even bring her to orgasm at all? He wanted to kill the guy. And he wasn't sure he wouldn't as soon as she told him who the fucker was.

In an attempt to remain calm and not scare her, he kissed her temple. "It's okay, baby. I've got you."

She calmed as the minutes passed, her body slowly relaxing in his embrace. Until heavy breathing next to the bed made her flinch. Then she giggled. "Thor."

Gage smiled. "Yeah. Lie down, buddy. Not enough space on the bed for you tonight."

His dog whined, but Gage heard him plop down beside the bed.

"Doesn't he need to go out or something?"

"Doggy door. He's good."

"But I'm in his spot."

"He'll get over it."

Thor sighed loud enough to make them both chuckle.

"You sure about that?"

"We'll see."

"Just when he was learning to like me. He's gonna hate me now."

"Nah. As long as you pet him, all will be forgiven." Gage stroked the skin under her breast. "Sleep, baby." He kissed her forehead and snuggled onto the pillow beside her. He'd never been so content. For a man who didn't have actual sex, it was amazing.

CHAPTER 10

Soft lips nibbled along Kayla's neck, making her moan. *Gage.*

She turned toward him, but he stilled her. "Stay asleep. I need to go to the gym."

"I can go home," she muttered.

"Nope. You can stay here. Sleep. I'll be back in a while. Help yourself to whatever you want if you wake up."

"'K." She couldn't argue with him. The thought of jumping up and heading home right then made her want to groan. Sleep sucked her back under...

Wetness on her neck again. This time too much of it. She giggled as she turned to find Thor licking her cheek. He lay sprawled out next to her on the bed, propped up on his front paws.

She wrapped her arms around him and burrowed in his soft fur. "Hey, buddy. You forgive me?"

The room was brighter than it had been the first time she roused.

Thor set his snout on the pillow beside her with a long

sigh as though he were willing to wait as long as it took, but when the hell was she going to get up already?

Kayla giggled again. "Did I sleep too long for your taste, Thor?" She pulled herself to sitting.

Thor lifted his ears in excitement. His tongue reached out, and he licked her again, slinking forward to nuzzle her thigh. He even batted his eyes.

"Kind of spoiled, aren't you?"

Kayla glanced at the clock. Ten. Wow. She couldn't remember when she'd slept that late. She moaned as she pulled herself out of bed and padded toward the bathroom. She assumed Gage wasn't back yet or the dog wouldn't be in bed with her, begging for attention.

Gage's master bath was luxurious. She hadn't seen a thing of the rest of the house yet, but if it matched this bathroom, it must be nice. Warm brown tiles covered the floor and the walls of the shower. A long vanity with two sinks had nothing on it except a razor and a toothbrush. Gage was a guy after all. What more did he need?

Kayla made her way to a small room with a toilet to the side, and then returned to flip on the shower. She didn't have clean clothes to put on, but at least she could wash away the results of last night's escapades. She shivered as she stepped inside, not from cold but from the memory of everything she'd experienced in the last twenty-four hours. She closed her eyes and tipped her head back to let the hot water cascade down her body.

It seemed cruel that she hadn't had sex with the man who'd given her two glorious orgasms. He was a magician with his hands and his mouth. In fact those same hands had been used to masturbate onto her belly. The memory of watching his intense stare and his stiff cock perform for her made her pussy come back to life. She almost reached down to stroke a finger through her slit before she remembered where she was. The last thing she needed was for Gage to walk in on her getting off alone.

Would he care? She relaxed her shoulders and set her forehead against the tile wall. The coolness felt good against her skin. Not that she had any interest in taking the risk of being caught with her hand between her legs strictly from the mortification standpoint, but Gage hadn't told her not to masturbate.

Simon had. He instructed her to keep her greedy fingers to herself at all times. Said her body was his to enjoy, and he would decide when and where.

Tears fell down Kayla's face as she compared Simon to Gage. Simon was a bastard. How had she not realized that? All those years. Wasted at his hands. He made her think his way was the way everyone behaved. He'd stolen a piece of her.

She righted herself and reached for Gage's shampoo. She wasn't going to let Simon steal one more second of her life. He was gone. She was free. And Gage was certainly not him.

Half an hour later, Kayla sat on Gage's back porch drinking a glass of orange juice.

Thor ran back and forth across the yard as though chasing some unseen alien being.

Kayla tucked her legs under her and leaned back. The only thing she wore was one of Gage's T-shirts. She didn't have clean panties, and the thought of putting on anything dirty made her cringe.

When the sliding glass door opened behind her, she twisted around.

Gage filled the opening, pulling the door shut behind him. His smile was huge. "Hey, baby. You're up."

"Yeah. Thor was tired of me sleeping the day away."

Gage scrunched up his nose. "Did he take my spot when I left?"

"Yep."

"Sorry. I should have warned you or shut the bedroom door." He straddled the end of the lounge chair she sat in and inched closer until he set his hands on her crossed thighs. His hair was damp, probably from showering at the gym.

"It was fine. We bonded. He might have forgiven me for making him sleep on the floor last night." She lifted her gaze from his waist to his face and squinted against the rising sun at his back. "How was your workout?"

"Good. Hope you weren't mad at me for running out on you like that." He leaned forward and kissed her. "Mmm, orange juice." He licked his lips. "Thanks for waiting for me."

"Exactly what other choice did I have?" She chuckled. "I don't have a car, or clothes for that matter."

Gage scooted closer until his thighs hit her knees. He leaned forward and set his hands on the back of the chair behind her shoulders. "Right. That was smooth of me, wasn't it?"

She smiled as his lips descended again, and he took her mouth in a long kiss that melted her insides and made her grip his forearms for support. He dipped his head to one side and deepened the tangle of their tongues, stroking his along hers until she squirmed at the thoughts his movements elicited.

He didn't pull away for several minutes, and then only an inch. "Delicious."

She shivered, squeezing his arms tighter, aware of two things—her nipples were hard rocks brushing against the cotton shirt, and her pussy was soaking wet between her spread legs.

And Jesus, Mary, and Joseph, she wanted this man to make love to her.

Heat crept up her face. "I should go home."

"Why?" He raised one eyebrow.

"Stuff?"

He snickered. "Do I make you uncomfortable?"

"Yes," she answered honestly.

He sat up, but the distance didn't help any because he set his hands on her thighs, pushing his shirt out of the way to grip her bare skin.

She closed her eyes, tipped her head back, and moaned as his thumbs brushed back and forth across the sensitive skin of her inner thighs. "Does this make you uncomfortable?"

She shook her head. "No, Sir."

He inched closer to her center until his thumbs pulled on the skin on both sides of her pussy, causing her lower lips to part and exposing her wetness to the cooler air. "Does this make you uncomfortable?"

"No, Sir." Her voice was lower this time as she fought to keep from oozing through the slats of the chair like jelly.

"How about this?" He dipped both thumbs into her pussy at once.

She moaned, so loud the neighbors surely heard. But she didn't respond.

"That's it, baby. Let it happen. You're long overdue for some intense orgasms."

He wasn't kidding. She rolled her head onto his shoulder and grabbed his waist with both hands while he fucked her hard with his thumbs. "Oh God," she mumbled, bracing her forehead against him.

One thumb disappeared to land on her clit.

Kayla squealed, her orgasm rushing through her so fast she couldn't stop it. She panted hard, not realizing for several moments that Thor panted next to her also. "God, Gage. Your dog is a voyeur."

"Haha. He's not used to so much activity here." Gage eased his thumbs from between her legs and sucked them both clean, one at a time.

Kayla watched him. It was so erotic when he did that. "Are you planning to keep me here indefinitely, half clothed and aroused?"

"Yep." He grinned. "Except when I have you naked and aroused, which I prefer."

Butterflies fluttered in her belly. She needed more. The orgasm felt fantastic, but her body craved a bigger fulfillment.

Before she could say anything, Gage stood, taking her hands and tugging her along with him. "I brought lunch."

Seriously? Was there anything this man did wrong? She followed behind him as they entered the house. Thor stayed on her heels.

When they got inside, Gage turned toward her and flattened her against the glass door. "Submit to me, baby. Give me the entire day. I promise I'll take you home first thing tomorrow morning, but I want this whole day and another night with you."

She sucked in a breath. He was overwhelming. Totally in her space and scrambling her brain. "Gage—"

"Don't say *no* yet. Let's eat. You think about it." He trailed his hands down her body until they reached the hem of his T-shirt at her hips. And then he flattened his palms under the cotton tee and shoved the material up her body. "Naked. Will you do that for me?" He asked the question as he pulled the shirt over her head and tossed it aside. His gaze went from her face to her chest, and so did his hands. He cupped both breasts, his thumbs grazing over the distended nipples that hadn't retreated since he'd arrived. "So sexy. I can't get enough of you naked."

Kayla bit her lower lip as he fondled her.

He lowered his voice. "Submit to me, baby."

"Aren't I?"

He smiled as he released her breasts. "Sit." He took her hand and led her to the table. He opened a brown paper bag and took out two sandwiches that smelled like heaven.

Her stomach rumbled.

Gage sat next to her. "Put your hands in your lap, baby, one on each thigh."

She did as he told her.

"Shoulders back. Head dipped slightly."

She flinched, the tightening in her belly going haywire.

He leaned closer. "Submit to me," he repeated.

She sucked in a breath and did as he requested, unable to do anything but.

"Good girl. Let me control you today. Leave all decisions to me."

"Why?"

He took her chin in his hand and met her gaze. "Because afterward you'll never want another Dom, and I aim to solidify that in your mind."

Her eyes widened as he spoke with such surety. Determination.

She nodded. "Okay." There was no other answer. And then she added, "Sir."

His smiled widened. "I'm not a stickler for the word Sir. You know that. If it makes you feel good, you may use it. But it's not imperative."

"Okay, Sir." She couldn't wrap her mind around submitting while not using the proper form of address. It came naturally in the role.

Gage opened the sandwiches and held one up to her mouth. "Bite?"

She reached for it, but he pulled it away. "Hands in your lap."

Her pussy clenched. He was going to feed her. No one had ever fed her. Someone had intentionally *not* fed her on occasion, but not this. This was fucking hot. She took the offered bite when the thick bread stuffed with meat and cheese returned to her mouth.

Gage took a bite of the same sandwich and then offered her another.

The flavors burst on her tongue. She'd never tasted food so thoroughly before. Something about her submission and the fact he controlled her intake made her notice more things about the meal. She moaned around the next bite.

"You're even sexy when you eat, baby." He wiped the corner of her mouth with a napkin and then set a straw to her lips. "Decaf, vanilla, iced latte."

She almost came at the idea of him remembering her preference and going out of his way to get her favorite coffee. She took the straw between her lips and sucked. When she was finished, he set the cup down and grabbed the sandwich again. He doted on her attentively through the entire meal, wiping her lips, offering her drinks at the right moments, and feeding her.

Halfway through the second sandwich, she was stuffed. "I'm full, Sir."

"Okay. Good girl." He continued, downing the rest of the food himself.

Kayla sat in the same position until he finished. He cleaned the table, wadding up the remnants of their meal and tossing it in the trash.

Thor came bounding through the doggy door at that

moment and planted himself on the floor next to Kayla. The way he stared at her made her feel awkward, as though he knew she was naked and questioned her motives.

Gage shooed him out of the way. "Go lie down, buddy." Gage quirked one side of his mouth up when he looked at Kayla. "I don't think he'll mention anything that happens here to anyone, if that's what you're thinking."

She flinched. How the hell did he know that? "Probably not, Sir."

"Come." Gage nodded behind him and headed for the living room. She'd wandered around his home that morning, taking in his space. His living room was warm, inviting, and masculine. The sofa was enormous, but so was Gage. And so were his friends.

He plopped on the couch and pulled Kayla between his knees. He lifted his gaze to hers. His hands landed on her thighs. He held her gaze.

He smoothed his hands up the front of her body. He paused to cup her breasts and pinch her nipples. Then he smoothed his palms over her stomach. "Your skin is flawless."

She inhaled a sharp breath. Everything he did made her feel alive, sexy, precious. So unlike her previous relationship. It was as if he knew that and was proving to her there was something else out there. And maybe he was right.

He worshipped her body with his gaze and his fingertips, leaning in to nibble her belly and then her nipples.

Simon rarely had her naked. He liked to bare her bottom for his whippings, but he spent most of the years she was with him ridiculing her for her looks.

Nothing about Gage said he found her lacking.

"Spread your legs for me, baby."

She stepped out, bracing herself with her hands on his shoulders. Moisture pooled at her entrance. She bit her lip, picturing wetness running down her legs any second.

"Do you realize how sexy you are?"

She paused. "No, Sir."

He trailed his fingers up and down her torso, crossing her nipples with each pass.

"I'm gonna change that answer to a yes."

How the hell did he think he could do that?

Suddenly, he released her and leaned back to look at her body.

She shivered at the lack of contact and the way he gazed at her.

He patted the couch beside him. "Lie down. Put your head on the far arm with your feet toward me."

She climbed onto the soft cool leather and leaned back as he'd requested. She bent her knees to keep her feet from landing on his lap.

Gage grabbed her knees. He gently parted them, pressing the one closest to the back of the couch against the leather. He tapped her other leg. "Let this foot hang off the side of the couch, baby."

She moved her heel that direction until it dangled down the side. The instant exposure was unsettling, and she crossed her hands over her belly.

"Arms above your head. Clasp them behind you on the arm of the couch."

Kayla couldn't breathe. Her chest rose and her knees shook. Her nipples chilled and puckered even though he was no longer touching them.

"Perfect." He twisted to face her more fully, bending his knee and leaning one elbow on the back of the couch. His face gave nothing away as his gaze roamed up and down her body.

She wished the field were even. She'd give anything to see his naked body too. But she wouldn't request such a thing. Especially not when he was dominating her.

"Talk to me."

What? Her mouth was dry. She could barely swallow under his intense gaze, and he wanted to talk? "About what, Sir?" If he thought he was going to grill her about the gap in her life, he would find her bolting from the couch and out the front door in two seconds flat, naked or not.

But he didn't mention any such thing. "How do you feel right now?"

She licked her lips, thanking God for his approach. "Exposed."

"Good exposed? Bad exposed?"

"Both, I guess."

He set one finger on her inner thigh and stroked a delicate path toward her center, but not close enough. "If I were to spread your pussy, would I find you wet for me, baby?"

"Yes."

"If I pulled the hood off your clit, would I find it swollen?"

"Yes." She squirmed, and he removed his finger.

"Stay still."

She moaned, almost willing to beg him to touch her again.

"What do you need, baby?"

"Touch me, Sir. Please." *God, anywhere, just touch me.* She craved his hands on her, or his mouth, hell even his cock, more than a dying man needed water.

"So, you're aroused?"

Heat raced up her chest and across her face. She knew

it would leave her with red splotches across her skin. "Yes, Sir."

"But I'm not doing anything."

She swallowed. It was true. And not true. In a way, he was doing everything.

He leaned in and set one hand on her belly. "What's happening in here?"

"Need. A tight ball that won't go away until you…"

"Until I what?"

"Fuck me, Sir." She turned her head to one side as she said the crude words that slipped out of her mouth nearly as a plea.

Gage wove his fingers into the hair at the apex of her sex. He tugged lightly, causing her clit to become exposed. With his other hand, he tapped her swollen nub.

She nearly shot off the couch.

He removed his hands immediately, leaving her panting, dying for his touch.

"Please, Sir."

"You're riding an endorphin high, and I'm not even doing anything." He leaned casually against his elbow on the back of the couch.

She met his gaze. What was he talking about?

"When I spanked you the first time, how did you feel?"

She closed her eyes and thought back to that day. It wasn't hard. It was embedded in her memory. The way he held her skirt up, exposing her bottom. The way he stroked her skin, massaging it, kneading it. And then he'd swatted her again and again, each pair of slaps increasing in intensity while she rose from her body and took in the pain…and the arousal. She hadn't been willing to admit to him, or even herself, how aroused she'd gotten that time, or the next time. But she had.

"Kayla?"

She opened her eyes. "Like this, Sir. High. Needy. Exposed."

"Good girl." He smiled in approval.

God, was it the same? How could she possibly get the same results without the pain?

One finger trailed down her inner thigh. One finger that made her hold her breath as he circled her pussy and grazed over her outer lips. One finger that teased her until she thought she would implode.

And he wasn't truly touching her anywhere specific. At least not where she most craved his touch.

"Please," she pleaded. She lifted her butt off the couch toward him.

He stopped. His finger disappeared. "Submit to me, baby."

He kept saying that. What more did he want?

"Ass on the couch, Kayla. Legs spread wider."

She settled back against the leather, glancing down to realize her knee had come away from the back of the couch. She pressed it open, gasping for air.

"Good girl." He set his palm on her knee and held it steady. "You stay still, and I'll take you someplace you've never been. Ride the high. But do it submitting to me."

Wasn't that what she was doing? *Not if you move, Kayla.* She nodded.

This time he held her leg open, not removing his palm spread against her thigh. With his other hand he stroked one glorious finger through her folds, finally.

As he opened her, she felt the cool air of the room hit her wetness. Her stomach dipped as she inhaled sharply.

"That's it. Just feel. Don't worry about anything except how good it feels to obey me."

God, his voice. It seeped into her skin, turning her to pudding. Her clit quivered, longing for his touch.

And then he was there, right below her nub, trailing her wetness up to the bundle of nerves that demanded attention.

"My baby is so aroused," he whispered. "I think she could come with just a command."

She moaned. He was right. She almost came at the suggestion of a command.

He stroked back through her folds, up and down, spreading her arousal, and then dipping his finger into her tight core.

She clenched his finger, wishing it was more.

"What do you need, Kayla?"

"God, Gage. I need to come so bad." Her legs shook. It seemed every time her blood pooled in her sex, she quaked.

"Do you want me to stroke your clit or your G-spot?"

She tipped her head back. She didn't care where he touched her as long as she came.

"Where, baby? Talk to me."

"My clit, Sir."

He suddenly pressed his thumb into the base of her clit and then just as quickly released it to pinch the sensitive bundle of nerves between his thumb and pointer.

Kayla tipped over the edge. The spasms started deep in her belly and spread outward.

And Gage didn't let up. He pinched and twisted with enough pressure to keep her high and needy even after the orgasm subsided. "Gorgeous."

She brought her gaze back to his to find him staring at her face. She struggled to speak.

"What else do you need?"

"Your cock, Sir. Please."

Gage stood and scooped her off the couch against his chest before she finished saying the words. He carried her to his bedroom in long strides and flattened her to the messy sheets, still scrambled from last night's antics. His lips landed on hers hard, taking her mouth in a powerful kiss that left her gasping for oxygen when he pulled back.

He lifted off her and stripped himself, dropping first his T-shirt and then his jeans and underwear. He turned to the bedside table and grabbed a condom from the drawer.

She watched all this with her eyes wide. The expanse of his chest and biceps and back were so fucking sexy covered in the intricate designs she'd only seen two other times. She wanted to run her fingers along each tattoo. Later.

She dug her heels into the mattress to push back and make more room for him. She spread her legs. When he had the condom rolled on, she reached for him. "Please, Gage. I need to feel you inside me."

He grabbed her ankles and spread her legs wider, meeting her gaze before he climbed into the V of her thighs. "Look at me, Kayla."

She did.

"Tell me you're sure about this."

"I'm so sure. Please, Gage." She repeated the plea. "Please, Sir. Fuck me."

"I'll never fuck you, Kayla. You're too precious to take like that. I might make love to you hard and fast, but it won't be fucking."

She nodded, another piece of her melting. She lowered her voice. "Take me. Make love to me, Gage."

And then he was over her, his cock nestled at her entrance, his elbows holding him above her body, shaking with the same need she felt.

She gripped his biceps and dug her nails into his skin.

Gage clearly gritted his teeth as he slowly eased into

her. He threw his head back and groaned as his cock filled her pussy.

And filled was an understatement. She was so tight after years of celibacy she felt stretched to the max. And it was wonderful.

"God, baby." His head dropped back down. "So fucking tight. I'm not going to last long. Hell, I almost came in my pants watching you orgasm on the couch."

She lifted a hand to his face and held his cheek, his soft beard beneath her palm. "I don't care. Do it."

He thrust the last few inches, groaning as his cock disappeared completely.

Kayla crested into a second orgasm as soon as he was seated and the base of his cock pressed against her clit. Her pussy pulsed around his length. There was no way for her to stop the freight train of sensation that coursed through her body.

And then he moved, pulling almost out and then pushing back in.

Her orgasm rode the friction like a roller coaster, shooting her back to the top of the world again in less than a second.

Gage lowered his body and took her lips, not moving his torso an inch as he did so. "Baby," he muttered against her mouth. "So good." He thrust again. And again.

And Kayla rose into the stratosphere with each pass of his cock against the sensitive walls of her pussy.

He thrust faster, stiffening as he did so. He sucked in a deep breath and groaned as he gave one final thrust to the hilt and tipped his face to set his forehead against her chin.

She could feel his throbbing cock as he filled the condom. Every pulse went with a jerk of his entire body.

And then he shocked her by leaning to one side and

dragging a hand down between their bodies to press his fingers against her clit. "Come again, baby. Now."

She flew with him, bucking upward, although she had no place to go. All she knew was the fullness of his cock and the black backs of her eyelids.

CHAPTER 11

Kayla smiled as she reached for her phone halfway through the morning on Monday. It may have been cheesy, but she'd given Gage his own text tone, so she knew it was him.

How's the front desk?

Good.

Swamped back here. Lunch?

Yes.

Noon.

K.

She set the phone aside, grinning at it like a teenager. Marci came in the front door from running an errand for the chief of police. She stopped at Kayla's desk and cocked her head to one side. "You're awfully happy today."

Kayla tried to rein in her smile. And failed. She shrugged instead.

"I assume this has something to do with a certain K-9 trainer?"

She shrugged again. "Maybe."

"Good. I'm so glad for you. It's nice to see a light behind those beautiful green eyes of yours."

"Thanks, Marci." Kayla dipped her head in embarrassment.

"You deserve it, girl." She tapped the desk and then went down the hall.

Did she? Deserve it? Deep down she knew she did. The happiness anyway. It was her turn. She was due for some fairy dust in her life.

But what about the chillingly haunting details of her past? Did she truly deserve to feel this close to a man while she never intended to divulge to him a word of what she'd been through? She couldn't. She couldn't ever begin to put those years into words. And she didn't want to relive the memories or spend the rest of her life looking into the eyes of someone who felt pity for her.

Whatever happened, being with Gage was invigorating. She was alive. It might not be fair to him, and that ate a hole in her under the happiness, but she'd warned him. The only way she would agree to this relationship was if he left her past right where it was, in the past. The second he started harping on her about it, she would bolt. And she meant it.

Saturday had been the best day of her life. Sort of like what a honeymoon should feel like. Gage had dominated her in his gentle way for twenty-four solid hours, barely letting her sleep even during the night. And he did it with kind, gentle words of encouragement. He hadn't spanked her once. Nor had he restrained her and tortured her into submission.

And still, he'd been on top the entire weekend. She rode an endorphin high for so many hours, she was still waiting for the crash. But it never came.

The only mar on the weekend with Gage was when he dropped her off at home Sunday afternoon, telling her he had some things to do. For some reason, his actions smarted. Just enough to make her wince. She couldn't put her finger on it, but a piece of her wondered what was so pressing and vague.

She shook off her doubts, telling herself she was being ridiculous and overreacting. After all, they'd only been dating for two weeks. He wasn't required to tell her every detail of his life. Still, the niggling sensation hovered in her brain. Something about the way he spoke sounded off. Or perhaps she read too much into it.

After Gage left her at home, she finally faced the pile of mail on her table, specifically the dreaded monthly envelope stuffed under everything. She picked it up and flipped it over. What if she ignored it? She shivered, knowing she had no option but to face the contents as usual. This was her life now. It would never change. Nevertheless, she stuffed the envelope back on the bottom of the stack and left it to deal with another day. She couldn't stand to dampen her excitement about Gage by opening that piece of shit.

Besides, she didn't need to open the envelope to know what was inside and deal with the damage. She stopped opening the damn things a long time ago.

She'd totally forgotten the envelope on her dining room table. That's how consumed she was with thoughts of Gage. And now it was Monday, and she passed the morning hours working steadily, which kept her mind from wandering too often. At noon, a wet nose landed on her leg. She turned to scratch Thor's head and leaned over to hug him against her body. "Hey, buddy."

"It's always all about the dog. Thor. Thor. Thor. Nobody ever greets me first anymore." Gage's voice was teasing, and Kayla lifted her face to grin at him while hugging his dog to her chest.

"What do you expect when you take a chick magnet with you everywhere you go?"

"You got an hour?" He leaned over her desk.

"Yeah."

"Let's go then." He clicked his tongue at Thor, who quickly ran to his side, amazing Kayla. No matter how much Gage grumbled about the attention everyone lavished on his dog, Gage himself was still top dog, literally.

Kayla rounded the desk, and Gage set a possessive hand on the small of her back as he led her out the door. Instead of heading to one of the restaurants on the street, he made his way toward his car.

"Where're we going?"

He smiled and winked as he settled her in the front seat and shut the door.

Happy tingles climbed up her arms. She had learned to let the man keep his secrets when it came to dominating her. The results were always beyond her dreams.

Five minutes later they pulled up to his house, and Thor bounded to the front door before them. The dog was probably excited, thinking he'd gotten a half day off work.

As soon as they were inside and Gage shut the front door, Kayla asked, "Are we eating lunch at home today?"

"Oh, yeah." He turned toward her, backed her into the door, and reached for the buttons on her blouse. His lips landed on hers as he pushed each disk through its hole, picking up speed as he went.

Kayla stopped thinking of anything beyond his hands, his knuckles brushing against her breasts, his knee pressing her legs apart, his mouth destroying her with that kiss. She grabbed his waist with both hands, but he tugged her shirt off, forcing her to release him.

He stepped back then, leaving her heaving for a breath as he stopped touching her.

A shiver raced down her body.

Gage reached out with one finger and traced the upper edge of her lace bra, the best one she owned.

She lifted an arm, and he gently grabbed her wrist and put it back at her side. "Stay still," he murmured. His finger dipped into her bra and flicked her nipple.

Kayla arched into him on a moan.

"So responsive. I love that about you, baby." He switched to the other breast, repeating his actions. And then both his hands went to the front of her skirt and slid around to the back to pop the button and lower the zipper.

The skirt fell to the ground, leaving her in the matching thong and bra.

"Love this pale pink on you." He leaned back again, his gaze roaming down her body, reverently, while she attempted to keep from moaning, her mouth pursed shut. "Spread your legs wider, baby."

She stepped out, glad she'd worn sandals today. In heels, she would have been less stable.

Gage lifted both hands and tugged the lace of her bra down so her nipples were pushed up and out, awkwardly squeezed. He cradled both and dipped his head to suck first one and then the other bud into his mouth.

Kayla grabbed his head and held tight.

He stopped, tipping his gaze to hers. "Hands at your

sides, baby." He righted himself and left her to walk across the room. "Come here."

Kayla followed, her steps wobbly, her uncertainty growing. She stopped several feet from him.

"Lean over the coffee table, Kayla. Hands planted flat. Legs straight and separated."

She paused a moment and then shuffled closer to the table. Was he mad? He didn't seem angry. His tone was even, but commanding. No vein of disapproval bulged in his head. No hand twitched at his side. His eyes weren't large and fierce. The only way she knew he was dominating her were his words.

"Do it, baby." He pointed at the table.

She decided to obey, but her heart beat faster.

Gage sat on the couch and leaned back. She could see him between her legs as she lowered her face. He sat casually behind her ass, staring at her. Finally he sighed. "I want you to listen to me closely." His demeanor seemed foreboding. She'd never seen him disappointed. And that's how she would describe his stance.

"Yes, Sir." She wasn't sure she spoke loud enough for him to hear.

"Here's what I know, Kayla."

Fuck. What does he know? She didn't like this already.

"I know that some jackass royally fucked you over. I know that he beat you hard enough to scare the shit out of you. It's surprising you don't have scars."

She sucked in a sharp breath. How did he know all this? And Jesus, he was spot on about the scars. She'd been shocked a few times herself. Especially when Simon drew blood.

"Relax. It's not that I've unearthed your deepest secrets behind your back. I'm just observant."

"Yes, Sir." That was an understatement.

"I know that he restrained you when he beat you."

She flinched.

"I know that because of that, I'll never lay a hand on you again." He paused for a long time.

She controlled her breathing, acutely aware of the change in her stance as her shoulders slumped. She let out a long exhale, unaware until that moment how much those words meant to her. Unaware, in fact, that she didn't want to be struck again. Believing until he uttered that important sentence, they had been working up to such a scene. Actually certain he had been about to strike her now.

"Kayla."

"Yes, Sir."

"You were abused."

She hesitated, drawing her slack shoulders up higher once again. And then she chose not to respond. It wasn't necessary really.

"No one can ever hit you again. The damage is too severe. It will bring back memories you don't want to picture with another Dom."

God, the man was psychic, and brilliant in his assessment.

"Here's the problem with that."

Shit.

"I'm a strong Dom. I've always enjoyed having a sub give herself over to me in such a way, trusting me to pinken her flesh to just the right temperature. I can't do that with you."

Was he going to break this off? Before it had barely started? Her face flushed, heat rising to match the pink he preferred to see on his submissives' asses. She couldn't give him that. He needed it. Why, then, did he insist on telling her all this while she displayed herself almost naked and so open and vulnerable?

"So, I need a different approach. I've thought a lot about this. I did some research last night after I got home. I've decided, for as much as you need release that doesn't come from being struck by anything, I need to dominate you in a way that doesn't come from striking you."

What was he suggesting? Quick shallow breaths while she processed his words.

He set his feet firmly on the ground and leaned his elbows on his knees.

She couldn't see his face, but between her legs she could make out at least his stance.

"When we're in the role, I need your obedience so you can come quick and easily from my words. Understood?"

"Yes, Sir." Her voice cracked.

"So, how am I going to attain that goal without spanking you?"

"I... I don't know, Sir."

He stood. He circled around her.

She could feel his gaze everywhere. Her nipples, having slipped back behind the lace, abraded against the material. Her pussy dampened her thong. She curled her toes under, anything to abate the pressure building inside.

"What do you want most from me, Kayla?" His tone was gentle, and he set a finger on her spine and traced it up to her neck.

She dipped her back under his touch. "Ummm. I'm not sure, Sir." She couldn't grasp his meaning.

"Really?" He stepped between her legs and flattened his cock to her ass, the bulge, even through his cargo pants, making her lick her lips. His hand reached around her waist, and he swiped his fingers through her folds. "No idea?" He plunged two fingers into her without pausing.

Kayla moaned. Oh, yes. She knew.

The fingers disappeared. "Need more suggestions?"

"No, Sir." She shook her head.

"What do you need most from me?"

"Release."

"From spanking?"

"No. From orgasm, Sir."

"Uh huh." This time he lightly palmed her hips and caressed his fingers up her body until he held her breasts, cupping them where they swayed. He pinched both nipples at once. "So, what if I were to do this?" He pinched harder and then released them.

Kayla moaned, swaying forward in an effort to retrieve his touch, just out of reach.

"Frustrating, huh?"

"Yes, Sir." She couldn't think of anything but the need for him to continue. She actually ached for more of whatever he would give her.

Instead, damn him, he stepped away, circled her again. Leaned in to her ear without actually making contact. His breath hit her warm and moist as he whispered, "What do you need?"

"To come, Sir." She spoke definitively that time.

"I see. Who decides if you come or not?"

"You do, Sir."

"And what happens if you can't obey me, Kayla?"

Her head shot up. She couldn't stop herself from meeting his gaze. Her mouth hung open. No words came out.

Gage smiled. "I think you're catching on to the new plan, baby."

Oh God. They'd spent so much time together over the past few weeks. They had sex all over his house for two days. No, they made love. Right? Like a boyfriend and girlfriend. Except with some bossiness. And some dominance that curled her toes and made her long for more.

Gage sat on the coffee table, inches from her face so they met eye to eye. "So, here's the plan. You obey me, or you don't come." He smiled. "When we're in the role," he added.

She gasped. She knew that was what he would say. He made it clear with his one-way chat, but saying it out loud like that was...totally fucking hot, sexy, and arousing. And annoying.

He continued to smile. "Deal?" He raised an eyebrow. "Gives me the sense of dominance. Gives you the sense of submission. Win win."

She swallowed and slowly nodded.

Gage stood.

Kayla didn't move, except to lower her head back to the table. He hadn't suggested she should.

"Take your bra and panties off, baby." He circled behind her.

Kayla stood and followed his instructions. He'd left her so needy, and the feeling lingered as a hard knot in the pit of her stomach. When she popped the front clasp on her bra, she turned toward him. Next, she dipped her fingers into her panties and lowered them also, stepping out of them and leaving them on the floor at her feet.

"Lie on the coffee table, baby. On your back, legs spread wide."

She did so, the coolness of the top of the table shocking her warm skin. As she let her knees fall open, she watched his face.

"Masturbate for me, Kayla."

She stiffened, gripping her thighs with both hands. She rarely masturbated alone. And she'd never done so for someone else—except in the car the other night, and that time she hadn't been permitted to finish. She almost cringed, fighting an image of Simon hovering over her. He never gave a flying fuck about her needs. Not a chance in hell he would have cared to watch her masturbate.

"Stroke your fingers through your pussy, baby." He stood at the end of the table, watching her.

She didn't miss the fact she was naked and he was fully clothed. She glanced at his cock, stiff inside his pants.

"This isn't about me this time. It's about you." He kneeled on the floor between her thighs, his face so much closer to her sex. "Masturbate," he commanded again.

Her fingers shook as she lowered them to her pussy. *He's crazy. This is so not going to work.* The pressure to perform alone would kill any arousal she brought to the table, literally. But she was shocked by the first touch to her pussy, flinching as her fingers spread her lower lips and dipped between them. Oh my God.

She actually moaned as she reached inside, gathering her wetness and spreading it wantonly around the entrance.

"That's my girl. See? Not hard at all." Gage grabbed her thighs and held them farther open, close to her knees. "Use both hands. I've got you."

Kayla's eyes closed as she tipped her head back. His commands were so fucking hot. She never would have believed she could arouse herself so thoroughly in front of someone. Emboldened, she used one hand to lift the hood off her clit and the other to stroke it, her arousal lubricating everywhere she touched.

"Kayla, that's so sexy." His voice was deeper, softer.

She flicked faster, her clit swelling beneath her touch, begging for release. She was so aroused before touching herself, it only took a few minutes for her ardor to rise higher than before. So close…

"Stop."

She froze. *What?*

"Remove your fingers. Look at me."

Kayla dipped her chin, widening her gaze. "Sir?" She breathed heavily.

"How do you feel, baby?" He caressed her inner thighs as he spoke, not reaching anywhere close to her sex.

"So close," she croaked. "Please, Sir."

"Who controls your orgasms?"

"You do, Sir." She gulped.

"Do you feel dominated right now?"

"Yes, Sir." *Hell, yes.*

"Do you need me to spank you?"

She furrowed her brow. "No, Sir." She shook her head.

"How about a flogging. Do you need that to get off?"

"No, Sir," she whispered.

"So, you're super aroused. You need to come. You would beg me to let you come right now, right?"

"Yes."

"Then I'd say I'm a pretty effective Dom without striking you at all, right?"

"Yes. Please." Her legs shook. He held them wider, but they shook anyway.

"Kayla."

One word, and she came to attention, focusing on his face again.

"Finish." He smiled.

She exhaled and moaned softly as she resumed stroking herself, her fingers rougher this time, her need that much more urgent. She pinched and pulled on her clit and then thrust two fingers into her pussy and stroked across her G-spot. It was fast and furious. She came hard.

It wasn't enough. It wasn't nearly as satisfying as when she came at Gage's hand, but it took the edge off. And she was grateful he hadn't left her hanging as she came down from her high.

He released her, stood, and leaned over to kiss her lips. "Fucking hot, baby. Get dressed." He glanced at his watch. "If we hurry, we can grab something at a drive thru on the way back to work."

Oh God. Work. She scrambled off the table, her body protesting every movement. Her weird lunch hour left her humming with more need than it had started out with.

Gage was full of surprises.

As she dressed, he went out back to get Thor.

She grinned. That dog was not real. He was too easy. Had he gone straight out the doggy door when they arrived?

On the drive back, Gage was good to his word. He stopped to grab them a quick bite and then chuckled. "You look a little peeved."

She realized her face was tense. "Maybe."

He took her chin and lowered his face to kiss her lips. "Good. I'm going to assume that means you didn't get quite what you wanted without my hands on you."

She nodded against him. "True."

"Remember that when you sub for me." He kissed her forehead. "There's a new game in town, and I think my girlfriend likes it."

She wasn't nearly as sure as he was, but she did like the way he said *girlfriend*.

When they got back to the precinct, Gage let Thor out of the back seat and led them back inside. "I'm gonna meet Zane at the gym after work. You want me to come by later?"

"Sure. You want me to cook?"

"You want to kill me?"

She grinned. "Maybe you should bring takeout."

"Maybe I should." He squeezed her hand as they entered the front door, but left it at that.

She was glad. She wasn't sure yet how she felt about the entire police academy being privy to their relationship. Sure, everyone probably already had the gist of it, but that didn't mean she wanted to start flaunting excessive PDA.

Gage was perfect.

CHAPTER 12

"How're your parents?" Zane asked as Gage set the weights he'd been curling back on the rack.

"Good. The same." He shrugged. Of all the guys, Zane knew the situation with his parents the best. He was the EMT on call when his dad had his stroke.

"Did you see them Sunday?"

"Yep. Same as usual."

"Did you take Kayla?"

Gage frowned. "Hell no."

"What do you mean 'hell no?'"

"She doesn't even know where I was. Not ready for that." He shook his head. No way in the world he was going to bring Kayla over to his parents' house yet. Wasn't on his radar. Though he had felt a cringe of weirdness when he told her he wouldn't be with her on Sunday.

"Seriously? Dude, you two are like an item. A thing."

"Yeah. So?"

"So, your mom has been waiting for this day for years. Why would you leave them guessing? They're gonna love Kayla."

"Yeah. I know. But I'm not ready."

"Ready for what? An invitation? I'm not following." Zane stepped around the weight rack and got in Gage's space. Too close.

Gage backed up. Zane was a close friend. Super close. But he was on Gage's last nerve. "Kayla needs a firm Dom right now. She's been through some serious shit. It would be confusing to her to see me in a different role yet."

"What the— Are you for real? What's confusing about having dinner with a man's parents? She totally digs you, man. I can tell by the look in her eyes that you walk on water for her. I don't think she expects to submit to you in front of your parents. She's not stupid."

Gage turned to another weight machine, preparing to work his thighs. He knew that. It had nothing to do with her submitting to him. "You know how I am with my dad," he muttered.

Zane hesitated.

Gage hoped Zane was done with his tirade.

"How's that, Gage? Loving? Doting? Scared?"

Gage flinched. "Yeah, that." Shit. What was Zane driving at? He wasn't ready to share that side of himself. What was wrong with that?

"You need to rethink this, dude. I'm not kidding. You're wrong. I don't care what Kayla has been through, and I'm not even asking. I'm just saying, she's a smart girl. You won't fuck her up by letting her see your softer side."

Gage pushed his leg out and breathed through the maneuver. Those words rang in Gage's head as Zane gave up the cause and walked to another machine. Maybe Zane was right, but it wasn't a chance Gage was willing to take yet. Besides Kayla being used to seeing him as a firm Dom with all his ducks in a row, unflustered by anything, he had to admit a part of him was simply unwilling to open himself up to that level of vulnerability. The kind of vulnerability he felt when he sat with his dad, talking to him for hours, fighting back tears a man shouldn't have to shed for his parents.

He wasn't ready for her pity or the looks. It made his stomach clench thinking about it. Besides, it was a lot to ask of a woman to visit his dad. It wasn't pretty. It was excruciating. He'd only been dating her for a few weeks.

But you know damn well those few weeks were fast paced and catapulted you forward quickly.

Kayla was a little confused on Wednesday afternoon when she got a text from Gage saying he would be busy that evening, but he would see her tomorrow night.

Unease crept up her spine as she set the phone on her desk. She'd brushed off her concerns on Sunday, but again on Wednesday? He didn't say he was going to the gym or even the club. He gave her that same vague "busy."

On the one hand, she knew she was being unreasonable and needed to lighten up. And she flat out refused to consider the idea he might be lying to her by omission about something important. On the other hand, why did he persist in giving her such vague details? Sure, they hadn't been together long, but was there more to Gage than met the eye? Even though they'd only been dating a few weeks, she'd been with him nearly every moment they weren't working since Friday night—except during his vague Sunday disappearance—and now this.

When five o'clock rolled around, she walked out front with Marci. Gage was nowhere in sight, and his Jeep was gone.

Marci smiled. "What are you lovebirds doing tonight?"

Kayla cringed. "Apparently nothing. He's got other things to do."

"What other things?" Marci's brows furrowed.

"Good question," Kayla muttered. She lifted her gaze to Marci, squinting one eye at the sun going down behind her. "Does it seem strange to you he has twice this week told me he needed to do some *things* without explaining what they were?"

Marci pursed her lips and tipped her head back to stare at the sky for a moment. When she brought her gaze back to Kayla's, she cocked one hip and blew out a breath. "A little weird, yes. But Gage is a good guy. I'm sure he has his reasons. I can't imagine him doing anything that would jeopardize his relationship with you. It isn't like him."

"Yeah. I'm just being paranoid." Kayla shuffled toward her Camry. "See you tomorrow, Marci."

Kayla drove home tense. Her chat with Marci hadn't helped. Clearly even Marci found his behavior odd.

Nerves ate a hole in her while she waited to see if he would text. Flashbacks of her past drove her to ball up on the couch and sit in the silence. She hated where her mind went as the sun went down and she was left in the dark. She didn't care. She rocked back and forth with her arms around her knees.

She never should have gotten involved with Gage in the first place. She wasn't ready. She knew that. She also knew she would never be ready to get into another serious relationship. And she didn't care. That's how damaged she was. She could even acknowledge that, and it didn't change anything.

When Simon swooped into her life, she'd been alone, scared, vulnerable, and desperate. He'd filled every void. He was the perfect gentleman. He convinced her to move halfway across the country with him within a week. Too fast.

Warning bells had rung, but she'd ignored them. With her dad gone, the only real support she had in the world was the chief of police. Chief Edwards had been like an uncle to her for years, and he did everything in his power to ensure she was taken care of after the funeral. He gave her a job and paid her tuition at the local junior college.

And she threw all that away without glancing back. Part of her knew she was making a mistake from the moment she'd consented, but the rest of her ignored the feeling. Simon was her everything, or so she thought. She ignorantly allowed him to whisk her to a twenty-four-hour chapel in her own town where she married him with stars in her eyes before following him to the naval air base he was stationed at in Mississippi.

He'd been on leave, vacationing in Vegas when they met at a local pizza parlor. She was there eating alone, studying for a history exam, when he slid into the booth next to her and smiled so broadly, she almost swallowed her tongue. Rugged. Handsome. And in uniform.

She was barely twenty and a virgin. Simon was twenty-five and horny as hell.

From the moment she set foot in Mississippi, she'd been filled with dread. But she wasn't a quitter. And determined to make the best of her situation, she forced herself to be the perfect wife. The job wasn't easy. Simon changed his tune the second they arrived. His on-base apartment was cramped. Kayla didn't know a soul. And he insisted she stay home during the day, taking care of lists of things he left her. He didn't want her making friends and "dallying around with the other lazy wives on base."

Within a month, Simon introduced her to the life of dominance and submission. She was scared out of her mind at first. But Simon had lit up when she consented. She wanted to please him so badly, anything to keep him smiling and happy. The task was monumental. Nothing made Simon happy. Ever. Not blowjobs, not sex, not submission, not house cleaning, not hot meals.

He needed more and more intense dominance to get off as the years passed. Kayla had let him. The first time he spanked her, she cried the entire next day. They'd been married over a year by then. The transition to hard-core BDSM had been gradual. When Simon got home and found out she hadn't completed all her tasks, he beat her again, stripping her naked and tying her to their bed on her belly.

After that, Kayla learned to go into her head when he spanked her, what she now knew was a subspace. She even learned to enjoy it. And he always fucked her hard afterward, not a care in the world for her release. He was the only one who mattered. The spanking had been a turning point. After Simon had a taste of hitting her, he became insatiable. He stopped seeing to her pleasure all together and seemed to only get off and relax after taking a hand to her. And then he started seeing other women.

She shivered, leaning back against the couch and staring into the darkness. The first sign she had that Simon was unfaithful was his unexplained absences. Simon would leave her alone on the naval base for hours when she knew he wasn't at work. He would come back late at night, smelling of booze and perfume. When she questioned him, things really went south. That night was the first time he broke her skin. He beat her with his belt, leaving abrasions all over her ass and thighs that kept her from sitting down for days.

He apologized afterward, the one and only time he ever did such a thing, and only because she threatened to leave him. Instead, he insisted he would get help, which meant he spent even more evenings away from home under the pretense of going to counseling.

Ironically, Kayla learned to enjoy being beaten. Twisted. Absurd. Stupid. But she taught herself to escape under his hand or his flogger, and the euphoria she experienced was better than sex. By then, he often didn't fuck her afterward. He said she was too dry anyway. He wasn't about to put his cock into her frigid cunt. If she couldn't manage to get wet for him, he wouldn't fuck her.

And that was fine with her. Besides, she knew he was fucking any number of other women. The last thing she wanted was a venereal disease at the hands of her husband.

The best day of her life had been the day he came home and announced he was being deployed to Iraq. She would never forget the elation she felt hearing that news. It lasted about two seconds, however, when he informed her he would be taking her to live with his parents in the most rural, godforsaken part of the South she'd ever visited.

She'd met his parents on eight occasions by then, none of them joyous. Every Christmas and one week in July Simon had driven them two hundred miles to Alabama to visit his parents in their rundown shack on several acres of wooded property. She knew within minutes of the first visit where Simon got his cruel genes. They came honestly, from both parents.

Kayla rolled onto her side, still in a tight ball, tears now running down her face as she forced herself to remember the details of her former life. She had learned from those mistakes. Right? Her inherent distrust for men was at the top of the list.

And the bottom line was she needed to take stock of her relationship with Gage. She was on the same path of destruction as before. Even though she'd known him for two years on the periphery, and he was a member of law enforcement, she didn't know him well enough to have gone all in. *Stupid. What were you thinking?*

Gage was still a man. Sure, he seemed kind and loving. But so had Simon at first. And she couldn't ignore the fact Gage was in the military himself before she met him. Maybe the dominant mindset was something men picked up from that experience. It wasn't farfetched. After all, it was easy to see why a man who spent all day taking commands from others might want to escape in the evening and dominate his wife or girlfriend.

She never should have gone to Extreme in the first place. It was like a drug to her. She spent months avoiding the lifestyle after returning to Vegas. But the pull was always there. She longed for the euphoria that came from being spanked.

And it was her own fault for not keeping it simple. She never should have let Gage get into her head. Had she learned nothing from Simon? This was exactly how things had started to go downhill with Simon. He gave her vague, lame excuses for not being home. It took her a while to find out he was cheating on her.

When her arms started hurting from holding herself in such a tight ball, she finally uncurled and stood on wobbly legs. She padded to her room in the dark, used the bathroom, and climbed into bed with no more than the light from the moon through her partially open blinds. She hadn't eaten, and she didn't care.

All she wanted was to escape. And since spanking wasn't a remote possibility tonight, she took the next best choice—sleep.

CHAPTER 13

"Where's Kayla?" Gage leaned over the counter the following morning, facing a frantic Marci, who held up a finger as she explained to someone on the other end of the phone she held against her shoulder that they'd most assuredly gotten the police academy, not the actual precinct. Kayla's desk was littered with papers in front of Marci, and she reached down to tap on the mouse in front of her computer as she spoke. Multi-tasking at its best.

Finally, she hung up. By then Thor had rounded the desk and brushed his head against her leg. "Hey, pal. Want to help out at the front today?" she asked the dog.

"Where's Kayla?" Gage repeated.

"Called in sick." She cocked her head, her brows furrowed. "You haven't spoken to her?"

He shook his head, unease making him stiffen. "I was out kind of late last night. Didn't get to talk to her." He pushed off the desk and pulled out his cell, texting quickly before he finished talking.

Marci spoke again. "Yeah, she mentioned you had other things to do last night."

He lifted his head as he finished the text to Kayla.

"Gage." Her voice was kind of stern.

He met her gaze. "What?"

"I think you hurt her feelings. Were you at your parents' house?"

"Yeah." He furrowed his brow. "Why?"

"Why didn't you just tell her that?" Marci bit her lower lip and shook her head. "Never mind. It's none of my business." She turned her gaze away from him.

"No you don't. What were you going to say?"

Marci blew out a breath. "Look. I shouldn't have brought it up."

"But you did. So spit it out."

Marci hedged, finally slumping in her chair. "Gage, why haven't you taken her with you? And why have you left her to wonder where the hell you go when you're at your mom and dad's?"

Gage sucked in a breath. *Shit.*

As secretary to the chief of police, Marci knew about Gage's dad. It wasn't a huge secret, but he'd been pretty quiet about it anyway. Besides Chief Edwards, Marci, and Rider, Gage didn't think anyone else at the precinct knew about his family situation.

Gage stared at her. "What's up with you people?"

"Pardon?" She lifted both brows.

Gage felt a little ganged up on between Zane and Marci. "My friend Zane asked me the same thing. Can't a man visit his parents without taking his new girlfriend?"

"Sure, unless his new girlfriend has tipped his world upside down and is with him nearly every other waking hour at work and at home, and I'll venture to guess some of the sleeping hours also. Then *no.* It's a little odd."

"And she mentioned this?"

"Yes."

164

"Damn. Was she mad?"

"No. I'd say hurt. Confused. Leery."

"Leery? Why would she be leery?"

"I have no idea. Why don't you ask her yourself, Gage?" Marci's tone was a little snippy, but she smiled at the same time, trying to lighten the blow.

Gage turned and walked away, somewhat confused and totally nervous.

He texted Kayla three times. She never answered. He decided if she really was sick, she might be sleeping. So he bit his tongue and stayed at the academy the entire afternoon. As soon as it was five o'clock though, he hustled Thor to his Jeep and beelined for her place.

She wasn't there. Or she didn't answer. He couldn't be sure since her car could be in the garage. Either way, he didn't have a good taste in his mouth. Was she really that pissed at him for being busy last night? Why not just say something?

Gage took a deep breath and did the only thing he could think to do—he headed for the gym. It was always his salvation. And he needed to stop worrying. She'd called in sick. Maybe the woman was sick. Maybe there was no correlation whatsoever between her apparent inquisition about his whereabouts and her absence the next day.

A quick stop by the house to drop off Thor and Gage entered his home away from home in no time.

Gage would have loved to spar with Rider, but the man worked second shift. He would be on patrol. Instead, he took his chances and found Conner in the locker room when he arrived. Conner was the oldest one of the group at thirty-eight. And the craziest bastard Gage knew. He was a conundrum. The guy was so mild-mannered in general, a college literature professor, for heaven's sake. But when the gloves were on—Conner was unstoppable.

They referred to him as "The Gladiator." No one had yet to beat him. And for all that, he had no desire to go pro. He saw the entire thing as a hobby. A way to stay fit.

"Gage. Perfect," Conner said. "Zane was supposed to spar with me but something came up. He's stuck at work."

Gage smiled. "Lucky then, because I was in need of a partner."

"Joe's gonna work with us. Already booked the ring with him."

"Awesome." Gage quickly changed and met Conner in the cage within minutes. He set his gloves down and stretched while Joe ambled toward them.

"How's the girlfriend, Mr. I'll-never-fall-for-a-woman?" Joe smirked as he stepped into the cage.

"Ha ha." Gage winced at the mention of Kayla, but didn't elaborate.

"Taking a night off?" Joe asked.

"Apparently," Gage mumbled.

"Uh oh. Trouble in paradise." Conner socked Gage in the bicep playfully, his gloves already in place.

"Nah. She's just sick."

"Sick?" Conner asked. "What is that code for these days? When my college students are sick, they're usually hung over."

"You guys are so funny." Gage started bouncing as he loosened up, pulling his gloves on at the same time.

Luckily both men dropped the subject, and Joe fired off a few instructions. "Let's practice a few jabs first, then move on to some kicks. Gage you've been weak on the left hook lately. Get several of those in. Conner...well, I can't think what you're weak in, so just do your thing."

Gage would have been miffed if he didn't know Joe was dead correct. Conner was weak at nothing. The man was a god. That's why they dubbed him "The Gladiator." That's also why the local Russian underground wanted him to fight for them. He was worth a lot of money, and he had no interest in earning that money, not through legal means by going pro, and certainly not from illegal means by fighting underground.

Two hours later, after the hardest workout Gage had engaged in for a while, he showered, changed, and jumped back in his Jeep. He drove by Kayla's condo, but all the lights were out, and there was still no sign she was inside.

"Fuck." He hit the steering wheel as he drove home. Something was off. No doubt about it. He couldn't grasp that she would shut him out without a word over something as ridiculous as not being invited to dinner with his mom and dad.

He drove home, threw a stick with Thor for half an hour, fixed himself a sandwich for dinner, and then plopped in front of the TV. Nothing good was on, and all he did was scan through the channels over and over until he gave up and flipped it off.

He checked his phone for the hundredth time. Nothing. No response to any of the three texts he sent her earlier in the day. And there was no way he was going to keep sending her messages. If she wanted to ignore him, he wasn't about to beg.

At least not anymore today.

He dragged himself to bed earlier than usual and flopped onto his back.

When his phone rang less than ten minutes later, he bolted upright and grabbed the cell from his bedside table, completely expecting it to be Kayla, chock full of reasons for not speaking to him for twenty-four hours.

His shoulders fell immediately when he saw the caller ID. He answered the call quickly, damping down his disappointment. "Hey, Mom. How's it going?" It wasn't unusual for his mom to call a few times a week, and often in the evening after his dad was asleep, with a rundown of the day's improvements, which were few and slow.

"Gage?" Her voice was off. And there was noise in the background. "He had another stroke." She sniffled into the phone and then let out a sob.

Gage jumped to his feet, grabbing his jeans and hopping on one leg to get them on while he held the phone at his shoulder. "Mom? Where are you?"

"The hospital. I called an ambulance. And then I had to follow it. I didn't have a chance to call you until I got here." Her voice cracked as she spoke. "I'm scared, Gage."

"I'll be there in fifteen minutes, Mom. Hang tight."

"'K, but drive carefully, Gage. It won't change anything. Be safe."

"Of course, Mom." He ended the call and tossed the cell on his bed to grab the shirt he wore earlier. He tugged it over his head while he toed on his shoes and stomped into them without untying them.

In less than a minute, he was in the Jeep, pulling out of the driveway, and praying he made it to the hospital in time.

When he arrived, he pulled into the first spot he saw and jogged to the emergency room entrance. His mom was pacing by the window, eyes red and puffy, a tissue clutched in her hand.

"Mom." He went straight to her and pulled her into his embrace.

～

On Friday, Kayla pulled into work shaking. She hadn't answered any of Gage's texts the day before, and in retrospect, she thought perhaps she was overreacting. Or at least behaving childishly. She needed to face him and tell him straight up what she thought about his nebulous absences. It didn't really matter if she was oversensitive. That was her personality. He could take it or leave it. If he had a legitimate explanation for his mysterious jaunts, fine. Or at least sort of fine. If he didn't...hell, if he was lying to her...she needed to know that sooner rather than later. One thing she was sure about—never again would she fall victim to another con man.

She didn't see Gage all morning, and unlike the previous several days in a row, he hadn't left her an iced latte. He had a right to be put off by her not taking his calls, though, and she didn't really want to exchange words with him at work, so she waited until lunch to seek him out.

He wasn't there.

She headed to Marci's office next, but ran into Chief Edwards in the hall. "Oh, hey. Do you know where Gage is?"

The older man furrowed his brow and frowned. He looked kind of shocked. "He took some time off. He didn't call you?"

"He *what?*" She nearly shouted the question, shaking her head. "No." But she'd hardly given him the opportunity.

"A week probably. Called me last night." Chief Edwards still frowned, concern etched in his face. "You two okay?"

She stood there stunned, processing. She nodded, and then she reconsidered and shook her head. "No. I guess not. I think we had a misunderstanding."

"Kayla, I'm sorry. Text him. I'm sure you'll work it out."

Kayla lifted her gaze to his. "That's all you know?"

He took a breath. "No. But I'm not at liberty to tell you any more than that. I would extend you the same courtesy."

"Right. Of course." She turned and walked numbly back down the hall.

After work, Kayla drove straight to Gage's house. No sign of him. Then again, she pulled the same shit on him yesterday. She'd listened to him knocking and ignored him entirely.

But she was determined to face him. There was no way in hell she could go home and do nothing. She'd never be able to sleep. So instead, she plopped down on the glider on his front porch and sent him a text.

I'm on your front porch. Not leaving until you either let me in if you're home or come home if you're out.

That was all she said. And then she waited. For two hours. It was late and growing dark before a car pulled into the driveway, and it wasn't Gage's Jeep. Not even close. It was a white F150.

She held her breath as she watched a man Gage's size step down from the cab, not exhaling until Zane stepped into the ray of light coming from the street.

"Kayla." He looked sorrowful as he stepped onto the porch.

"What are you doing here?"

"Gage sent me."

"Oh." And then, "*Oh*. For me?"

"Yes." He sat next to her and gave the glider a slow shove, making it rock back and forth. Finally, he met her gaze. "I told him he was going to fuck this up if he didn't let you in."

She pursed her lips, having no idea what he was talking about.

"His dad had a stroke last night."

"Oh God." She straightened her spine and grabbed Zane's arm. "Oh God," she repeated. "Is he okay?"

"He didn't die if that's what you mean. But he's far from okay. He was far from okay before the stroke, because it wasn't his first."

"Oh." She sucked in a breath. "I didn't know."

"Yeah. That's why I told him he was gonna fuck this up." Zane smiled now. "He had some macho idea that if he took you to his parents', you wouldn't see him the same way."

"What way is that?"

"Strong. Firm. A Dom. What he thinks you need."

She breathed harder and gripped the arm rest tight. "Are you telling me he didn't want me to see him…human?"

"Yes." Zane smiled again. "Exactly. Thought it would confuse you, he said. Although I think deep down he just doesn't want anyone to know he's vulnerable. He's very close to his dad. This thing is killing him. He hates it. He goes to visit twice a week and spends several hours sitting with the man, talking, watching sports, stuff like that. But inside, Gage is torn up because his dad isn't the same anymore, and his mortality is choking Gage."

"Oh God. I was such a bitch yesterday." *And the entire week….*

"Not your fault." Zane shook his head. "Hell, even *I* saw that coming. Man doesn't hook up with a girlfriend and make her the center of his universe, and then repeatedly leave her at home while he goes to his parents'. It isn't right."

"That's what I thought. I've been a little bitchy about it, I'm afraid."

"Understandable. I warned him."

Kayla twisted around. "Where's Thor?"

"My place."

BECCA JAMESON

"Ah."

"I'm sure he'd be happier with you, though." He lifted one side of his mouth in a small smile.

Kayla grinned back.

"Listen. Go home. Sleep tonight. You look like shit."

"Thanks." She punched his arm, though she knew he was right. "I didn't sleep much last night."

"They're moving him to a regular room tomorrow." Zane reached into his front pocket and pulled out a card, which he handed to Kayla.

Her fingers shook as she glanced down at it. "Think he would mind?"

"Well, probably, but I told him I was personally going to put an end to this madness. So, if he's mad, it will mostly be at me. And if he's any kind of friend, he'll forgive me for barging into his life and talking to his woman behind his back. A conversation he should have had himself. I'm gonna cut him some slack for being in a confused state of grief. So he'd better cut me some slack for being right."

Kayla chuckled at that. "Good point. I'll go tomorrow."

"I think that's the best plan."

"Thanks, Zane. You're a great friend." She leaned toward him and wrapped her arm around him in a sideways hug.

He did the same in return. "Nothing I wouldn't do for any of The Fight Club. We're like brothers."

CHAPTER 14

Kayla walked into the hospital and headed for the front desk. "Hi. I'm looking for Jed Holland."

The woman scanned her computer and glanced back up. "I can't give you his room number. It's listed as confidential. Are you a family friend?"

"Yes."

The woman smiled warmly. "His wife and son are in the family waiting area. I saw them a few minutes ago." She pointed to the hall to the right of her. "Go down this hall and take the first left. You can't miss it."

"Thank you so much."

Kayla tried to relax as she made her way toward the waiting area. She hoped his dad hadn't taken a turn for the worse. In either case, she needed to be there for Gage. And he was going to have to get over himself and let her.

As soon as she stepped into the room, she swallowed.

Gage sat in a plastic chair, horrifically uncomfortable looking considering its location in a waiting room, his head dipped to the floor, elbows on his knees.

A woman sat next to him, undoubtedly his mom. The

woman glanced in Kayla's direction. She smiled, and the smile grew as though she knew exactly who Kayla was. In fact, without removing her gaze, she grabbed Gage's arm and tugged.

Gage turned his face toward her and then followed her line of sight. For a split second, he stared in confusion, and then he righted himself and stood, rubbing his hands on his jeans. "Kayla."

She came into the room farther, hesitantly. She didn't want to upset anyone, especially his mother.

If she was truly unwanted, she would leave.

But suddenly Gage came toward her, picking up speed as he moved. And then his arms were around her, and he pulled her into his embrace, burying his face in her neck and clutching her a bit too hard. "You came," he mumbled into her hair.

"Of course I came. And I would have been here sooner if you hadn't been so pigheaded." She tried to sound teasing.

Thankfully, he didn't take offense. He pulled her away from his chest and looked her in the eye. "I'm sorry, baby. It was stupid." He led her from the room, holding on to her arm on one side. They retraced the steps she'd taken to get to him, all the way out the front door.

"Do you want me to leave?"

He looked at her quizzically. "No." And then he glanced around. "Oh. I just thought we could talk in private for a minute."

She nodded, relief making her slump her shoulders. "Zane came to me."

"Yeah. I figured he would. I mean I asked him to go handle things when I saw your text. I'm sure he told you more than he should have."

"Don't be mad at him. He means well." She grasped his hand as she spoke.

"I'm not." He let out a long breath. "And I'm sorry I tried to keep this part of me separate from you."

She leaned into him and wrapped her arms around his middle. "We all have vulnerabilities, Gage. It's nothing to be ashamed of. I'm choked up that you love your parents this much. It doesn't make you less of a Dom. It makes me think even more highly of you."

He wrapped his arms tight around her also and kissed the top of her head. "I should have given you more credit."

"Yes. You should have trusted me. I'm not a total bitch. You don't have to keep things from me or coddle me. I can handle a little stress and a man with a soft spot for his dad." She grinned, but he wasn't smiling back.

"Like you trust me with your secrets?"

She stopped breathing.

Fuck.

Seconds passed.

She blinked, but his words dug deep, and she had trouble processing or deciding how to respond.

Finally, Gage glanced away on a sigh. "Uncalled for. I'm an ass."

She shook her head. "No. You're right. Totally. I deserved that."

Silence stretched. When he looked back at her, he changed the subject. "The timing sucks, and my mom is a wreck, but do you want to meet her?"

"Sure, unless you'd rather wait until some other time. I don't want to intrude, and I don't want either of you to be uncomfortable."

Gage rolled his eyes. "Baby, if I don't bring you back inside to meet my mom, she will personally kill me right here, and that will be awfully messy inside the hospital."

Kayla nodded. "Did you tell her about me?"

"I did. We've had a lot of hours to kill in the last two days."

Kayla smiled. He'd told his mother about her. Her heart beat hard, her chest swelling. "I'd love to meet your mom."

～

Sunday morning Gage walked into his dad's room and froze two steps from the doorway. He held a cup of coffee in one hand and an iced latte in the other. It wasn't exactly what Kayla normally ordered, but it was the best he could do from the cafeteria.

Kayla didn't notice him yet. She was holding his father's good hand and talking to him in hushed tones. His dad was unresponsive. He hadn't regained consciousness since the stroke. It was too early for the doctors to know how severe the damage from this second stroke might be.

Gage almost dropped the drinks. How could he have been so stupid as to keep this from Kayla? She was strong. Clearly stronger than himself. As he inched closer, he saw that Kayla caressed the back of his dad's hand with her fingers.

Tears gathered in Gage's eyes, and he fought to keep them from falling.

"Hey. I brought coffee." She glanced his way, and he handed the iced cup to her as she twisted toward him. "Are you telling Dad all my dirty secrets?" He grinned and set his cup of coffee down on the table by the bed, his hand landing on Kayla's back and stroking up to wrap around her neck. He leaned over her from behind. "You know he can't hear you, right?"

Kayla frowned. "You can't know that for sure. He needs to know people are around him and rooting for him."

He kissed her forehead, swallowing the lump in his throat as she tipped her head back to meet his gaze. "Where's Mom?"

"She went home to change and hopefully take a nap. I told her I would let you know when you got here."

"How long have you been here?" He'd only gone to the cafeteria. After another night slumped in a chair in the corner of the room, he was stiff and uncomfortable. He needed sleep himself. He'd introduced Kayla to his mom yesterday and they'd bonded over vending machine snacks in the waiting room. But seeing Kayla with his dad took his breath away.

"I must have arrived right after you went to the cafeteria." She smiled.

Gage took his father's palm from Kayla and squeezed.

He sat on the side of the bed and rubbed his dad's leg under the blankets. For the first time in his life, he felt the weight of the world lifting. Even though his father's condition was uncertain, Kayla was his. And she was a gem.

They sat like that for a few hours, Kayla never seeming interested in leaving. The two of them bantered with each other, talking to his father as though the man could hear them.

When his mother returned, she looked slightly refreshed. She hugged Gage and then Kayla. "I still can't believe he was keeping you from us," she teased. "He's lost his marbles." His mom leaned down to kiss her husband's forehead.

Gage's chest tightened. His parents had always been so close. This had to be hard on both of them. And it got harder every day. The future was uncertain, but after this second stroke, it seemed unlikely Jed Holland would ever return to normal.

His mother pointed at the door. "Go. Both of you. Gage, you need sleep. We're fine here. I'll call you if there's any change. It could be weeks before he improves. You know that."

Gage hesitated, but when Kayla wrapped her arm around his and hugged him close, he knew he needed to be alone with her. It was true he needed sleep, and the only way that would be restful was with her at his side.

Gage squeezed his father's hand and led Kayla out of the hospital. When they stepped outside, the fresh air made him tip his head back and take a deep breath. "Follow me?"

"Of course," she whispered, leaning up on her tiptoes and kissing him on the lips, a soft kiss that promised him she was at his side.

When they arrived at home, he kicked off his shoes and padded through the quiet house, tugging Kayla behind him.

"Should we get Thor from Zane?"

"Later. Zane will take care of him. I need sleep. And I need you with me."

"Okay."

In his bedroom, he turned toward her, took her face in his hands, and kissed her long and deep. His eyes slid closed as he stroked her tongue with his own, reaching for the hem of her shirt. He broke the kiss to see what he was doing.

Gage tugged her shirt over her head and proceeded to remove the rest of her clothes. "God, baby. You take my breath away every time." He stepped back and divested himself of everything he wore also. And then he led her to his bed and pulled her into his embrace as he covered them. With both arms wrapped around her, he settled her back against his front and kissed her neck. "You smell so sweet. Never change this shampoo."

She giggled as his breath hit her skin, squirming in his embrace.

But he held tight. "So tired, baby. Give me some time. Please don't leave."

"Never," she whispered, her hands settling over his and squeezing him with reassurance.

Kayla fell into the most peaceful sleep she'd experienced right alongside Gage. She woke before him and watched the sun fall in the sky while he continued to inhale and exhale the shallow breaths of deep sleep.

Watching him was the best thing in the world. He still touched her in several places, but when she'd awoken, she found herself on her back. He had one muscular leg nestled between hers and a hand lying on her belly. The sheet had slipped down so her breasts were exposed, the nipples puckering the instant she woke up to see his face next to her.

She'd been dreaming, and now that she saw her surroundings, she understood why. Her pussy was wet, drenched in fact. Not surprising considering the way her legs were pressed open by the giant thigh between them.

Her breathing increased as she tried to remain still and enjoy staring at the man who was beside her. He'd given her so much in such a short time. And yesterday he gave her the last piece of himself, his vulnerability.

She'd watched him with his mother and then with his father, Aletha and Jed, and understood immediately what Zane told her. Gage's parents were beyond important to him. He loved them deeply. And he ached just as deeply for what they were going through. That sort of raw exposure would be difficult to share with the woman you'd been seeing for such a short time.

Of course, she knew their relationship had escalated fast. She could barely recognize herself from a few weeks ago. And she knew deep inside she owed him information about her past. It would be painful reliving the details, but it was only fair. His words about both of them keeping something from the other had made her cringe. She hadn't been able to shake the uneasy feeling she'd had about the imbalance of their relationship since then.

She hadn't expected to ever be this intimately involved with a man again in this lifetime, but now she was. There was no denying how she felt every time she was with him, or even when she wasn't.

Suddenly, Gage's knee shifted upward, pressing firmly against her pussy. At the same time, his hand skimmed up her belly to cup her breast.

Kayla moaned and turned her face toward him. Her body was instantly on alert. He hadn't made love to her for a week. She wanted to feel him inside her again.

He was smiling at her through hooded eyes. "Best sleep ever," he mumbled. His cock grew rapidly against her hip, and he leaned his face into her neck to nibble a path toward her ear. He pressed his entire frame closer, squeezing her breast and pinching her nipple. His lips met her ear. "Open wider for me, baby."

She bent her knee and let it fall to the side.

Gage kissed a path down her body, sucking her free nipple into his mouth on the way. He climbed between her legs, slunk down lower, and pushed her thighs wider with both hands. His face disappeared between her legs before she knew what was happening. "Mmm." His hum against her pussy made her buck into his mouth.

He backed off, lifting his face to meet her gaze. "Baby, stay still. Ass on the bed. Hands above your head."

She lifted her shaking arms up over her and grabbed the rungs of the bed. It was easier if she grounded herself like that. Less tempting to release her fingers and reach for him. And God how he loved to have her sprawled out like a feast before him.

"Can you stay still?"

"I'll try, Sir."

He grinned. "We'll see." And he lowered his mouth to her pussy again, licking a path up to her clit and then circling the swollen nub before flicking his tongue over it rapidly.

Kayla stiffened, working hard to remain still. She closed her eyes as she concentrated on his talented tongue. Within a minute she was on the edge.

"Don't come, baby." He lifted off her again.

She gasped, biting her lip to keep from begging him to let her come.

Is this how it would always be with him? Gage dominating her in bed, and her enjoying it immensely. Her fear of being harmed was dissipating. He was nothing but tender and attentive. At no point had he shown signs of turning on her.

It was hard, letting him in like that. It took herculean effort to trust, but it was getting easier every day that went by as Gage proved himself over and over.

"Flip over, baby."

She lifted her head off the pillow. "Sir?"

"Onto your knees." He lifted from between her legs and grabbed her waist to help her.

She released the rungs of the bedframe, surprised by his maneuver. Before she could wrap her mind around his intent, she was on her elbows and knees, her ass in the air.

Her nipples grazed the sheet beneath her, stiffening with every movement as Gage nudged her knees apart and settled on his between her thighs.

His hands were on her everywhere. He flattened his palms and caressed them up her back and down again. "I love the way your back dips right here," he said as he thumbed the small of her back, making her squirm.

His hands landed on her ass next, massaging the globes and pulling them apart.

Kayla held her breath as his thumbs grazed down the crack between her cheeks. "Kayla, I need to know if you've ever been taken here." He tapped her puckered hole as he spoke.

Kayla flinched at the contact and then shook her head. "No, Sir." She wasn't at all sure she was interested in such a thing.

His hands left her butt to circle around and dance up her belly until he cupped her breasts. He toyed with them until her nipples were ultra-sensitive. "I love the way your tits respond to me." He pinched the hard buds in emphasis. And then he released her and leaned across her leg to one side. He opened the bedside table and righted himself behind her.

Something soft landed on her back, dragging up her spine until it met her neck.

"I want you to let me blindfold you, baby."

She flinched. The idea scared the fuck out of her.

This is Gage.

He tapped her hand on one side of her face. "You aren't restrained, baby. If it gets to be too much, all you have to do is tug the material off your eyes."

True. But in the meantime, she worried she might freak out on him.

"Trust me, baby. Every time you push yourself to step

outside the box, it makes me so fucking hot my cock aches. You know I won't strike you just because you can't see me."

True again.

"There's no correlation. I'm just asking you to eliminate your sense of sight. Have you ever been blindfolded?"

"No, Sir."

"Good." He wove his fingers into her hair and lifted her head. "I love that I have the privilege of being your first at so many things. I won't let you down. Ever. That's my promise to you."

"Yes, Sir." Her voice was weak.

"Safe word?"

"Red, Sir."

Gage leaned over her and slid the silky black material of the blindfold over her eyes. "Breathe, baby. Nothing has changed. I'm still the same man behind you. You have full control over the situation."

"Yes, Sir," she whispered.

One finger grazed down her spine until she wiggled. "So sexy." His finger hit the top of her crack, making her press her ass out toward him. He chuckled. "You like the idea of having me touch you here." He tapped her forbidden hole again.

She squirmed, battling a moan that leaked out anyway. She had no idea whether she would enjoy having something in her ass or not, but Gage could suggest anything in the world to her, and she would probably readily agree just from listening to his persuasive tone.

"That's my girl. Relax your cheeks." He circled the rim of her hole and tapped again.

Holy hell she was aroused. Nothing he did dampened her need.

Gage released her ass where he gripped it with his

other hand and reached for something next to her. What else had he set there?

A pop sounded, and moments later something cold and wet landed on her rear entrance.

"Gage…" She lurched fully to attention. Lubricant. Whatever he had planned, her comfort was his top priority, and the idea made her moan in satisfaction.

"God, baby. You're such an open book. I can read the raw emotion coming from the tiny sounds you make. Does it intrigue you to have my finger at your back entrance?" At the end of his question, that finger dipped inside her just enough to force her to concentrate on the sensation, ignoring his question.

Gage chuckled, a lower, deeper pitch than usual. He also slipped his finger in deeper as she relaxed into his touch. He twisted his wrist in both directions, making her hyper-sensitive nerve endings come alive.

Never had she considered that ass play would turn her on. She always imagined guys liked it because asses were usually tighter than pussies. So she was in no way prepared for the firing of synapses that made her press her butt toward Gage, squirming for more attention.

"That's it, baby. Let it feel good. Your tight hole is grasping my finger so hard my cock is pulsing at the idea of taking you here."

She concentrated on his fingers, stroking her in a place no one had ever touched. With her vision blocked, it was easier, just as Gage had insinuated. Nevertheless, she wasn't mentally prepared for him to fuck her there yet.

"Not going to take your ass today, baby. Just giving you a taste. I'm going to replace my finger with a plug now. It will fill you so when I enter your pussy, you'll experience double penetration."

God. Would he please stop talking? Did he have any

idea how his voice affected her? His gentle play by play was enough to make her come.

The second his finger popped out of her, something cooler hit her hole. He swirled the plug around the entrance and then pushed gently. "Only slightly larger than my finger, baby. Relax for me. Let it slide in." He gripped her hip with his free hand to hold her steady.

Until then, she hadn't realized she was rocking back and forth.

"That's my girl. Trust me, baby." Every time he used that word, trust, she worried about how deep she was falling for him. So deep she'd give him anything he asked for.

And that was exactly what she'd done with Simon until he'd taken advantage of her and twisted everything about their relationship into something ugly.

"Kayla, come out of that dark place. Listen to my voice. I'm not him. I'm not going to hurt you or pressure you in any way. You know that."

She swallowed and licked her lips. "Yes, Sir."

"Do you need me to stop?"

She hesitated briefly. "No, Sir."

He squeezed her cheek with one hand and pulled it away from the other, spreading her open more. "Take the plug in for me, baby. Breathe through it." He applied a slight pressure, awakening her puckered hole further.

The second she unclamped her cheeks, Gage pushed the plug home.

Kayla moaned. He twisted the knob outside her body in both directions, making every nerve ending come alive. Her pussy clutched as if it were the hole being filled, and all she knew was the overwhelming need for that to be true.

She got her wish. Gage's touch disappeared. She heard the distinct ripping sound of the condom, and then his hand was on her hips again, his cock lined up with her entrance, the tip grazing between her lips until she went mad with the need to be filled. "Gage…"

"Baby. So sexy. Your little whimpers drive me crazy." On the end of that sentence, he drove into her, clutching her hips with both hands and then holding her steady.

Kayla screamed. She shot so close to orgasm, it unnerved her.

"Go ahead, baby. Come for me. And then I'll make you come again." He thrust in to the hilt and held steady.

With both holes filled, her arms shook, and she thought she would collapse. And then the orgasm ripped through her, claiming her with its force. The same way Gage claimed her with his cock.

Before she finished pulsing around him, he moved, stroking in and out of her body, giving her not a second of reprieve before one orgasm turned into two.

Fuck. The high was amazing. She let the waves crash through her body. She lost the battle to hold herself off the bed and set her forehead on the pillow.

Gage pumped faster, harder. He'd never taken her like that before. And she liked it. Liked it so much her pussy continued to grip him even after that second orgasm washed through her. It should have left her sated, but instead she felt the need rising again. She fisted her hands at the sides of her head, almost heedless of the blindfold by that point. Who cared if she could see? As long as Gage consumed her so thoroughly, she knew she was well taken care of.

He held her firmer. She knew his release was close when he grunted and sucked in a sharp breath, only to hold it. And then he came.

She felt his cock pulse inside her, and when the base of

his dick hit her clit, she was swept over the edge a third time, following Gage into the abyss.

She breathed so heavily as she came down from on high she thought she might hyperventilate. Instead, she found herself flattened to the bed as Gage nudged her knees and eased her onto her belly.

He set his lips on her neck, raining kisses across her shoulders as he pulled out of her and lowered himself to one side. He tugged the blindfold off her eyes.

When she met his gaze, she found him smiling. He touched her face with his fingertips as though afraid if he didn't memorize her features before the end of the hour, she would vanish and he would never be able to remember her face.

CHAPTER 15

Kayla stared at him for an eternity, hardly blinking, not wanting to let the moment pass. She couldn't move anyway. Her limbs shook from the strain of holding herself up.

Gage's breath came heavy on her cheek, slowing gradually. He groaned when he finally pulled off her and made his way to the bathroom. Moments later, he returned, having cleaned himself up and carrying a washcloth.

Kayla finally mustered up the energy to flip onto her back and spread her legs for him. Gage eased the plug from her tight ass as she winced. Then he cleaned her with the cloth until he was satisfied.

"We have to eat, baby."

Her stomach growled at that moment, as though recognizing his words. She giggled. "I guess so, but not if it involves moving. I can't do that. You've killed me."

Gage grinned down at her. "Don't move. I'll be right back." He turned and padded from the room, still naked, his fantastic firm ass and the red, white, and blue tattoo on his shoulder giving her the best view.

The room was quite dark by then, the sun having slipped behind the horizon. She felt two conflicting sensations that made her somewhat nauseous at the thought of food. The sense of peace she had in Gage's bed, in his house, in his life, was enough to make her grab on to that lifeline and ride it to the end of the Earth.

On the flip side, she needed to talk to him, and she wasn't looking forward to the conversation. She knew in her heart her resolve to keep those four years buried for the rest of her life would no longer work. Not with the way she felt about Gage. Not after what he'd given her of himself. Not after the look she saw in his eyes every time she met his gaze.

He deserved to know.

But what happened after that? What if he looked at her differently?

Kayla turned over again and moaned into the pillow. She knew Gage was bringing food, but it would have to wait. There was no way she could swallow a single bite with this weight on her shoulders. She pulled herself to sitting, grabbed the blanket from the foot of the bed, and wrapped it around her.

She found herself drawn to the window, the rays of light coming in from outside pulling her for some reason. Or perhaps it was the window itself that called to her. It was an inviting bay window stuffed with pillows in a variety of dark colors, almost feminine in an otherwise masculine room.

She smiled as she settled into the space, wondering if Gage's mother, Aletha, had helped him decorate. She leaned against the wall, drew her knees up, and hugged herself in the cocoon of blanket, pillows, and moonlight.

"Baby?"

She hadn't heard him enter. Surprising. But then again, her mind had gone to another time. When Kayla turned her head to see him, he was arranging several plates on the bed. He took one step toward her.

"Don't."

At her one word and the undoubtedly commanding tone, he froze. "Kayla?"

She turned her head back to the window and watched the tree limbs waving back and forth gracefully in the breeze. All she could hear was the rustle of the branches and her own breaths for long moments.

Gage had taken her advice. He didn't move another inch.

She didn't look back toward him. She took a deep breath finally, and started, "His name was Simon." She squeezed her eyes closed, cringing at the sound of the bastard's name. When she opened them again, she was ready to continue. "I met him here in Vegas. At a pizza joint, actually."

She thought she heard Gage settle onto the bed. He didn't say a word, for which she was grateful. She needed to get this out and not be interrupted.

"His smile when he slid into my booth froze me in my tracks. I couldn't even swallow the bite I was chewing. I was barely twenty years old. My father had just died. I was working for Chief Edwards and going to school. I was actually studying in that booth when he took over my life.

"And that's about how it happened. One minute I was me, and the next minute I was some other person, unrecognizable. That's the pull he had on me.

"I fell fast and hard. Stupid." She paused, pursing her lips while she tried to pull herself together and keep from letting her emotions rush in. "In less than a week Simon managed to convince me we were destined for each other. And I fell for it. He whisked me to a chapel right here in my own town, slapped a ring on my finger, and then packed me up and moved me all the way across the country to a naval base in Mississippi."

Gage gasped at that, but he held his tongue. Thank God.

She'd never told him a thing about Simon. Everything he knew he'd pieced together for himself, but that hadn't included the fact her previous Dom had been in the military. There was no way for him to know that.

"It was sunshine and roses at first, but not for long. Simon isolated me. He didn't want me to leave the base apartment. He didn't want me to meet the other wives, not even those of his friends. He said they would taint me with their lazy greed. He seemed to think all of them had married their husbands to get a cushy life of luxury. As if life in a dinky apartment on a naval base was so wonderful.

"I tried to be what he needed. Honestly I did. But it was hard. By the time I realized what a huge mistake I had made, it was too late. I should have gone home. I could have called Chief Edwards and asked for help or money, but my stupid pride got in the way. I was embarrassed. And as my problems mounted, it only got worse.

"There was no way to please Simon. He belonged to a fetish club, and he started bringing me there. The first time, I was scared out of my mind. He chose what I wore and set down rules I couldn't begin to remember all at once.

"And then he would punish me. At first he did so by making fun of me in front of his friends at the club. He would taunt me and laugh at me. He would expose me to anyone he wanted. I was so innocent that I nearly died of embarrassment. And then when he couldn't get off from that alone, he started spanking me and later escalated to beating me." She paused, ducking her head and staring at her knees, trying to gather her emotions so she could continue.

Gage whispered through the darkness. "Baby, you don't have to—"

"No, I do," she interrupted. "Let me finish." She lifted her gaze back to the moonlight and continued. "The first time he spanked me was at home. I'm not going to sugarcoat it. It wasn't pretty. He was mad about something I did or didn't do that day. I have no idea what it was. It was always something. The lists he left me each morning were ridiculous and long.

"My butt hurt so bad after that beating, I couldn't sit down the next day. And this made him delirious with laughter. When he spanked me at the club, he did so for an audience. He would strip me, attach me to a bench or cross, and whip me just enough to keep people from questioning him. How he managed to avoid drawing blood when we were in public I have no idea. But he saved the real beatings for the house."

Deep breaths. Kayla thought back to those times and cringed. "No one at the club knew what happened in our home in private. He was very careful that way. And I was learning. There were rules in that lifestyle. If you bent the rules, you wouldn't be permitted to enter the club. So, Simon followed the rules, skirting the edges when we were in public.

"I watched the other interactions at the club. Month after month, year after year. I longed for the type of relationship other women had. I saw Doms that took care of their submissives like they worshipped them. I craved that. I never had it, but I craved it.

"I wouldn't have said I was submissive before I met Simon, but years of submitting to him opened my eyes to what others had. I sat for many an hour on my knees in a corner of that club and witnessed. And then I learned to take something from the spanking and flogging I was subjected to. I learned to withdraw from this world and enter a different space while Simon's hand tormented me.

"Instead of concentrating on his intentions, which were all ill-conceived, I let myself slip into a sort of subspace that released me from this world in a way. I learned to like it. I learned to crave it. When Simon beat me, I escaped. Those were the best times, and I looked forward to them, as sick as that may sound.

"Even at home when he hit me hard enough to draw blood, I escaped. He rarely fucked me after the first year of our marriage, saying I was dry and frigid. And he was right. There was no way for me to get aroused at his hand. He was a sick bastard. I know this now."

She sucked in a deep breath and let tears run down her face. There was no way to avoid them. She wiped them with the back of her hand.

Gage moved. She didn't stop him. He came toward her slowly. She heard every footstep. She knew he did this on purpose to keep from scaring her. Finally, he was behind her. He set his hands on her shoulders, scooted her forward, and climbed into the window seat at her back.

When he pulled her into his arms, wrapping her tight in his embrace, she knew she would be okay. She leaned her cheek on his arm. They sat in silence for a while. There was more to say, but she needed this time to just *be* first.

Minutes went by. "You left him." It wasn't a question. Gage was simply prodding her for the rest of the story.

She shook her head. "I'm not sure if I ever would have left him. I was too far gone. I was lost. But I got lucky. He was deployed to Iraq. Or I thought I was lucky. Instead of leaving me in peace at the naval base, he dragged me to a remote area in Alabama and left me with his parents.

"I'd met them many times. We visited them twice a year. And I'd known from the first moment I met them where Simon got his nastiness. They were awful humans who saw about as much value in me as Simon did. He dumped me at their cabin and warned me to behave and do as they said, or I would pay big time when he got back."

Gage stroked her head with one hand, brushing her hair from her face. He kissed her gently over and over on her forehead, but didn't interrupt.

"The situation with his parents was worse. I was like a living Cinderella immediately. But for some reason I started to grow a spine. These people were nothing to me. Why the hell would I stay and take their abuse? It was one thing to live with an abusive husband. It was another thing to live with his vile parents.

"It took months. They had no Internet. No cell service. I decided the best tactic was to pretend to be the best daughter-in-law I could be. This earned me privileges. As soon as his parents decided they could trust me to behave, they started sending me into town to the store or the post office. And that was when I got my break. I watched people. I made acquaintances. Eventually, I befriended an older woman at the grocery store who knew Simon's family. I could tell by the way she looked at me that she knew. She *knew*. Estelle Forester saved my life.

"She was so kind, and I finally opened up to her over a cup of coffee on one of my trips to town. She immediately helped me get a lawyer in town who started divorce proceedings. I was ecstatic. It took another few days, but the second I had the paperwork signed and delivered, I didn't return to the house. Copies were sent to Simon overseas and to his parents. I thought I was free. All I needed was enough money to get out of Alabama and I could return to Vegas.

"Mrs. Forester let me stay with her. I hid at her home, actually. No one knew where I was. I didn't want to risk any wrath coming her way in town, so I hid. I gained strength while she took care of me. Simon's parents asked around for me, but no one breathed a word. The only people who knew where I was were Estelle and the lawyer.

"The Bollings found their car in town, but they finally assumed I had run away. All the while I was right there in Mrs. Forester's house." Kayla took a deep breath and relaxed farther into Gage's embrace. He held her tight. She let relief sweep over her.

"So eventually you got the money to come home to Vegas?"

"Not exactly. It was even better than that. I was waiting on the papers to be served. It takes time when someone is overseas to accomplish that. And then I got a lucky break." She shivered, well aware how insane it was that she considered Simon's death to be a blessing. But it was. "He was killed in combat."

"Jesus."

"Yeah. Roadside bomb took out everyone in his Hummer. There wasn't even enough left of him to send home. All the Navy had was DNA evidence that he'd been there.

"And I was free."

"God, baby." He twisted to one side and turned her face to his. "I'm so sorry."

She smiled wanly. "It's over. I'm safe." *Sort of.* She wiped her eyes again. "I rented a car, went back to the base, settled everything with the Navy, and cleared out the savings account. It wasn't much, but it was something. I never even entered the apartment we shared. I then got on the first flight to Vegas."

"My God. So, Simon never signed the divorce papers?"

"Never even saw them."

"So all the benefits are yours."

She nodded, but dipped her head. She couldn't meet his gaze. Telling him that saga was all she could manage for today. The rest would have to wait.

He squeezed her tighter until she couldn't breathe. "You're an amazing woman."

Those words shocked her. Not what she'd expected. She didn't consider herself amazing. She was simply a survivor, and at that she had been lucky more than anything else. No telling what might have happened if Simon had lived to see the divorce papers. Her life might have been easier if he'd signed them, cutting her loose.

Gage scooted them to the edge of the window seat and lifted her into his arms. He walked across the room and deposited her on the bed, shoving the plates of sandwiches and chips to one side. He hovered over her, his body smashing her to the mattress, his hands cupping her face. "I love you."

She gasped, her mouth falling open.

"I mean it. Don't say anything now. I know it's soon. But I wanted you to know. If you thought anything you just told me would turn me away from you, you were wrong. I love you, Kayla. And we'll work through all of this and come out victorious."

She nodded, another tear slipping free to run down her cheek.

Gage wiped it away, kissed her gently, and held her tight until she fell back asleep. Food could wait. She was exhausted. Years of stress had slipped from her body, leaving her depleted. The last thing she knew as she drifted off was Gage's soft mouth on her cheek.

CHAPTER 16

Warm lips touched hers, nibbling a path to her ear. Panting and wetness landed on the other side of her face. Kayla smiled as she realized Thor was next to her. She opened her eyes a slit to find the dog watching her intently. "When did you get here, big guy?"

She lifted an arm to wrap around his softness.

The voice from her other side was teasing. "Ah, I see how I rate now. Not, hey Gage. Not even a kiss." He chuckled.

"Mmm." Kayla buried her face in Thor's neck. "That's about how it is. Dogs are more loyal. They love you unconditionally."

"I'm loyal. And I promise to love you unconditionally."

Kayla stiffened. Was it really possible for Gage to be in love with her so soon? Of course, it wasn't really soon if you considered how long they'd known each other. But their relationship hadn't been at a measurable level until a few weeks ago.

"Zane brought him over a little while ago. He bounded

right into the bedroom and took up a spot next to you. It's like he's some sort of protector."

"He knows who loves him and gives him the best treats."

"You've been feeding my dog treats behind my back?" He chuckled again.

Kayla turned to face Gage with a grin.

"You need to get up, baby. You need to eat. You haven't had a bite all day."

She pulled herself to sitting. She was still exhausted from the great reveal, but she felt a sense of relief also. The bulk of her secrets had been revealed. She cringed as she admitted to herself that she still carried the most important one of all, one Gage wouldn't be remotely happy to hear about. But that was precisely the reason she would keep it to herself. "Feed me," she announced as she stood on wobbly legs. "What time is it?"

"Almost midnight."

Thor jumped to the ground beside her, his head rubbing against her leg.

"That dog is spoiled." Gage came around to her side. He'd pulled on a pair of jeans that sat low on his hips and left his delicious broad chest open for perusal.

Kayla licked her lips and leaned against his pecs.

"Uh uh." Gage took her shoulders and held her back. "Don't start that. Food first and then I'll think about claiming my dessert from between your legs."

Kayla shivered as he spoke. The idea of Gage settled between her legs, his lips on her pussy, made her grow automatically wet with need. But she couldn't deny she was hungry, and the smells coming from the kitchen made her mouth water. "You cooked?"

"Yep." He took her hand and tugged her toward the door.

She tugged back. "I need clothes."

He firmed his grip. "No you don't." He turned his head and winked. "I like you naked."

"Not while I eat."

"Yes, while you eat. And if you don't stop arguing, I'll make you sit on the table with your legs spread and feed you myself."

She clamped her lips shut and followed him, knowing he would do such a thing, and not entirely sure she wouldn't enjoy the idea.

An hour later, she was once again in his bed. She couldn't lift her arms off the mattress because all her energy had been depleted by his dessert. The man had spread her wide and laid claim to her pussy as though he were starving and hadn't just eaten the most delicious spaghetti she'd ever tasted.

After bringing her to a quick delightful orgasm with his tongue flicking over her clit, he now plunged that tongue into her channel, fucking her rapidly while managing to stroke across her G-spot.

"Gage..." She couldn't take much more. She was too sensitive.

His response was to hold her tighter, his hands grasping her thighs above her knees and pressing them higher and wider. And then he sucked.

She nearly shot off the bed when he added that pressure. She burrowed her hands in his hair and tugged, but he didn't relent. His mouth and lips and tongue moved everywhere, eating her so thoroughly her vision blurred. It was too soon. She'd come less than a minute ago.

He didn't see it that way. In his book it was never too soon for a second orgasm. And he intended to deliver.

Kayla stiffened, her hands no longer pulling on his head, but switching to holding him down as her arousal peaked again. "OhGodohGod." She twisted her head to one side and tried to catch a breath, but that tongue...

Gage shifted so his shoulder held her leg open. He sucked her clit into his mouth and used his free hand to thrust a finger into her pussy.

If she could have lifted her body off the bed, she would have, but he was stronger, and she was occupied with too many thoughts of floating to get her leg muscles to listen to her brain cells.

When Gage's finger trailed down the space between her pussy and her ass, she moaned. She should be embarrassed to find his touch so arousing, but she couldn't remember how to find anything he did mortifying. Two seconds later, her arousal shot out of this world when his finger pressed into her ass and stroked upward toward her channel.

Kayla moaned long and loud as her second orgasm washed through her body. It lasted forever, the pulsing of both channels clenching at Gage's finger and tongue. She was lost. Totally and irrevocably a goner to Gage Holland.

Kayla woke up early the next morning before Gage, little wonder considering how long she'd slept the day before. It was still dark outside. In fact, she had no idea what time it was, but there was enough light to assume the sun was thinking about making an appearance. She could hear Thor rustling around on the floor, and she was glad he hadn't decided to sleep on the bed with them this time because she had plans that didn't involve his furry self getting in the way.

Gage's huge frame was snuggled against her, as usual. The man was hot and suffocating when they slept. He had one leg tossed over hers, as usual, and one arm draped over her belly, as usual, his hand cupping her breast in a way that made her immediately come alive. In fact, his thumb rested on her nipple by coincidence, though Gage clearly had no idea because he was breathing heavily in deep sleep.

Kayla shifted slowly out of his clutches, biting her lip to keep from moaning as his thumb dragged across her erect nipple. She had no idea how she managed to accomplish it, but somehow she nudged Gage onto his back and slithered down his body, taking the sheet with her until she could see his entire glorious frame at rest.

Normally there was no way she would be able to accomplish such a thing. Gage didn't seem like the kind of guy who slept hard. He was often jumpy and alert way before her, but luck was on her side this morning, and she made her way down to his cock.

For a minute she stared at him, amazed at how erect he could be in sleep. He wasn't completely engorged—she'd seen him enough times to know that much—but not far from it. She hesitated longer than she wanted to admire his damn fine body.

What she ever saw in Simon, she had no idea. Simon had been fit for sure. He was a military man after all, but he was nowhere near as ruggedly built as Gage. Nor had the asshole engaged in any unnecessary extra exertion. He did what was strictly required by the Navy and nothing more. He sure wouldn't have mustered up the energy to spend his off hours fighting in a ring. God forbid he get hit by someone else. No. Of course not. The only person swinging punches in Simon's life was Simon.

Kayla shook the unwanted images from her mind and focused on the fine specimen in front of her. She tentatively set the tip of one finger on Gage's length and stroked from the base to the tip. Precome leaked from the slit, shocking her an instant before his deep rumbly voice interrupted her perusal. "You gonna look at it all day, or do I get the privilege of something more than that?"

She jerked her gaze up to meet his. She should have known better than to think she had the upper hand for once.

He stared down at her, his mouth curved in a smile, his eyes twinkling with amusement.

"I thought—"

"Baby, I'm never fully asleep when you're in my bed. But I've enjoyed allowing you to think I was."

She rolled her eyes. "Seriously? That's fucked up." She swatted his chest with her hand, her forearm brushing against his engorged head.

Gage moaned and grabbed her under her arms to haul her up his body until she lay on top of him. He cupped her face and took her mouth in a kiss that made her forget her frustration in less than a second. When he finally released her, he nodded toward his cock. "What did you have planned after show and tell?"

She shrugged and lowered her face to lose his gaze. "That was all. Just wanted to look," she lied, testing him.

"Really? Huh. Didn't look that way from where I was. If you had licked those lips one more time, I thought I might come from that alone."

She lifted her gaze to his again, knowing her eyes were wider this time. "No way."

He nodded.

She licked her lips again, aware of the effect and using it to her advantage.

Gage's cock, nestled between her belly and his, jerked. "You're killing me here." He moaned and tipped his head back, his hands gripping her biceps.

Kayla giggled as she decided to put him out of his misery. She wiggled her way down his body, planted herself between his thighs, and took his length in her hand. She wanted to control this blowjob. And she sincerely hoped Gage would allow it. Sure, normally he was the Dom in bed, or even in the house. But for this she needed some leeway. Hopefully he could recognize that and give her the time she craved. Then again, not verbalizing that need was stupid and could lead to discomfort on her part.

Kayla lifted her gaze to him again. "Babe, I need you to, um…" God, how did she tell him something she couldn't even form into words in her head?

Gage wove the fingers of one hand into her hair and stroked her cheek gently with his thumb. "I know, baby. I won't move a muscle. Take all the time you need."

She exhaled slowly and nodded, fighting the tears that threatened to fall. This Dom of hers was perfection. He knew when to control her, how much, and how often. But better yet, he knew when to back off and let her have her way.

Simon would have slammed her face onto his dick and forced her to swallow his come. Gage showed no signs of anything similar. In fact, he lifted both arms and tucked his hands under his neck.

Kayla turned her attention back to the cock in front of her and licked through the slit at the top. She tasted his come for the first time and brought it into her mouth. Salty, but also flavored with the heady taste of Gage. She trailed her tongue down his length next and then back up to the tip.

He moaned softly, breathing rapidly, but he said nothing and didn't move a muscle, other than to flex his cock, which might not have been voluntary.

When she sucked his length into her mouth, she didn't hesitate. She sucked hard, drawing him deep, taking as much of his length as she could and swirling her tongue around his shaft as she did so.

Gage's thighs flinched, but other than that, he made no move. She thought he held his breath since moments ago she'd heard his deep heavy inhale of arousal.

When she drew off him and kissed the tip, he exhaled sharply. "Oh God, baby. That's so fucking amazing." His legs squirmed on the bed beside her, but he kept his hands under his neck.

And Kayla continued, sucking him into her mouth again, deeper this time. Not all the way to the back of her throat, but close. She wasn't comfortable enough not to gag, but she'd never enjoyed a blowjob before this morning either. The idea that she made Gage lose a piece of himself was intoxicating. She did this to him. She made those sounds escape his lips unbidden. She made his legs stiffen and shake at her sides. And she wanted more.

She set up a rhythm, bobbing on and off his cock, increasing the speed and intensity as she went. It didn't take long for him to pant and lose control.

"Kayla, baby. I'm gonna come."

Wasn't that the plan? She would have laughed if she hadn't been so otherwise occupied. Instead she sucked him harder. When he finally bucked his hips up a few inches, she knew he was close. And seconds later, he came, his orgasm shooting into the back of her mouth. She swallowed rapidly, trying not to lose any drop of him. It was no hardship since she wanted that with him more than she'd ever wanted anything with a man.

When she finished and his cock lost the tiniest bit of its erection, she released him from her mouth with a pop and set her face on his thigh. So many times Gage had taken her. So many ways he'd made her feel special. She hoped this one little act could convey how much she appreciated him without words. Especially because she wanted to do that again. Soon.

Suddenly, Gage hauled Kayla off his thigh and flipped their position so that she lay on her belly. He massaged her back up and down her spine. She couldn't control the noises she made at the simple touch of his hands. "Baby, stop moaning. I'm trying to rub your muscles. I can't do that with you whimpering every few seconds."

"Mmm. Why is that?"

He pinched her ass playfully. "Imp. It's hard enough to control my cock around you. When you make those noises, I can't be held responsible for my actions. So, unless you want me to fuck you again this morning, I suggest you stop that."

Kayla smiled into the pillow. Was that a challenge? She knew she should be sore from the number of times and ways he'd taken her in the last twenty-four hours, but she didn't care.

Gage suddenly stopped and slid down next to her. He brushed her hair from her face until she met his gaze. "I need to go see my dad."

"Of course." She cringed at her insensitivity. She was monopolizing his time and meanwhile his parents needed him. She moved to lift herself off the bed, but Gage held her steady with a hand at the small of her back.

"Stay." He kissed her temple. "Please. I know it's too soon, and I won't freak you out by asking you to move in with me, but I want you here in my house in my bed. Stay?"

"I need to go home, Gage. You need some time with your parents, and if I don't hurry, I'll be late for work."

"Lord. It's Monday."

She nodded and cupped his face with both hands. "I don't even have clothes and my mail is probably piling up. I haven't been home for days."

He kissed her again, lingering around her ear lobe until she squirmed. How did he manage to affect her like that so easily, even after more orgasms than she could count? "Come back after work then," he requested in a tone that straddled the line between a command and a plea. "Please?"

She nodded, swallowing the lump in her throat.

His smile was supreme. "I'm gonna take a quick shower, feed Thor, and get to the hospital. It's early. Take your time. Rummage around in my kitchen for food."

Thor jumped onto the bed on the other side. The dog seemed to know when it was his turn. He lay down next to her with a sigh.

Kayla giggled and wrapped an arm around his huge body.

"You're in good hands. Apparently my dog knows when to step up to the plate. It's like he senses you need him." Gage cocked his head to one side and then shook it as he walked away.

CHAPTER 17

Kayla settled into a new reality with way too much ease, and that made her nervous. She worried constantly. For one, she didn't trust fate to be so kind to her, and she fought to keep from worrying that Gage would turn on her at any point. He'd shown no signs of being the asshole Simon had turned into within a week. But still...

Gage had a full plate. Between work, the gym, and visiting his dad, they rarely had time to go to the club. Which was fine with Kayla. She enjoyed getting to know Gage's mom and spending time with his dad during his slow recovery. It had been so long since she'd been part of a real family. She prayed the bottom didn't fall out and leave her lonelier than she had been before dating Gage.

He hadn't mentioned her condo, which was a relief. She wasn't even close to prepared to give it up. It was a lifeline in her mind. Someplace she could fall back on when everything went to shit. And Gage was smart enough to know it. She was sure that was why he never brought it up. He insisted she stay with him, and he drove her to her place a few times a week to check on things and grab her mail, but he never pushed the issue of her keeping the place.

His dominance was the perfect balance. Kayla worried herself sick that he had been a firmer Dom than she could ever tolerate before she'd come around. After all, he was a master at spanking and flogging. Submissives had requested his attentions for years at the club. She'd seen him do scenes with dozens of women. Nothing sexual, just submissives that enjoyed his touch.

The second week after she'd started staying at his place, she questioned him about it. They were at Extreme, sitting in a booth talking to his friends. Harper, the head bouncer came over and spoke in Gage's ear. Gage shook his head and glanced at Kayla. Harper smiled and nodded. He walked away before Kayla had any idea what he said.

Later, on the dance floor, Kayla tipped her head back and asked Gage about it. "What did Harper want? You stiffened at his suggestion."

"He asked if I was available to flog another submissive who requested me."

"Oh." She let her mouth hang open for a moment and then swallowed. "Do you want to do that?" She should let him. She knew it. Especially if it was something he needed. She winced inwardly, concerned she wasn't able to fulfill his needs herself. Maybe in time she could, but he wouldn't hear of it yet.

Gage reared back and narrowed his gaze. "Hell no. Kayla, I'm not doing scenes with other women. I'm with you now. That would be awkward."

She shrugged. Her voice was weak when she spoke, but she forced the words out anyway. "Lots of Doms do scenes with other women even though they're in a committed relationship. It's not unheard of, Gage." She gripped his shirt in the back with her fists. "If it's something you need…"

He furrowed his brow further and backed her quickly off the dance floor. She knew this maneuver. Every time he needed her undivided attention, he tugged her into a dark corner and pressed her against the wall. It made her so horny she couldn't breathe. She grabbed onto him to hold steady.

"Baby," he took her face in his hands and forced her to meet his gaze, "I'm not doing scenes with other women. I'm not 'lots of Doms.' I'm me. And the me that I am would find it distasteful. We've been through this. I don't need that. I don't have some latent need to flog a woman to feel fulfilled. I have you, and what matters is filling *your* needs. It's more than enough for me. Are we clear?"

"But—"

Gage rolled his eyes and lowered his lips to take her mouth and cut off her sentence. When he pulled back, he set his forehead on hers. "Are we going to discuss this every few weeks for the next fifty years?"

She held her breath and bit her lower lip.

"I hope not. It will get old fast. Have I given you any indication you aren't enough for me?"

"No, Sir."

"Do I dominate you enough to make you feel fulfilled?"

"Yes, Sir."

"Do you understand that it makes my cock harder than ever when you kneel in front of me?"

She swallowed.

"Your naked body spread out at my command makes me so close to coming I have to grit my teeth to stave off the inevitable." He kept talking. "When you grip the headboard of *my* bed in *my* bedroom in *my* house and keep your hands there at *my* command, I become putty for you. Do you get that?"

She nodded, barely.

Gage cupped her cheeks, tipped her head back farther, and wove his fingers into her hair. "I'm so fucking in love with you, I can't see straight. You're perfect for me in every way. I need nothing else. Not for one second since we started dating have I considered wanting to lay a hand on another woman."

She opened her mouth, but he cut her off before she could begin.

"And baby, don't even mention again that you want to try enduring a spanking or a flogging. It's out of the question. You have to let that go. It died with your ex. When you bring it up, it makes me think you aren't getting what you need. So, unless that's the case, the subject is closed." He narrowed his gaze in question.

"No, Sir." She shook her head. She'd never been more fulfilled in her life, nor had she ever expected to be as consumed with another human in this lifetime. Gage was everything to her and more. She hadn't told him she loved him yet, even though he mentioned it so many times it was becoming casual conversation for him. But she would. Soon. As soon as she had the balls to reveal one more tiny detail about her past that haunted her still every single day of her present.

She shook the thought from her mind.

"No, you aren't satisfied at my hand? Or no, you don't need more than I give you?"

"Sir, I'm beyond satisfied."

"Does your pussy get wet when I command you to obey my wishes?"

"Yes, Sir."

"Does your pussy clench when I stare at your naked body beneath me?" He leaned in closer.

"Yes, Sir." Her words were softer, breathy.

"Is your pussy wet and clenched now?"

"Yes, Sir." She barely heard her own voice that time.

He held her gaze while he removed one hand from her face and jerked it down to her skirt. In less than a second he had the material gathered in his fingers and lifted to expose her thong beneath. One second later, his finger shoved the scrap of lace to one side and plunged into her wetness.

Kayla moaned, gripping his arms tighter as her knees buckled at the contact.

Gage shoved one knee between her thighs and held her up. His finger fucked her hard, one becoming two and then two becoming three. His thumb landed on her clit. He pressed in and then rubbed rapidly.

Kayla came so fast the world spun.

He smiled. "Baby, I think we're good here."

She nodded, unable to speak over the pulsing of her pussy around his fingers. Her eyes were wide. She couldn't breathe. He held her close as she came down, not removing his fingers until her breathing steadied.

"Let's go home. It turns out I don't want to be in public tonight after all."

Kayla's cheeks burned as he dragged her through Extreme. After that intense orgasm, she knew she was in trouble. If Gage didn't want to be in public, it meant only one thing…

～

Three weeks later, Kayla went with Emily to watch Gage

fight. The arena was farther away than the last time, and Katy and Jenna had begged out.

Emily was excited, though. And that excitement rubbed off on Kayla. By the time they arrived, Emily had talked her ear off all the way there. Kayla knew much more about the sport this time around.

Gage hadn't been in a great mood. Apparently his opponent was someone Gage didn't feel confident about beating. He left right from work with the guys, leaving Kayla to come with Emily later.

The arena was small and packed. Kayla's adrenaline spiked the minute they walked inside. Something about the noise level and the smell of a fight excited her. It was crazy. Who would have thought she would find it enjoyable to watch her boyfriend kick someone's ass in the ring? Or worse yet, get his own ass kicked.

But, God almighty, all those firm masculine bodies without an ounce of fat on them... What was not to like?

Kayla followed Emily to a spot near the ring when they announced the middleweight division. Rider was in the third group, and Emily stood on her tiptoes, her hands fisted in front of her for the entire match. Kayla didn't think the woman breathed.

And Kayla couldn't blame her. Rider was impressive. He had the upper hand for the majority of the three rounds, clearly earning more points. When he won, Emily finally exhaled. "Lord, that's stressful."

It was. Kayla could feel the tension in the air. Every match, even between competitors she didn't know, put her on edge.

Two more matches went by before Gage, who came out bouncing. Kayla's turn to freak out. From the moment the bell sounded, things didn't go his way, however. The other guy swung several punches right at the beginning. Two of them hit Gage in the side of the head. Kayla winced.

Gage recovered, but he never got the upper hand for the first round. He landed a few kicks, but his opponent landed more and got him in a neck hold once. Gage didn't go down, but he struggled.

The second round wasn't better. Byron, the corner man, had dabbed at Gage's left eye during the one-minute rest, and when the bell sounded for round two, Kayla could see his eye was swollen. She cringed, praying silently he would be able to pull it together. Tonight the other man was a few inches taller and quicker on his feet.

Gage attempted to take the guy down several times, swinging his leg out to hook a knee. His opponent jumped out of the path every time. Gage landed a few uppercuts, but the other guy seemed unfazed. The announcer droned on and on, and the crowd got louder with every hit.

Sweat poured off Gage's chest and face as he plopped down in the chair for the second break. Byron shouted instructions Kayla couldn't hear, but she stood riveted, watching Gage's chest rise and fall with his heavy breathing. He didn't look her way. He probably didn't even know where she was in the crowded arena. It was just as well. She didn't want to distract him.

Her heart sank as the third round began. She worried he would be disappointed. She hadn't seen him lose yet. Granted she'd only been to the one fight, but according to the other women, the members of The Fight Club were a tough group known for far more wins than losses.

Suddenly, Gage hooked the guy's knee and knocked him to the ground. The man looked stunned as Gage straddled his chest and pinned him. Moments later, Gage had him across the neck, cutting off his airway. The man struggled, clearly fighting to right himself. He bucked, but

Gage was too strong now that he was on top and the man was down.

The referee leaned in close, bouncing around on the floor. Kayla gasped as she waited for someone to end the match.

Finally, after what seemed like an eternity, although probably only had been a few seconds, the man tapped the mat and Gage jumped off him.

"God," Emily said, "incredible. Been a while since I've seen a man tap out."

"What does that mean?"

"It means the guy was out of fight. He knew he couldn't win, so he gave up."

The other guy crawled to his knees, gasping, and then stood on wobbly feet. He looked confused and angry with himself as he shook his head and left the ring.

"And the winner is Gage 'The Ranger' Holland," the announcer shouted to the crowd. The man sounded as shocked as everyone else seemed to be. The audience roared. Women from all around the ring leaned closer, grabbing the fencing with both hands and screaming like groupies.

Gage's gaze landed on Kayla without missing a beat, however. He winked and nodded.

Kayla's cheeks flamed. She'd had no idea he knew where she stood. And she was beyond aroused by his actions.

The women closest to her turned to gawk. A few of them looked disappointed, their shoulders drooping as Gage turned and left the cage.

"Shit. I think your man just lit a few panties on fire."

Kayla smiled at Emily. "Hey, as long as he never sees any of them, I'm good."

Emily laughed, and the two of them wormed their way

through the crowd and back to the lobby. Emily knew exactly where to go, and she led Kayla to a door around the side marked employees only. "They'll come out through here."

Within a minute, in fact, Rider pushed through the door. He took Emily in his arms and hugged her close, kissing her forehead.

"Awesome, babe. Loved it."

"Yeah, I hear Gage ended up pretty good himself." He lifted his gaze to Kayla.

"Yep. Didn't look so good at first, but he pinned the guy finally," Emily said.

The three of them leaned against the wall and waited, Emily wrapped in Rider's arms, her back leaning against his front. Kayla felt like a third wheel as she stood next to them. And it took another half hour for Gage to surface.

Kayla winced. She moved into his arms, her face lifted to his. "Ouch." His eye was swollen and red.

He grinned. "Yeah. Looks worse than it feels. Won't be pretty tomorrow, though." He nodded at Rider. "Thanks for waiting with Kayla. Appreciate it."

Since Emily had driven Kayla, Gage had driven Rider. That way each couple had a car. The four of them made their way to the exit and stepped out into the warm evening air, typical of Vegas.

Gage turned to Rider. "I'm beat. I think we'll head home. You guys going to Extreme?"

Rider nodded. "See you tomorrow. Work out at ten?"

"Yep. Sounds good."

Gage fell asleep almost as soon as they got home, mumbling his apologies to Kayla. He was exhausted from weeks of juggling work, the gym, the club, his dad, and his woman. And he'd never been happier. But it was taking a toll on him.

When he opened his eyes in the morning, it was to find Kayla wrapped around him, covering as much of his body as she could with her small frame.

She was watching with a smile. And she reached to stroke his cheek as he roused. "Hey, babe. You feel better?" She let her fingers dance over his swollen eye. "You have a black eye."

"Mm hm. It happens. I'll live." He wrapped his arms around her and dragged her over his body.

"I fed Thor and he went outside."

"Thanks, baby. I'll feel even better as soon as you mount me."

Kayla grinned. "I might be able to do that." Her teasing smile warmed his heart. God, he loved this woman.

Gage held her arms and pushed her up until she sat astride him. "You might, huh?" Her pussy snuggled against his cock, making him stiffer by the second.

"Perhaps." She pushed against him, wetness coating his dick as she rocked over his length.

He moaned. "Baby…" They'd stopped using condoms a few weeks ago when Kayla went on the pill. Gage still couldn't believe how much more intense she felt wrapped around his naked cock.

Kayla rocked again, immediately sending him from half asleep to totally ready to fuck. "Need you." He lifted her hips, letting his cock bob upward. And then he settled her pussy over the tip and tugged her down.

Kayla moaned as he entered her from beneath. Her hands flew out to brace herself on his chest.

Gage held her body against him, controlling her

movements even though she was on top. "Don't use your hands, baby. Let go of me."

She looked at him quizzically, one eyebrow rising.

"Let go. I've got you."

She tentatively released her grip on his pecs, clearly unsure he could hold her.

"So little faith, baby. Use those hands on your nipples. I'm pretty sure I'm strong enough to hold your sweet ass over me," he teased her.

Her hands came up to cup her breasts, and she tipped her head back on a moan. Sexiest creature on Earth.

His cock jumped inside her. "Pinch your nipples, baby. Make them hard for me."

Kayla gripped each nipple between her thumbs and pointers. She whimpered as she did what he said.

"Twist them. I like the way your pussy tightens around my cock when you add a little pain." It was hard to keep up the monologue, but totally worth it. Even though what he really wanted to do was fuck her fast and hard, he so enjoyed watching her writhe, he made himself wait.

Kayla twisted, her body stiffening, her thighs clutching his hips. She sucked her lips between her teeth.

Gage watched her perfect pink nipples pucker and stiffen. And then he lifted her torso several inches and slammed her back down.

Kayla leaned forward, her eyes opening wider to match her mouth.

"I've got you, baby. Trust me. Don't let go of your nipples, or I won't let you come."

She nodded, her lips back between her teeth in concentration.

He controlled her movements, fucking himself with her body as she moaned and gripped her nipples. She swayed forward a few times, but he didn't let her fall. And then he had the idea to tempt her. It had been a few days since he'd thoroughly dominated her. Even though he was usually on top and commanded her in the bedroom most of the time, some nights or mornings he made love to her without requiring much submission.

Gage let her rock too far forward on the next thrust, causing her to release her tits and throw her arms forward to stop herself against his chest.

"Oh, baby. So little trust." He couldn't keep the mirth from his voice, and he knew she wouldn't believe for a minute his actions weren't contrived.

She gaped at him and swatted his pecs. "You made me do that."

"Mmm. Is that so?" He lifted her off him and switched positions so fast she gasped. Seconds later he had her on her hands and knees, her thighs spread wide. He thrust into her tightness from behind, noticing how much wetter she was at the sudden change.

Her head dipped, and she moaned loudly.

Instead of reaching around her body to rub her clit, he held her hips and closed his eyes, ensuring he came fast and hard, leaving her needy.

He got his wish. With his sub beneath him, it was an easy feat. He loved taking her from behind. He didn't usually leave her hanging, but toying with her this morning seemed like fun.

As soon as Gage emptied himself inside her, he pulled out.

Kayla shook. When he flipped her onto her back, her legs open to his gaze, her eyes were wide. She opened her mouth but didn't speak. Her hips lifted off the bed, and she grabbed for him to gain purchase.

"Arms above your head, baby."

Kayla released him as though he were on fire and she'd

just noticed. She tossed her arms over her head, but met his gaze. "Gage, please…"

"Baby, you didn't trust me."

"I did. I lost my balance, Sir."

"Ah. Is that so?" He held her legs wide with both arms and let his gaze roam up and down her body. Finally, he released her. "Don't move an inch," he said as he crawled off the bed to clean himself and bring a cloth for her.

When he returned, she was shaking with need. Her nipples were still puckered from her pinching them. Gage wiped her pussy clean of his come without taking time to arouse her further. He tossed the washcloth aside and spread his palms on her belly.

"Sir…" Her head rolled back and forth. Her word was clipped and soft.

He lowered himself between her legs and held them wide. He loved looking at her in this position, her hands raised, her body submitting to his commands without need for restraints or punishment. She thought she was doing him a disservice by keeping him from enjoying a spanking scene with other women. But she was wrong. It was far headier watching his woman intentionally obey him than any flogging scene he'd ever participated in.

Her clit was swollen and distended enough the hood was retracted. Gage tapped it once and then watched her buck her hips. She panted as she eased back onto the bed.

"You aroused, baby?"

"Mmm." She didn't meet his gaze. Her pussy was pink and swollen from his cock. Her lower lips begged him to stroke them, but instead he blew on them.

"I need to take a shower, baby. How about you lie there and don't move an inch while I'm gone."

She met his gaze this time as he lifted off the bed. Her eyes were wider than he'd ever seen them.

He stroked her breast, grazing over her nipple enough to make her shiver. And then he left her there.

And she thought she wasn't submissive enough…

Gage showered quickly, dried off, and returned to the room with his towel around his waist. "Ah, what a good girl. I'm proud of you." He glanced at the night stand. "I need to meet a few of the guys to work out this morning."

She whimpered, lifting her head slightly toward him.

He sat on the edge of the bed and flicked his thumb over her closest nipple. Immediately it pebbled. "So submissive. My sweet girl obeys me so well." He flicked the other nipple next. "Do you need to come, baby?"

"Yes, Sir." Her voice cracked as she spoke.

"Hmm, but I'm already cleaned up." He stood, dropped the towel in the corner of the bed and pulled on shorts and a T-shirt for the gym.

When he finished, her facial expression was one of murderous intent.

He sat on the end of the bed this time. "I have an idea. How about I make you come without touching you?" He lifted his hands. "That way I won't get all messy before I need to leave."

She let her mouth fall open.

Gage stood and went to the bedside table. He opened the drawer and pulled out the vibrator he'd been saving for weeks. He watched Kayla suck in a breath as he opened the package. "My little sub likes the idea." When he had the thick rubber in his hand, he climbed up between her legs again. "Hold yourself open for me. If you close your legs, I stop. If you can keep them wide, I'll let you come."

Kayla's hands came from above her head to grasp her thighs. She spread her fingers and held tight. Her pussy was so wet, he could see the arousal building on her lower lips.

At first, he pushed the vibrator inside her without turning it on.

Kayla flinched. She was wet enough, but the dildo would be cold against her skin.

"Don't let go. I would hate to leave you here horny and needy all morning." He slowly turned the dial with the dildo deep inside her. As the vibrations increased, so did the humming sound coming from Kayla's mouth. Gage tipped the vibrator down, pushing the part inside her against her G-spot.

Her noises got louder.

As soon as he had the vibrations turned up all the way, he pulled the dildo from her pussy and flattened it to her clit.

Kayla bucked, her hips coming so far off the bed he had trouble keeping the vibrator in place.

"That's it, baby. Hold your legs wide for me, but buck all you want. I love watching you fuck into the toy."

Kayla shook violently as she lowered her hips and then raised them once more. Her feet remained planted on the mattress. Why had he waited so long to use the vibrator on her? It was like his own personal perfect show. One he intended to enjoy far more often now that he knew how much Kayla liked to writhe against a vibrator.

Finally, she screamed, her release coming so loud, he stifled a chuckle. She never had any idea how loud she screamed when she came hard. Her voice was glorious music to his ears. When she came so violently, he knew he was doing his job as a Dom.

As soon as she settled back against the mattress, gasping for breath and still not meeting his gaze, Gage removed the dildo and leaned forward to kiss her clit. He sucked the swollen nub between his lips and flicked it fast with his tongue. Kayla lifted her ass back off the bed, angling closer to his mouth. But she still held her legs open for him, so he drove her back to the peak and over the top once more with his lips and tongue.

He licked his lips, savoring her sweet taste as he pulled away from her sensitive pussy. "So fucking sexy, Kayla. I think I'll set you up for disobedience more often." He leaned over her and kissed her lips.

"God," she mumbled. "You make me lose my mind."

"Good. That's the plan." He cupped her breasts. "I gotta go."

She nodded and licked her lips. "I need to go by my place today. I'll do that while you're gone."

"'K. I'll meet you here for lunch then? I'll bring Chinese."

She smiled. "Sounds good."

CHAPTER 18

When Gage finished working out, showering, and dressing, he grabbed his phone and found a message from Kayla.

Car won't start. Ugh. Would you please grab my mail?

Gage secretly hated the car. It was too old and unreliable. Even with the new battery, she'd had problems. When he asked her about getting a new one, she told him she couldn't afford it. That seemed ridiculous to him, but she said she was saving every dime to go back to school.

With the military checks she got as a surviving widow, she shouldn't have been struggling so hard. But he left her alone about it, at least he had so far. Some people really preferred to have a huge nest egg in the bank for a rainy day. He couldn't fault her that, but this was getting absurd. He couldn't stand the idea of her getting stranded someplace with a car that wouldn't start.

Gage swung by her place, grabbed a pile of mail from her box, and then hit their favorite Chinese for takeout.

When he got home, he dropped the mail on the table, and they settled down to eat. He broached the subject of her transportation again. "Baby, your car."

She held up a hand. "I know." She rolled her eyes. "I'll start looking for another vehicle. But I was hoping not to have to replace it yet."

"If it's the money—"

"Don't even think about it, Gage. I'm not discussing money with you yet. It's bad enough you let me stay in your house and don't let me contribute to anything, not even the groceries. If you so much as mention helping me with a car, I'll hurt you." She turned back to her fried rice and scooped another bite.

Gage leaned back in his chair, having finished eating before her as usual. He spotted a package amongst her pile of mail and pulled it free of the stack.

Kayla's gaze lifted. She jumped to her feet and yanked the package from his hands so fast, he was startled. She stomped to the trash can and tossed the fatter-than-normal envelope into the bin.

"What the hell?" Gage sat up straighter.

Kayla paced.

"Kayla? What's the package? And why are you tossing it without looking at it? Shit. You didn't even open it. How do you know who it's even from?"

Kayla turned toward him, her hand running through her long hair on top. "Leave it alone, Gage. Please. For me."

He stood. "What? Are you serious?"

"Yes." She stood her ground between him and the trash, visibly trembling. "Please."

He narrowed his gaze. He didn't want to get crazy stupid angry and scare her with his actions, but she was out of her mind if she thought he could drop something like this without a word. He stood very still for a long time, reining in his frustration and dragging his hands through his hair in much the same way she had done. Finally, he took a deep breath when he knew he could be reasonably calm. "Kayla, talk to me."

"Gage, I'm begging you to let this go."

"And I'm telling you there's no fucking way."

She met his gaze, her upper lip trembling. Her eyes glazed with tears before she wiped them away and turned her face to the floor.

Gage was on her in an instant, pulling her into his embrace and wrapping his arms around her. "Baby." He rocked her gently, staring at the ominous trash can behind her back, knowing instinctively he was not going to like what was in that package.

He decided the best thing to do would be to separate her from the source of her obvious stress. He led her away from the kitchen with an arm around her shoulders. When he reached the couch, he sat, taking her with him and settling her on his lap.

She leaned into him, making him hope there was a possibility this would not go as badly as he thought.

He thought wrong.

Kayla sobbed against him. She lifted her face and clutched at his T-shirt. "I'm so sorry." Tears ran down her face.

Gage swallowed fear. He wasn't going to like this. And he wished for a moment he could undo the existence of the package and go back to the way things had been right before he touched it.

"I-I—" She nearly hyperventilated trying to catch her breath and get a full word out. "I'm such a bitch. I didn't want you to know."

She wasn't making any sense, and he stiffened, waiting

for her to say more. When she didn't continue, he lifted her chin and looked her in the eye. "Tell me."

She inhaled slowly and pushed the breath out. "Simon's parents have been blackmailing me for two years."

"What?" The word popped out fast as though he hadn't understood her correctly even though she'd been very clear. He held her away from his chest and looked her in the eye. "How? Why?"

She trembled. "They have…videos…of me…" Her voice fell to a near whisper as Gage began to shake. His head pounded at her admission. *That fucking asshole.*

"Kayla. Tell me everything. And do it now before I explode."

She sniffled. "I'm sorry, Gage. I never wanted you to know."

"Why, baby?" He tried to calm his voice at the very least.

"Why? Do you have any idea what's on those videos?" She jumped from his lap and backed away.

He had a pretty good idea of course.

"Simon… He…" She straightened her spine and twisted around in a circle as though looking for answers. And then she faced Gage again. "He fucking taped me. Apparently dozens of times."

Gage gritted his teeth. He didn't move. If he did, he was afraid he would throw something across the room.

"I had no idea he'd done it so often," she continued, her voice shaking. "But apparently he got his rocks off watching me fight against him. So, he taped me while he beat me. He taped me while he fucked me. He taped me in the shower. He had fucking surveillance all over the apartment, and I never knew." She stiffened, her hands fisted at her sides. "I'm so fucking stupid that I didn't notice fucking cameras everywhere in my tiny fucking apartment."

She seethed with anger. It rolled off her in waves, making Gage calm by default. There was no reason to be furious on her behalf. His sweet Kayla was angry enough for both of them. And she was the one who starred in the videos. Not him. And his poor girl had endured two years of torment as a result.

She stomped around the room now. "I thought about telling you ten thousand times. But I didn't have the guts. And I didn't want you to intervene."

"Why, baby?"

She stopped and faced him. "Because if I stop sending his parents the money, they will send my embarrassment to every social media venue on the planet. They've even threatened to send the disks to various porn sites." Her voice rose until she was screaming. When she finished, she sank to the floor in tears.

Gage jumped up then and came to her. He wrapped his arms around her shaking body and pulled her close. He kissed the top of her head and amazingly convinced himself to calm the fuck down. She needed him. She didn't need him to act like a raging lunatic. She needed him to hold her and get her through this fucked-up thing.

When her sobs turned to whimpers and then sniffles, he lifted her off the ground and carried her back to the couch. He still held her tight, stroking her hair away from her face. He waited to speak when he knew she was calm enough to hear him. "I love you, baby."

Kayla inhaled sharply and cried some more.

Thor wandered in from outside and plopped down next to his distressed woman, clearly feeling her pain and hating it as much as Gage did.

He rocked her shaking body as she let it all out. Two years of dealing with this alone. Two years of catering to these fucked-up humans who thought they could wring every dime from his woman. It stopped today. He would do everything in his power to put an end to this insanity and get Kayla free of these assholes.

"I love you," he repeated. "And we'll work through this."

"How?" She lifted her gaze. "Don't even fucking sit there and tell me to stop sending them money, because the risk is tremendous." A tremor shook her frame. He could only imagine what was on those DVDs.

Gage stroked her back. "Baby, you can't live your life this way. You must have been on edge for the last two years, waiting for a ticking bomb to go off."

She nodded.

"Let me help you. We'll find a way." He hugged her against him again. "First thing we need to do is call Chief Edwards and get his advice."

She pushed away from him, shaking her head. "No. Gage. God, no. Chief Edwards is like a father to me. This would kill him."

"I know, baby." He kept his voice calm. "But he knows you better than anyone, and we need his help. I work at the police academy, but I'm not a cop. I don't know how things like this should be handled. We have to bring him in and get help. He'll know what to do. You don't have to live this way."

She stared at him.

"Trust me, Kayla. Please."

After a long pause, she nodded, but new tears fell.

His chest ached for her. How many things would happen to open that festering wound again and again? Dozens over the next few days probably, but the blackmail had to stop.

~

Kayla sat curled up on the couch, her knees against her chest, a blanket tucked around her as she waited for the chief of police to arrive. Thor sat at her feet, his head propped on her legs, watching her. Gage had called Chief Edwards and asked him to come to the house. It was a Saturday morning. The man didn't work on Saturdays usually. But Kayla knew he would drop everything and move heaven and earth if she asked.

She still trembled as though she had a fever. Nothing would keep the images from her mind. She hadn't seen more than a few minutes of the DVDs, but it didn't take any imagination to know what was on them. She'd lived those home movies personally. Every single one.

Chief Edwards arrived, his knock making her flinch.

She listened as Gage opened the door and whispered to her closest friend in the world. She couldn't hear the words, but she didn't need to. Moments later, the older man kneeled in front of her, took her in his arms, and gave her a tight hug. "Why didn't you come to me, Kayla?"

Tears fell again. "I didn't want anyone to know." She heaved for air. "It's bad. Worse than you can imagine. I never wanted you to know about what I endured. I was so stupid to fall for that bastard, and I've paid dearly for so many years." Her voice lowered to a whisper. "I'm tired, Chief Edwards. So tired." She leaned her head back on the arm of the couch and didn't even bother to wipe away the line of tears running across her cheek.

"I bet you are. Let's figure this out and put a stop to it. Now. It ends today. Right now."

She nodded, having no faith anyone could truly help her. But even with all the pain she felt, amazingly a weight had lifted in its wake. Her chest felt lighter. The two men closest to her in the world cared enough to handle this. She didn't really believe they could prevent the inevitable. But the fact they were willing to try gave her hope. "There's a pile of letters in my condo. Top shelf in my closet. Blue shoe box."

Gage sat next to her. "I'll get them, baby." He set a hand on her thigh and squeezed.

"How much money have you sent them?" Chief Edwards asked.

Kayla explained the thousands of dollars she'd sent to Simon's parents in the last twenty-four months. She had no idea how many disks they had, but each month they sent her one DVD in exchange for payment. Each month they also sent a note warning her what they would do if she ever went to the police or stopped paying them.

Kayla had only watched the first few minutes of the first couple of disks they sent, enough to ensure herself they weren't fucking with her. They were pissed that Simon had died before signing divorce papers, leaving them without a dime and Kayla with all his DIC payments, Dependency and Indemnity Compensation. Pissed was too mild a term, actually. They were psychotic lunatics who would stop at nothing to humiliate Kayla over and over until she either died or the DVDs ran out.

She'd considered going to the police, and almost told Chief Edwards on more than a few occasions, but every time she pictured her naked, exposed, violated body slapped all over social media, she kept her mouth shut. She'd spent countless hours trolling the Internet to make sure the Bollings kept their word. She'd even gone so far as to hit several sex shops and peruse the video aisle to make sure she wasn't featured on any of the covers.

Gage left her with Chief Edwards for just long enough to run to her house and grab the box of letters. When he came back, she was still lying in her tight ball answering the unending line of questions from her boss and friend.

Her neck hurt. Her arms hurt. Hell, her entire body felt like it had been beaten with giant balls of hail, and she'd been caught outside in a storm being pelted to death by the chunks of ice.

When Chief Edwards thought he had all the information he needed, Gage lifted her off the couch and carried her to the bedroom. He set her on the mattress as gently as she'd ever known him to be. "Stretch out some, baby. You're gonna ache later."

Kayla unfolded as he pulled the covers up to her chin and tucked her in tight. He stepped to the bathroom and returned with two ibuprofen and a glass of water. He held her head up for her to swallow. And then he stroked her hair, sitting on the side of the bed until sleep graciously sucked her under.

CHAPTER 19

Gage paced a hole in is living room while Chief Edwards went over the pile of letters Kayla had saved. There was also a pile of disks in the bottom of the box that made Gage cringe. He retrieved the envelope from the trash can and added it to the stack.

"Jesus." Chief Edwards was pissed, at least as pissed as Gage. He kept sliding his reading glasses on and off his face until Gage thought he would surely break that pair.

They managed to keep their voices down so Kayla could rest, but barely.

"I can't believe she kept this from me." Gage paced.

"Oh, I can. I'm sure one look at those tapes and it would be crystal clear."

Gage would never in this lifetime open one of those disks, but he would forever be haunted by the possible images they contained. "How much of this did you know?" he asked Chief Edwards.

Chief Edwards leaned back in his chair. "Nothing about the extortion, if that's what you mean. I did know about her marriage to this asshole and most of the details about her divorce proceedings and then his death. She contacted me from Alabama after she left the Bollings, and I helped arrange for her to come home."

Gage watched the pain on Chief Edwards's face as he spoke, the same pain Gage had felt since Kayla had opened up to him about Simon. Chief Edwards had lived with that for two years, six if he worried about her the entire time she was gone also.

"Got to call this in to the local police in Alabama now." Chief Edwards stood. He pulled his cell from his pocket. "If we're lucky, they can head out to the Bollings' home and arrest them within the hour. There's enough evidence here to lock them up for a long fucking time. I just wish Kayla had realized she had other options sooner than now. That poor girl has been through more than most women could handle in a lifetime."

Gage agreed. And he also knew she was the strongest woman he'd ever met for surviving years of torture and abuse followed by years of extortion and threats. It was a good thing Nevada was not close to Alabama, or he would probably have stomped to those mother fuckers' house and killed them with his bare hands.

Things moved fast. By the end of the day, the Bollings were in custody and their house ransacked for any evidence. Unfortunately, as stupid as those idiots were, they had covered their asses concerning the disks. The police in charge of the case found absolutely nothing inside the house, and the Bollings weren't cooperating with authorities. They insisted they knew nothing and hadn't ever bothered "that poor girl."

The rage that boiled beneath the surface made Gage antsy. It wasn't as though the couple would be set free without physical evidence from their house. Hell, there was enough evidence on Gage's kitchen table to light a bonfire. However, it would certainly have been tidier if they'd fucked up a little more and had the disks in the house.

The rest of Saturday and all of Sunday were tense. Kayla sat curled in a ball on the couch staring at nothing. She chewed her lip for so long, Gage kept cupping her face and tugging the poor flesh loose. He gave her space, only encouraging her to eat and drink, but she said little. All she did was sit and stare at nothing and occasionally wipe a line of tears from her face.

Thor understood Kayla better than anyone. That dog was sharp as a whip. He spent the entire day curled up next to Kayla, his jaw on her leg, as though ready to pounce if anyone upset her. He even followed her to the bathroom.

Gage ached for her, but she needed time to process what had happened. He imagined she'd spent the majority of the last two years stuffing her feelings deep inside and ignoring them. A coping mechanism.

"Come to bed, baby," he prodded Sunday night.

She nodded and lifted herself off the couch as though she weighed four hundred pounds.

It was early. Barely nine o'clock. Gage held her in his arms and stroked her face as they snuggled under the covers. "It's going to be okay," he reassured.

"How do you know? You can't be sure of that." She lifted her face, her eyes watery and wide. "Until the police find those disks and destroy them, I can't rest."

"I understand, baby. And believe me, I agree. And the local police are doing everything in their power to locate the disks."

They'd grilled Kayla for any possible solution. She knew nothing. As far as she was aware, the Bollings had no safety deposit box or secret safe anywhere. They lived so far from town they didn't even have friends. She'd learned from her time with Mrs. Forester that most people didn't like the Bollings and steered clear of them. They had one other son, older, but Kayla had never met him. He lived somewhere else in the South.

Gage wished he could jump on a plane and head straight for Alabama, but he would never leave Kayla to do so, and furthermore, he wasn't a cop.

Thor leaped onto the bed and snuggled in on Kayla's other side. Normally Gage didn't let the dog sleep on the bed when both he and Kayla were there, but Kayla seemed to calm every time Thor touched her, so he pulled her closer, scooted them across the mattress, and let Thor claim his spot.

Kayla's heart rate slowed with Thor at her back. Her breathing evened out as she leaned against Gage and fell asleep. For the first time in two days, she slept without jerking awake in a panic or flinching her muscles in her sleep.

Gage hardly slept, preferring to watch her rest and play with her gorgeous blonde curls. He brushed them back against the pillow so many times, it was a wonder he didn't have a handful of her hair.

He finally closed his eyes and rested, only to jolt awake some time later, instinctively knowing he was alone in the bed. He sat up quickly and scanned the room. Kayla wasn't in sight, but he could hear the shower running.

The clock showed seven thirty. He crawled out of bed and headed for the bathroom. He smiled when he found Thor lying next to the shower door, his head on his front paws.

Kayla turned and smiled at him through the glass door.

"You feel better, baby?"

"Yes. Thank you." She shut off the water and stepped from the shower.

Gage handed her a towel and watched her dry. "You don't have to push yourself if you want to stay home, you know." He worried about her. She was too calm.

"I know. But it will be better for me to go to work and have a normal routine. The police may never find those disks, and I need to accept that possibility and move on." She wrapped her hair in the towel and stood before him naked and sexy as hell.

He stepped forward, pulled her into his arms and kissed her soundly. "You're an amazing woman, and I thank God every single day for putting you in my path."

She blushed, her face turning every shade of red. "Gage…" She pushed on his chest, never one to easily accept his praise and admiration.

He trailed his hands up her warm back and wrapped one around the back of her neck. "I mean it." He pinned her with his gaze. "I love you, and we'll get through this and come out stronger."

She opened her mouth, hesitated, and then spoke. "What if the disks get leaked? What if my face is plastered all over social media or on a porn film? Worse yet, what if my entire body is displayed for the universe at large? I don't think I can live with that, Gage. And I sure don't intend for you to."

He closed his eyes for one second and then whisked her off her feet, carried her cradled in his arms to the bedroom, and dropped her unceremoniously on the bed. He came over her without a pause, his body pinning her to the mattress as the breath whooshed from her lungs. He grabbed both her hands and tugged them over her head to hold her down. "Listen to me, baby. There isn't one scenario or resolution to the case that will end with me not in your life. Do you hear me?"

She didn't move. Her eyes were wide, but her mouth was pursed.

"I don't give a fuck if I have to spend the rest of my life chasing loose videos of you across the entire planet, collecting them, and getting them off the streets. I will do so until I die. So, don't look at me again and suggest you'd leave me over this. It's not going to happen, and frankly it's insulting. I'm a bigger man than that. A few naked videos is not going to stop me from loving you to pieces. Ever." His voice rose. "Don't insinuate otherwise again. Are we clear?"

She nodded. Tears fell again. Finally, she opened her mouth and gave him what he'd longed for for weeks. "I love you too, Gage."

A smile formed on his lips and spread so wide it felt like his cheeks would split. "Then that's settled." He leaned closer and took her mouth in a long, thorough kiss that led to him sliding into her warmth and them arriving several minutes late to work.

The morning went smoothly. Gage tried not to think too hard about what was happening in Alabama, and he only buzzed Chief Edwards once an hour for an update. Chief Edwards's voice grew leery with each call, but Gage was undaunted. He wanted answers, and until he had a satisfactory resolution to this topic, he wouldn't rest easy. For Kayla's sake. And for his own.

It was almost lunch when Marci came running into his side of the building and stopped, heaving for breath as she interrupted his class. "Gage. She left."

He dropped the papers he was holding and jumped off the edge of his desk where he'd been perched. "What? Who left? Kayla?"

"Yes. She tore out of here like the hounds of hell were on her heels. Chief Edwards is up front."

Gage ran after Marci with Thor on his heels. He ran out the front door and joined Chief Edwards where he found him in the parking lot. "Where did she go?"

Chief Edwards spun around and faced Gage. "No idea. She didn't say a word. Did she have her car?"

Gage glanced at the parking lot. "No. She took mine. She has her own keys."

"Do you suppose she couldn't handle the pressure of being at work?" Chief Edwards asked.

Gage's heart beat faster. He shook his head. "Not buying that. She was fine this morning. Better than she has been for two days. Something must have happened. No one saw anything?"

Chief Edwards shook his head. "No. Nothing. She was alone in the front, and suddenly she jumped up and tore out of here. A few of the guys saw her from next to their cars where they were getting ready to patrol." Chief Edwards nodded toward Rider coming from across the parking lot. "Rider saw her peel away and called me on the radio."

Rider jogged forward. "What happened?"

"No idea," Chief Edwards said.

"I've got to go find her." Gage spun in a circle, realizing he had no transportation.

"I'll take you." Rider turned on his heel and headed for a patrol car.

Seconds later the two of them were speeding down the road with Thor in the back seat, alert and sitting upright. Rider had the lights on, but not the siren.

"Where do you think she would go first?"

"Drive by my place." Gage grabbed the handle above the door and held on as Rider took a corner, hugging it tight.

It took only five minutes to get to Gage's house with Rider driving, and there was no sign of Kayla. "Her place next." He gave Rider the directions, and they took off again. Gage dialed her phone over and over, but she didn't answer. He texted her also. Nothing.

When they pulled up to Kayla's condo, he sensed immediately that something was off. His jeep was in the driveway, askew as though she'd parked and exited hastily.

Thor jumped out of the squad car the second Rider opened the back door. That dog could sense even more than Gage or Rider. Thor followed Gage toward the house, his ears standing up, his tongue wagging.

Gage pushed the front door open with Thor right beside him.

And what he encountered when he entered the house and slid to a halt made his heart stop.

Kayla stood in the center of the room, but she wasn't alone. Some jackass had his arm around her throat and a gun to her head.

Thor growled low and menacing.

"Call your fucking dog off now, or she's dead."

Thor didn't speak asshole, so he kept growling. The dog was smart though and trained to handle this sort of situation. Gage knew Thor was waiting for the signal to pounce. Gage would wait for the perfect moment and then give Thor the command to take this motherfucker down.

And the best part? This son of a bitch didn't know that.

Gage could sense that Rider hadn't entered the house behind him. Which meant he was either lurking outside the door waiting for an opportunity to shoot first and ask questions later, or he'd circled to the back of the house.

Gage lifted both arms in the air. He wished he had his .38 on him, but it was in the glove compartment of his jeep. As a civilian, he couldn't carry a weapon inside the police station. Rider was somewhere nearby, and that man was indeed packing.

Who was this asshole, and what did he want with Kayla? Gage wished there was some explanation that didn't involve the Bollings, but the likelihood of that was slim. The coincidence the dude happened to be in the house for a random robbery was nil.

"What do you want?" Gage asked.

The guy snarled. "Money, dickface. What do robbers usually want?"

"Money, as in a roll of twenties from the underwear drawer, or money as in extortion and revenge?" Gage didn't bother mincing words. "I suggest you put that gun down now before you find yourself in more trouble than you're already in. If you add homicide to extortion, you'll serve life without parole."

"Fuck you."

Gage shuffled slowly forward, still holding his hands up.

"You think you and Fido here are going to take me out?" The fucker laughed sardonically as if he had the upper hand.

Gage did nothing to insinuate this shithole wasn't far from the truth. As long as he held a gun to Kayla's head, he did indeed have Gage by the balls.

Kayla held on to the fucker's forearm, tears streaming down her face, her eyes wide, and her mouth open. She wasn't getting enough oxygen. Her feet barely scraped the floor.

Moments of silence as Gage angled to one side, trying to get out of the way in case Rider planned to get by him. He moved right, forcing the asshole with the gun to follow him with his gaze.

"Stop fucking moving, dickface." He gripped Kayla tighter, making her whimper.

A shot rang out behind Gage, but that wasn't what took this jackass down. The distraction was exactly what Gage had been waiting on. He gave Thor the signal, and the dog leaped into the air and clamped his jaw down on the fucker's forearm while the guy looked in the direction of the shot. In less than a heartbeat, Kayla was free, the gun went flying across the room, and the jackass went down, screaming in pain.

Thor did not release. He was trained to incapacitate. One word from Gage and he would do just that.

Rider came around the corner on the next heartbeat, gun raised. He made his way across the living room, grabbed the jackass's free arm and slapped a cuff on him.

Gage hesitated, letting Thor continue to grip the man's arm tight. He knew it had to hurt like a son of a bitch, but all the more reason. He still didn't say a word when Rider glanced back.

Finally, Rider lifted an eyebrow. Calm as could be, he announced," I've got this, Gage. Call him off."

Gage took a deep breath and transferred his gaze to Thor. "Release."

Thor dropped the man immediately and turned toward Kayla.

The squirming asshole on the floor flailed, screaming about his arm, but Rider set a knee on his chest and then flipped him to his front, locking his second hand to the first behind him. Next, Rider pulled out a radio and hit the side button. "Need backup at two seven five Maple. Man in custody." He put his radio back in the holster and inserted his knee in the center of the fucker's back.

Gage took three long strides to get to Kayla, who sat choking on the ground, her sobs mixing in with her erratic breathing. Thor nuzzled her arms, trying to get her to look at him. The dog was a genius.

Gage bent down and gathered Kayla in his arms, lifting her and turning to go outside, Thor on his heels. He didn't want her witnessing another second of that man's face. He went straight to the squad car, opened the back door, and slid inside, still holding her cradled in his arms. When he was seated, Thor jumping into the open door on the other side, he brushed her hair from her face. "It's over, baby."

She shook violently and sobbed harder.

Not surprising considering what she'd been through.

He let her cry, listening to the sirens as they came closer. It seemed like an eternity, but probably only lasted about three minutes. After all, the entire precinct had been aware of the situation before it went down.

Kayla heaved deep breaths as two squad cars squealed to a stop in front of her condo. Gage blocked her from the view, hoping to calm her. It took forever for her to speak. "Oh my God, Gage. If you hadn't…"

"I did, baby." He held her closer, kissed the top of her head. "I'm here. I'll always be here. It's over." He lifted her chin to meet his gaze, hating the number of times he'd seen her in such pain in the last few days. "Talk to me, baby."

"I never met Simon's brother."

"That was Simon's brother? Fuck."

She nodded. "He wasn't too pleased that his parents were arrested, and he demanded fifty thousand dollars or he would turn the entire stack of disks over to the highest bidder. The box of DVDs is in there. He actually brought them." She sobbed again, fighting to control herself enough to continue.

"Baby, why on earth did you come here alone?"

She inhaled sharply. "I didn't know he was here, Gage.

I'm not that stupid. All I got was a series of e-mails that shook me up. I just wanted to get the hell out of there."

"Baby…" He stroked her hair again and then rubbed his thumb under her eyes to wipe away the tears.

"I'm sorry. It was stupid. It never occurred to me he was here in Vegas. I just opened the e-mails and saw his name. He ranted about what a bitch I was and how he was going to make me pay. I had no idea he was here in my condo."

Gage pulled her head in to his chest and blocked the commotion behind him. He watched Thor nuzzle her from the other side and wiggle his face into her lap.

Kayla reached out and clutched his fur. "Your dog is the bomb."

"Yes he is, baby."

"He saved my life."

"Mmm hmm. That's what he's trained to do."

"How did he know?"

"No idea what goes on in his head, but he loves you to pieces and won't tolerate any threat to you. He knew before we got in the house."

"Amazing." She leaned down and held him closer, kissing his fur and squeezing him tight. "Perhaps you wouldn't mind if he stayed with me twenty-four seven from now on." She grinned.

"Wish he could, baby. Close. But he does work in my part of the building. He's a great watch dog, but he sucks at front desk work."

Gage held his dog and his woman close, taking deep breaths and thanking God for both of them.

EPILOGUE

One month later...

Kayla cupped her hands over her mouth and shouted through the crowd at Gage. He'd taken several hits to the head and chest, but none powerful enough to throw him off his game. He was clearly the better contender in this fight. "Go, Gage. Come on, babe. You can do it."

Jenna stood next to her, chuckling. "Lord, we've created a monster."

Kayla glanced at her and grinned before turning her attention back to the cage.

Katy spoke next. "I blame Emily. She's a bad influence in the fighting department."

Emily hip-butted Katy to the right of Kayla. "Don't listen to them. They don't appreciate good masculine sweaty chests when they see them."

"Oh, I appreciate the chests all right. I just prefer mine to be dry and clean and hovering over me in bed. The bloody parts make me squeamish," Jenna said.

Gage threw a serious leg kick, landing on the other guy's side and making him buckle. They were only two or three minutes into the first period, but Gage took the opportunity, swept the guy with one leg, and forced him to his knees. He then grappled for a dominant position and knocked the poor guy out with one direct hook to the face.

That part Kayla hated. She cringed when someone was seriously injured. And she held her breath waiting for the guy to get off the floor even though her man had won the fight.

She finally let out an exhale when the opponent stood on wobbly feat and nodded at Gage.

But Gage, Lord he was magnificent. All firm muscle and sexy tattoos. She loved to trace the lines of the words across his abs and on his biceps with one finger while they lay in bed on a lazy day.

That didn't happen often, though. Gage was a busy man. Between work, the gym, the club, and making Kayla's eyes cross with need, he didn't have much time for lazy.

Kayla didn't either. She'd signed up for two on-line classes the week before, and she was loving getting back into school. Gage had wanted her to quit working and go to school fulltime, but she wasn't ready for that much change yet. She'd only given up her lease last week and officially moved in with him. Letting him support her so fully made her nervous.

He shook his head when she expressed her feelings about that, but didn't argue. Instead he set his foot down. "One semester, baby. You can juggle these two classes and work for one semester, and then when you're comfortable and back in the swing, I want you to give up your job and concentrate fully on your studies."

She'd opened her mouth to argue, but he held up a hand. "We're a team. I don't want one member of my team too tired to have sex with me at the end of the day because she's burning too many candles."

"It's gonna be expensive, Gage."

"And we'll handle it."

Kayla could afford it, but she hated to chip away at her savings while not working. Without rent and utilities, she was in much better shape, though. And Gage hadn't permitted her to give him a dime to help out with his house yet. She was still negotiating that one. Although, Gage was not so much.

By the time she had everything settled concerning her finances, she wasn't in too bad of shape. She no longer had to make enormous monthly extortion payments, and there was a chance she might recoup some of the money she'd lost for the last two years. The Bollings, including their son, were in jail without bond awaiting trial.

Oh, and the new car in the driveway gave her peace of mind. Gage had done that behind her back also. She'd shot daggers at him with her eyes for two hours when he came home with it, but he did nothing but chuckle at her ranting and raving until she gave up and thanked him with her lips and her body.

She was the luckiest woman on Earth, and she didn't hesitate to thank Gage every single day.

Kayla waited for Gage outside the locker room at the arena. Some of the women she saw even went into the locker room. She cringed every time she noticed. Gross.

He came out fifteen minutes later, hair dripping wet and a smile spread across his face. He'd told her he had plans for her that night, and whatever his plans were, he was certainly excited.

She smiled as he lowered his face to kiss her. "Let's go, baby. We have stuff to do."

She'd already prodded him on the way to the arena.

There was no sense continuing along that path. Clearly Gage Holland wasn't a man to divulge his secrets.

Twenty minutes later they were back at home. Kayla lifted a brow as they pulled in the driveway. How was an evening at home so exciting? They did that every night. And it was always heavenly, but Gage had something else up his sleeve this time. And it was a Friday night. So, usually they went to Extreme.

Perplexed, Kayla entered the house, or rather was tugged inside by Gage's hand. The man was excited. His enthusiasm rubbed off on Kayla, making her giggle. "What the hell, Gage?"

He flipped on the light at the same moment Kayla heard a strange whimpering noise. She startled and glanced around the room. And then she doubled back when her mind caught up and realized she'd seen something that didn't belong. "Oh my God." Her hands flew to her mouth. Her eyes darted back and forth from Gage to the small cage sitting next to the kitchen table. "Oh my God," she repeated. "Gage?"

The man wore a grin wider than she'd ever seen on him. "Gotcha something. Happy birthday, baby."

Kayla whipped her gaze to Gage one more time. "You knew it was my birthday?"

He furrowed his brow. "Of course."

Tears came to her eyes. It had been so long since anyone cared about her birthday. And the man had gotten her a puppy. Best birthday present ever, hands down.

"You just gonna stand there?"

Kayla pecked him on the cheek and ran across the room. The cutest little fellow she'd ever seen in her life lifted his sweet face to her as she opened the latch on the little door. He came bouncing out and jumped into her lap.

His tiny body climbed all up her until he could lick her face, his paws on her cheeks. She giggled.

Gage kneeled beside her and stroked the little guy's fur. "You like him?"

"Do I like him?" *Crazy man.* "I love him to pieces. What's his name?"

"Whatever you want it to be."

Kayla glanced around. "Where's Thor?"

"He's with Chief Edwards for the night. Chief Edwards picked up this little fellow and brought him over and took Thor home with him. Just to give us some time before Thor gets all territorial."

"Oh, Gage. I love him so much. Is he the same breed as Thor?"

Gage nodded. "German Shepherd. We'll train him to be just as possessive, so you'll never be alone." He leaned closer and kissed Kayla on the forehead.

She snuggled with the puppy, burying her face in his fur while he squirmed in her arms. She finally lifted her face. "I love you too, you know."

He shrugged. "Sure. Whatever," he teased. "Finish playing with your little beast there and then show me how much you love me."

"Deal." She set him on the floor, and he trotted around clumsily, sniffing at everything in the vicinity.

"Better take him out to pee. That's the first lesson he needs to learn."

Kayla scrambled off her butt and went to the sliding glass door. As soon as she opened it, the little guy bounded out behind her, nipping at her ankles and doing nothing to avoid getting stepped on. "I think he likes me."

Gage followed her. He leaned against the door as Kayla took the puppy into the yard.

He ran circles around her with his boundless energy.

Kayla lifted her face and looked back at Gage. "Jove."

"What?"

"His name. I want to call him Jove."

Gage grinned. "The Roman equivalent of Thor."

"Uh huh. You like it?"

"Love it. It's perfect." He kneeled down to the ground. "Now, come on young Jove. Back in your kennel. I have plans for your mama that don't involve you peeing on her."

Jove raced across the lawn and jumped eagerly into his lap.

"Let's go, baby. You can play with him tomorrow. I want you to myself tonight."

Kayla followed Gage and watched him put Jove in the tiny cage. "He's not going to fit in that long."

"Yeah, but it's the only way to keep a puppy from peeing inside. They won't pee on themselves where they sleep."

"Oh." She was going to need a how-to manual for this endeavor. Although she did live with the latest version of the dog whisperer, so she was guaranteed a perfectly trained dog within months.

Gage shut the gate and led Kayla to their bedroom. He sat her on the edge of the bed and turned to light several candles around the room. The first addition Kayla had made to Gage's house was the candles. She loved the lighting and the way they made her feel.

"Strip, baby," he said as he rounded the bed to light the ones on the other side of the room.

Kayla stood and pulled her shirt over her head. Her fingers trembled as though she'd never slept with Gage before. She had no idea why she was nervous, but with the way he was acting, she had a suspicion she would need every nerve she had.

She unbuttoned her jeans and wiggled her hips to lower

them. When she stood in her bra and panties, he stepped in front of her. He reverently reached with one finger and stroked along the upper swell of her breasts. "I'll never get enough of you."

"I hope not," she whispered.

"Do you realize how much I love you?"

She nodded.

"Happy birthday, baby."

"You've said that."

He grinned. "I've also told you I love you. Is once enough for a lifetime?"

"No." He had a point. She shivered deep inside every time he said it.

Gage popped the front clasp on her bra and slid it down her shoulders to drop it on the floor with her other clothes. Then he hooked his fingers in the sides of her panties and lowered them also. He kneeled in front of her to tug them off and then smoothed his hands up her legs as he rose to his feet again. "Spread your legs wider, baby." He tapped her hip.

Kayla did as he said.

"Submit to me, Kayla."

She nodded and swallowed. "Yes, Sir." It had become their way. She knew when it was time to play because Gage always began with that line. *Submit to me.* Whenever he said that, she fell into the role for him, assuming the proper stance he preferred and using the reverent term of Sir when she spoke to him. It worked for them. She didn't submit to him twenty-four seven, but he did enjoy requiring it most evenings and sometimes before they went to work in the morning.

At other times, no one would know about this side of them. They were just a regular couple in a committed relationship.

"I'm going to push your boundaries tonight, baby. I think you're ready."

She stiffened. "Yes, Sir." Her head dipped lower than necessary to stare at the floor.

"Do you trust me?"

"Yes, Sir."

"Implicitly?"

"Yes, Sir."

"You understand that I'll never strike you for any reason, right?"

"Yes, Sir."

"I want it to be clear. At no point in our lives am I going to spank or flog you. Not for play. Not for sex. And not out of anger."

She nodded. He'd said that many times.

"But I want to restrain you."

She swallowed. Secretly she'd wanted that too for several weeks, but she hadn't been able to ask for it. She suspected he would balk at the idea and turn her down, and she didn't want to hear his refusal. "Please, Sir."

"That appeals to you?"

"Yes, Sir."

"You're an excellent submissive in complete control of keeping your hands and feet exactly where I demand them to be. But being restrained is an entirely different element, a deeper level of obedience."

She trembled, more with need than fear. Her body was so alive, her pussy already pulsed with the thought of coming.

"Safe word?"

"Red, Sir."

"Do not hesitate to use it."

"I won't, Sir." They'd also had several lengthy discussions about using her safe word. Gage had been almost overbearing with his need to make sure she wouldn't let things go further than she could tolerate. If she freaked out on him like she had at Extreme that night several months ago, he would be destroyed. She knew that. And she never intended to make him feel that way again. First of all, there was virtually nothing he could do that would cause the same sort of fear to enter her mind again. Gage was Gage. He wasn't Simon. She'd stopped comparing the two of them a long time ago.

Kayla trusted Gage implicitly. She knew she would even survive a spanking or flogging from him. But that would never happen.

"Climb on the bed and spread your arms and legs toward the corners."

Kayla crawled up and lay on her back in the center. When she reached her arms toward the corner of the headboard, Gage took the first one and wrapped her wrist in a Velcro cuff. He attached the other end to the bed. Instead of circling her body and repeating the action on her other limbs, he stroked her skin, slowly trailing his fingers down her arm from her palm to her shoulder. He breezed over her nipple and then circled it with the tips of his fingers.

"Your tits are so fucking hot, baby." He cupped the globe and weighed it in his hand. And then he danced his fingers down her belly toward her pussy. He didn't linger. He barely touched the hood of her clit and passed through her folds, and then trailed the rest of the way down her leg until he reached her ankle. He wrapped her ankle in another Velcro cuff and affixed it to the footboard. Not satisfied with the amount of leeway she had, he tightened the attachments and pulled her leg straighter. If he did her other arm and leg the same way, she wouldn't be able to lift even her hips, splayed for his view and pleasure.

Gage circled the bed and wrapped the Velcro around her other leg. He caressed up that leg and back through her lower lips until he flicked his pointer over her clit.

Kayla squeezed her eyes shut. Already she was so aroused. The restraints he'd been afraid to use on her for weeks on end were making her so aroused, she couldn't think.

Up her body, he trailed, tickling her belly and then teasing the swell of her breast. And finally her nipple.

When she bucked her chest the few inches left to her, he stopped and pulled her arm tight toward the last corner to join all of its mates in restraint.

"So sexy, baby. You have no idea how horny it makes me for you to let me tie you down. It's humbling to have your trust like this."

Did he not have any idea how aroused she was right alongside him?

"Don't move." Gage turned and left the room, chuckling under his breath. He jerked his shirt over his head with one hand while he walked and dropped it on the floor.

Kayla rolled her eyes and squirmed to see how much room she had. Almost none. She couldn't control anything enough to prevent him from doing whatever the heck he chose. Even her pussy didn't have more than an inch of space wiggling in either direction or up into the air. She was well and truly secured for Gage's pleasure.

At least that's what he thought. In truth, the pleasure would be all hers.

When he returned, Kayla jerked her gaze to follow him into the room. He held several items that made her heart rate soar as he set them on the bedside table.

The first thing he picked up was the jar of marshmallow cream.

She bit her lip to keep from giggling. This was not

meant to be funny, and even her body agreed there was nothing remotely humorous happening between her legs right then, but she couldn't help it.

He twisted the lid off, and she flinched when the vacuum seal popped. He climbed up between her legs and got comfortable on his knees. He reached into the jar with one finger and drew out a glob of the sticky white confection. He slowly brought his finger toward her pussy, but at the last second he retracted and sucked the cream from his pointer, so provocatively her eyes widened. By the time he reached back into the jar for more, she was close to begging him to apply it to her. Anywhere.

Gage tapped a nipple first, and Kayla yelped. He grinned. "I've barely started, baby."

She held her tongue as he repeated the action on her other nipple.

He reached in for more and spread it around both stiff buds until little peaks of sticky cream highlighted her rosy tips. Shocking her, he spread a generous portion onto her entire breast until she was covered with mounds of white, hardly any of her skin showing.

And then the man leaned down and proceeded to lick every speck of the marshmallow off her tits. He intentionally lifted onto his knees so that no part of him touched her pussy, which drove her crazy.

By the time he leaned back and licked his lips, Kayla was writhing with need. Her nipples were sensitive normally, but that much activity was beyond anything he'd ever done.

And then he grabbed the jar of fluff and held her gaze while he scooped out another large glob. He kept staring at her as he dipped his hand to her pussy and spread the cream all around her clit and lower lips.

Kayla moaned. There was no stopping her mouth from emitting sounds.

Gage smiled broadly and then lowered himself between her legs. He held her thighs with both hands and licked her pussy from bottom to top, flicking his tongue over her clit.

"Oh my God. Gage." She fisted her hands and tugged on her wrists, but there was no way to move more than an inch in any direction.

"Yes, baby?" He lifted his face, a coy look of confusion hovering in his blinking eyes.

She stared daggers at him, but she doubted it came off that way. Her eyes were glazed, and she was torn between begging him to stop and begging him to continue.

He dipped low again and repeated the action. And then he sucked in earnest, feasting on every inch of her pussy. He even nipped at her clit and then held it between his teeth. When she stiffened, so close to coming she could think of nothing else, he stopped. "Not yet, baby."

Kayla moaned and rolled her head to one side. She gritted her teeth and tried to pull her legs in, but they wouldn't budge.

Gage wiggled so much between her legs that she twisted her head to see him. She watched as he tugged his jeans over his hips and shrugged out of them. Now gloriously naked, his cock bobbed in front of him, and he watched her face as he took the length in one hand and stroked himself. His breathing was erratic, much how she imagined hers was.

Suddenly he dipped one hand between her legs and thrust a finger into her pussy while he continued to work his cock with is other hand. "Oh, baby. So wet for me. I'm so in awe of your strength."

My strength? What was he smoking? She was two

seconds from spontaneously combusting and he wanted to point out her strength?

He smirked. "I love that look of shock on your face when I confuse you." He rubbed the tip of his cock with his thumb as she licked her lips, trying to concentrate on his words. "It took courage to let me restrain you like this, and you've gone above and beyond. You're so aroused, you could come with just a word. Right, baby?" He pulled his finger out to emphasize his point.

She swallowed. "Please, Gage. Oh God. I need you so bad. Don't leave me like this any longer."

He released his cock and leaned over her, planting both hands beside her shoulders and kissing her lips. "Since you asked so nicely, and since I can't stand another moment outside of you." And then he plunged into her, his lips brushing over hers as he did.

Kayla couldn't stop the tidal wave of sensation as he thrust in and out, not pausing to take her pulse. He took and he gave in equal measure, holding her gaze and communicating his love for her with his face alone.

"Come, baby. Come with me."

She shattered. Her pussy pulsed around his cock in rhythm with his own orgasm. She recognized every nuance of the way he came deep inside her. The way he held his mouth, slightly open. The way his arms stiffened at her sides. It took effort to watch him come while she herself was engrossed in her own orgasm, but she forced herself to witness his release.

It was a thing of beauty. And she never wanted the image to fade.

Luckily she would never have to.

When they were both spent, Gage leaned over her, his cock still lodged inside her where she preferred he stay. He ripped the Velcro from her wrists one at a time and then slumped onto her chest, holding himself up enough to keep from crushing her. He rained kisses along her neck, her throat, her face. And then he met her mouth and consumed her with a kiss that curled her toes.

When neither of them could breathe, he pulled back only enough for them to gasp for oxygen. "Happy birthday, Kayla," he repeated a third time. He kissed her nose then and set his forehead on hers.

"Can tomorrow be my birthday too?"

"If you'd like." He chuckled, his deep rumbles shaking her frame.

"I think I'm gonna like celebrating birthdays with you."

"I'll do my best."

"You do realize you've set a precedent, and it will be hard to top it each year."

"Challenge accepted."

Half an hour later, Gage had cleaned her up with a damp cloth and removed the binding from her ankles. He crawled over her body and snuggled up behind her to hold her back to his front.

She'd never felt so totally worshiped.

He nibbled around her ear. "I guess restraints are now on the yes column."

"Absolutely," she admitted.

Her eyes were heavy as she stared at the array of flickering candles still burning around them.

And then a faint whimper broke the silence.

Kayla grinned and popped into a sitting position. She twisted around to face Gage, suddenly forgetting how replete and sated she'd been two seconds ago.

"Would I be a bad mom and ruin our puppy if I took him out of his cage and played with him for a while?"

Gage laughed, his entire body shuddering with his amusement. He wrapped his arm around her neck and pulled her head down to kiss her lips. "Go get him, baby. I know you won't be able to sleep until you do. But I'm warning you, if Jove pees in my bed…"

She wiggled free of the blankets, not bothering to listen to the rest of his sentence. She didn't need to hear what he was going to say because she knew Gage. Even if that puppy did pee in the bed, he would roll his eyes and give Kayla whatever her heart desired. That's the kind of man he was. And she was damn lucky he'd fallen in love with her. She paused at the door and turned back. "We should take him to see your dad Sunday."

Gage smiled. "I'm sure he'd like that." They had moved Jed to a rehab center two weeks before. He was alert more and more often. He didn't speak yet, but it was clear he understood what was being said around him and managed to smile on occasion. Aletha firmly believed meeting Kayla and finding out Gage had a woman he was in love with gave Jed a reason to try. Kayla wasn't sure how all that worked, but she did know when they brought Thor to visit, Jed perked up even more.

Kayla jogged down the hall toward her new little bundle of energy.

She had every intention of bringing that sweet puppy into their bed. She just hoped Thor adored the puppy as much as she did and he didn't feel threatened. He'd earned his spot in the bed. She wasn't about to kick Thor out. There was room for one more, wasn't there?

Life was about to get very interesting.

Gage Holland was *hers* in every way. And she was one lucky woman.

AUTHOR'S NOTE

I hope you've enjoyed *Hers* from The Fight Club series. Please enjoy the following excerpt from *Want*, the next book in the series.

WANT

THE FIGHT CLUB, BOOK FIVE

Sabrina could not tolerate another minute of the intense scrutiny coming from across the room. She glanced up from her uneaten slice of pizza to verify that Professor Bascott was indeed still glaring at her. His expression was hard, his brow furrowed as though he was aggravated.

A chill raced up her spine, not for the first time.

Why was the infuriating man staring at her?

She shivered and squirmed in her seat, narrowing her gaze at Dr. Bascott. Something was different about the way he watched her today, his expression more intense than she remembered. If she didn't know better, she would swear he looked like he wanted to tear her clothes off and fuck her in the middle of the restaurant.

No way.

She shook the feeling from her mind and glanced at her friends.

Her friend Dana continued to yap about some sort of office gossip that meant nothing to Sabrina. Thank God Dana had a willing audience in their other two girlfriends at the table, because Sabrina had done little for the last half hour but monitor the gaze stabbing her from several tables away.

Dr. Bascott had been the bane of her existence for the entire spring semester. The man was unbelievably sexy with fantastic dark hair—shaved very short on the sides and left longer on top—and stunning blue eyes that could nail a woman to the wall and leave her speechless. He was fine to look at all right. Better than fine. He was built, his enormous chest bulging beneath every shirt he wore, and his ass a drool-worthy specimen half the student population ogled without apology—the female half. Or, truth be told, probably some of the male half also.

One literature class. That was all she'd taken at the university. It had been over for two months. She'd finally managed to get Dr. Bascott out of her head—sort of. And here he was at King Pizza, a favorite restaurant and bar among everyone she'd ever met.

Fuck.

Another glance.

Still he stared. Or glared. She couldn't decide which.

And she wasn't certain his look wasn't one of lust instead of aggravation.

Dr. Bascott also sat at a table of friends, most of whom looked like they must go to the same gym as him—or take the same steroids at least. All of whom appeared considerably younger.

She hated how badly she lusted after him. She'd hated it all semester. And she still hated it, sitting in her chair squirming against the pulsing of her pussy and the tightness of breasts that suddenly felt too large for her bra.

The problem was the man was a first-class asshole. He'd done little more than grunt at her like she had the plague for the entire semester. And by the looks of things, he didn't think any more highly of her now than he had then. Right?

Nothing she wrote pleased him. Nothing she said in class pleased him. Hell, she couldn't even please him with correct multiple-choice answers.

She cleared her throat and pushed back from the table. "Bathroom. Be right back." She took a deep breath as she walked from the room to the side hall, holding her head high and trying not to trip and fall.

She didn't exhale until she sequestered herself in the blessedly individual restroom and leaned against the door. She bent forward and set her hands on her knees, as though hyperventilating. She didn't need to pee. She needed to regroup, grow a spine, or at least get the hell out of Dodge so she could resume another two months of waking up panting over that damned exasperating man.

She moaned. That's what was going to happen. Seeing him in her favorite pizza joint had not only ruined her taste for the food there, but also set her back in time.

Unfortunately, she had forgotten to lock the door. It hadn't been the first thing on her mind, especially since she had no intention of using the toilet. She jolted forward as someone opened the door, pushing hard as though it was stuck. Not shocking.

Sabrina righted herself and grabbed for the handle, shocked to find a huge male body in her way, not a woman.

She gasped as Dr. Bascott pushed the door closed and filled her space, stepping around her, turning her, and pinning her against the door. He stared at her hard for several seconds, his brow still furrowed.

And then he smiled.

Sabrina was unable to utter a single sound. That's how shocked she was.

Stunning her further, he set his hands on her shoulders

and lowered his mouth to hers. He didn't hesitate. He met her lips at a slight angle and kissed her. He wasn't slow and gentle about it either. More like a starving man who had waited all evening for a taste, and finally getting his opportunity, ravaged her.

Sabrina melted into the door. Dr. Bascott could kiss. *Holy shit.*

She grabbed onto his biceps, forgetting entirely how pissed she had been two seconds ago with this very man. All thought fled her brain as his tongue slid between her lips, demanding entrance.

She freely gave him what he wanted, opening her mouth and letting him devour her.

He kissed with a high level of urgency, as though the world would self-destruct in a few minutes and they needed to hurry. And then he pressed into her, his hands wandering down from her shoulders to her waist. Without hesitation, he grabbed the hem of her shirt and broke the kiss to tug it over her head. He set it on the vanity next to her and met her gaze.

Sabrina hadn't breathed since he'd entered the room. She licked her lips, but then he was on her again, this time cupping her breasts while he tasted her mouth.

She moaned, and Dr. Bascott swallowed her sound. She could have sworn he smiled against her lips. Her breasts swelled as he squeezed them in his palms. When his thumbs tugged the cups of her bra down to flick over her nipples, she bucked into him.

The only word she could think was *more.*

After burning for this man for so many months, she needed him like she needed her next breath. Even if she was dreaming, she didn't care. It was worth it. For a moment she considered that perhaps she had fallen and hit her head and this was where her mind took her while she lay unconscious on the floor.

Totally worth it.

Her nipples continued to harden under his touch as he pinched them between his thumbs and pointers. And then his hands were gone, and she moaned again, hating the loss of his touch against her breasts.

But only for a second, because suddenly his huge fingers were at her jeans, popping the button and lowering the zipper. His lips trailed from her swollen mouth to nibble a path to her ear. "Stand still," he whispered. "Patience."

She hadn't realized she was squirming, wanting her jeans to disappear faster, needing his cock inside her.

Insanity.

She didn't give a fuck.

Insanity won.

She pressed her hips forward when his thigh landed between her legs, rubbing her pussy against him, burning with arousal.

Dr. Bascott set his teeth on the skin behind her ear and bit down, just enough to get her attention. "Stop."

She froze. Stop what?

He leaned back and met her gaze, his hands on the opening of her jeans. His face was fierce with concentration, his brow furrowed as he reprimanded her. "If you want this... If you want my cock inside you, you'll stop wiggling."

She held herself rigid; her nipples, pressing out of her bra awkwardly, pulsed with the need for more contact. Her pussy flooded at his demand. If she didn't know better, she would swear he was a Dom. But that was so unrealistic...

She had to be dreaming. Only in her dreams would her

perfect man also happen to be a Dom. Real life was never that kind.

She nodded, sucking her lower lip between her teeth.

Without dropping his gaze, Dr. Bascott lowered her jeans, tugging them over her hips until he had to squat to pull them off her feet. She stepped out of her flip-flops to help the process, and when he smoothed his hands back up her body from her calves to her thighs, she shivered.

He lifted his face to meet her gaze as he pulled her panties down next. Her cheeks burned as she watched him stuff her panties in his back pocket. She was essentially naked in front of him. And he was fully clothed.

And then his mouth was on hers again, her hands were lifted in the air above her head, and his thigh was between her legs, forcing them wider.

The instant her soaking pussy and aching clit hit the denim of his jeans, she rose on her tiptoes and moaned louder into his mouth.

Dr. Bascott pulled her lower lip between his teeth and nipped her enough to remind her of her role. *Stand still.* He didn't need to repeat the command.

The need was unbearable, but he didn't make her wait long. Shifting both her wrists to one hand, he used the other to pop his own fly and shimmy the jeans down enough to release his cock.

She could see nothing with his tongue dancing against hers, but she felt his cock bob against her belly as he pulled something from his back pocket. Undoubtedly a condom.

At least he had the sense to use one. In fact, with one free hand, he managed to open the wrapper and push the rubber down his cock, never breaking the kiss.

The air whooshed from her lungs when both his hands reached under her arms to lift her off the ground. She'd read about such a possibility in books, but never considered fucking someone against the wall as a feasible reality.

She'd been wrong. Dr. Bascott was tall and lean and muscular. It was clear he expended no effort hoisting her off the ground and forcing her to hover above his cock.

"Please," she mumbled. She was so wet and needy. She wasn't above begging.

"Ask for it."

"Please, Sir. I need your cock inside me." She grabbed his shoulders and dug her nails into his skin. She flinched when she realized she'd called him Sir.

He made no indication he noticed. "That's my girl." As soon as he finished speaking, he thrust into her, lowering her body at the same time he bucked forward to bring his cock into her to the hilt.

Sabrina inhaled sharply. So full. God, his cock was huge. And he knew how to use it. If only he would move...

No one had ever fucked her like this. No one had ever entered her without preparing her pussy first. Hell, no one had ever taken her at all before she'd dated them for at least a month.

This wasn't a man she was dating. He wasn't someone she even liked five minutes ago. And now his cock was buried in her, and all she could think about was how badly she wanted him to pick up the pace. So badly she almost missed the look on his face that attested to his lack of control.

The always stoic Dr. Bascott was closer to orgasm than he would like.

Just as quickly as he'd entered her, he lifted her up and let his cock slide out about halfway before thrusting back home.

Sabrina whimpered. She gripped his shoulders so hard there would be marks. She didn't care. She had never needed to come this badly in her life. "Please," she begged.

"Greedy girl," he admonished. But he didn't stop fucking her hard and fast against the bathroom door. Faster. Harder. Deeper. It seemed like he would split her in two. She willed him to do just that. Her orgasm was so close her vision blurred.

Dr. Bascott cocked his hips forward slightly, making her clit rub against him with each stroke.

That was all she needed. She tipped her head back. Her mouth fell open, but no sound came out. So close...

"Come for me, baby."

She obeyed, her orgasm ripping through her body, pulsing with the pent-up need she'd carried for months.

She moaned. One of his palms landed across her mouth as he released her hip. His cock remained buried deep inside her. "Shhh. Too loud, baby."

It took several deep breaths before she floated back down to Earth and realized he came at the same time she did. She'd been so engrossed in her own orgasm, she only caught the tail end of his pulsing cock inside her. That's how violently her pussy had grasped him.

She blinked and licked her lips as Dr. Bascott released her mouth and lifted her off his cock. He steadied her on the floor and then turned around to dispose of the condom.

Without saying a word, he put her clothes back on her, straightening her bra and pulling her shirt over her head first, and then leaning down to tap her legs one at a time until he had her jeans back in place also. He kept her panties.

Externally, she assumed she was back to rights. Internally, she was a hurricane. What the hell just happened?

Dr. Bascott finally leaned into her against the door. He gripped her chin, kissed her thoroughly but briefly, and then eased her away from the door. Before she knew what happened, he was gone.

Eyes wide, mouth open, she glanced around the room and met her gaze in the mirror. "Holy shit." She turned on the faucet and splashed cold water on her cheeks. She was barely composed, and definitely shaking, when she opened the bathroom door.

Thank fuck no one stood outside the room waiting. She'd have died on the spot.

The first place her gaze landed when she stepped back into the main room was Dr. Bascott's table. He was gone. In fact, his entire party was gone. A family of six now occupied the space.

Sabrina made her way back to her friends. Surprisingly, neither of them mentioned her prolonged absence. She was relieved there was no interrogation. The last thing she needed was the third degree. In fact, she grabbed her purse from the table without sitting.

"You okay, Sabrina?" Dana asked.

"Yeah. My stomach's a little upset. I'm gonna go ahead and go." Sabrina nodded toward the entrance, backing that way.

"Oh. Okay. Well, get some rest. I'll call you."

Sabrina turned and left without another word. She knew her minutes were numbered before she would break down in a shivering pile of tears.

Because what happened in that restroom wasn't a simple fuck against the door. Nope. It was a total act of domination, and Sabrina recognized she'd been in a sub space that was going to leave her in tears and then wrung out before she could drive herself home.

If she could just make it to her car...

She walked out the front door, half expecting the man who had rocked her world to be standing in the parking lot. But her wish was not granted. Dr. Bascott was indeed gone.

Whatever aftercare Sabrina needed, she was going to have to administer it to herself.

ALSO BY BECCA JAMESON

Hot SEAL, Red Wine

Hot SEAL, Australian Nights

Hot SEAL, Cold Feet

Dark Falls:

Dark Nightmares

Club Zodiac:

Training Sasha

Obeying Rowen

Collaring Brooke

Mastering Rayne

Trusting Aaron

Claiming London

Sharing Charlotte

Taming Rex

Tempting Elizabeth

Club Zodiac Box Set One

Club Zodiac Box Set Two

The Art of Kink:

Pose

Paint

Sculpt

Arcadian Bears:

Grizzly Mountain

Grizzly Beginning

Grizzly Secret

Grizzly Promise

Grizzly Survival

Grizzly Perfection

Arcadian Bears Box Set One

Arcadian Bears Box Set Two

Sleeper SEALs:

Saving Zola

Spring Training:

Catching Zia

Catching Lily

Catching Ava

Spring Training Box Set

The Underground series:

Force

Clinch

Guard

Submit

Thrust

Torque

The Underground Box Set One

The Underground Box Set Two

Saving Sofia (Special Forces: Operations Alpha)

Wolf Masters series:

Kara's Wolves

Lindsey's Wolves

Jessica's Wolves

Alyssa's Wolves

Wolf Gatherings series:

Tarnished

Dominated

Completed

Redeemed

Abandoned

Betrayed

Wolf Gatherings Box Set One

Wolf Gathering Box Set Two

Durham Wolves series:

Rescue in the Smokies

Fire in the Smokies

Freedom in the Smokies

Stand Alone Books:

Blind with Love

Guarding the Truth

Out of the Smoke

Abducting His Mate

Three's a Cruise

Wolf Trinity

Frostbitten

A Princess for Cale/A Princess for Cain

ABOUT THE AUTHOR

Becca Jameson is a USA Today best-selling author of over 90 books. She is most well-known for her Wolf Masters series and her Fight Club series. She currently lives in Houston, Texas, with her husband and her Goldendoodle. Two grown kids pop in every once in a while too! She is loving this journey and has dabbled in a variety of genres, including paranormal, sports romance, military, and BDSM.

A total night owl, Becca writes late at night, sequestering herself in her office with a glass of red wine and a bar of dark chocolate, her fingers flying across the keyboard as her characters weave their own stories.

During the day--which never starts before ten in the morning!--she can be found jogging, running errands, or reading in her favorite hammock chair!

...where Alphas dominate...

Becca's Newsletter Sign-up:
http://beccajameson.com/newsletter-sign-up

Join my Facebook fan group, Becca's Bibliomaniacs, for the most up-to-date information, random excerpts while I work, giveaways, and fun release parties!

Facebook Fan Group:
https://www.facebook.com/groups/BeccasBibliomaniacs/

Contact Becca:
www.beccajameson.com
beccajameson4@aol.com

- facebook.com/becca.jameson.18
- twitter.com/beccajameson
- instagram.com/becca.jameson
- bookbub.com/authors/becca-jameson
- goodreads.com/beccajameson
- amazon.com/author/beccajameson